A Bilingual (English-Bengali) Novel

SOUMYANETRA

Copyright © Soumyanetra 2023
All Rights Reserved.

ISBN 979-8-89133-742-8

This book has been published with all efforts taken to make the material error-free after the consent of the author. However, the author and the publisher do not assume and hereby disclaim any liability to any party for any loss, damage, or disruption caused by errors or omissions, whether such errors or omissions result from negligence, accident, or any other cause.

While every effort has been made to avoid any mistake or omission, this publication is being sold on the condition and understanding that neither the author nor the publishers or printers would be liable in any manner to any person by reason of any mistake or omission in this publication or for any action taken or omitted to be taken or advice rendered or accepted on the basis of this work. For any defect in printing or binding the publishers will be liable only to replace the defective copy by another copy of this work then available.

Contents

1. চিঠি

9th January

মা, it's been impossible without you... on the day of your funeral পিপিমণি and জেঠুভাইয়া and everyone came and I didn't even know what they had come for... তুমি চলে যাওয়ার পর থেকে বলি... তারপর থেকেই তো তোমার সঙ্গে কথা হয়নি.... কিছুদিন আগে থেকে বোধহয় তুমি আর থাকবে না সেটা বুঝেছিলে, না? ...

সেই আগের winter থেকে খালি বলতে না, 'বাবা মা কারুর চিরকাল থাকে নাকি? আমি একা বলে তুমি চিরকাল থাকবে নাকি? আমি তোমায় খুব ভালোবাসি বলে চিরকাল থাকবে নাকি?'... এখন মনে হয় মা বলি, যে তুমি না থাকলে কেমন লাগে ঢের বুঝেছি, এবার ফিরে এস ... সত্যি তাই বলে চলে গেলে?

11th August দুপুরে জানো তোমার চাহুনিটা যে কি অদ্ভুত লাগলো যে কি বলি... আমার দিকেই তাকিয়ে আছো... অথচ আমাকে দেখছো না... তখন জানো আমি চেঁচিয়ে উঠেছিলাম .... মা'র কিছু হয়েছে, মা'র কিছু হচ্ছে ... তুমি বলেছিলে না লেখা ছাড়বি না আর নাচ ছাড়বি না .... দেখো, লিখছি তাই ... চোখ ভিজে যাচ্ছে মা তাও লিখছি ... আর তো তোমার সঙ্গে কথা বলার উপায় নেই ... রোজ রাতে তোমার mobileটা পাশে বালিশে নীচে নিয়ে শুই ... ওটাতে তোমার স্পর্শ আছে তাই ... রোজ ভাবি আজ যদি একবার স্বপ্নে তোমায় দেখতে পাই ... কিন্তু কই আসো না তো?... আমি দেখি না তো?...

10th Jan

মা কাল তোমাকে আর বাবাকে স্বপ্ন দেখলাম ... বাবা না shave করতে করতে যেরম ভাবে আমার সঙ্গে এসে কথা বলতো সেরম ভাবে এলো ... তুমিও পাশে ছিলে ... একটা বাড়ি... পুরোনো মতো... সিঁড়ি আছে... তুমি সেই দিদানের সাদা শাড়ী পড়তে না সেরম পরেছিলে... আর কোথা থেকে একটা কালো কাঁকড়া

এসেছিলো ... কাঁকড়াটার পা টা আবার খুলে গেছিলো ... তারপর তুমি bend হয়ে পাশে কি যেন করছিলে আর বাবা সামনে থেকে এলো ... আর মেয়েটার কি একটা not well দেখলাম ... আর বাবা বললো বাবা তাড়িয়ে দেবে ... "One last টাইম" বইটা-এ ছিল জানো যদি dream খুব vivid হয় তার মানে it wasn't a dream… the spirit was actually visiting me… I am sure you were yesterday… and I am also sure you both are really together somewhere… thanks so much ma… আমি কালই লিখলাম তোমরা স্বপ্নে আসো না ... তাই বুঝি এলে?... তোমরা এই লেখাগুলো দেখতে পাচ্ছো না?... please দেখো ... it's really a letter to you…

মা তুমি ঠিক এটাই বলতে জানো ... দেখবি আমি চলে গেলে ও কত ভালো থাকবে তোদের নিয়ে ... আগে তুমি ওলি ঘুম থেকে ওঠার সময় এলে কেমন serious হয়ে থাকতো না ... সব সময়ই তো তুমি থাকলে যেন ওর সমস্ত আনন্দ চলে যেত ... আর bank-এর কাজ, online কিছু pay করা, even ড্রিমল্যান্ড-এর বাড়ির খবর - সব কিছুই কোনো বিরক্তি ছাড়া করছে দেখছি... ... আজকে আমি কয়েকবার বলতেই City Cleaners দের-ও ডাকলো জানতো (আলো লাগানোর জন্য)... সেদিনকে online আলো order দেবার জন্য বললাম... order দিয়েও দিলো সঙ্গে সঙ্গে ... ভাবো!... তুমি থাকতে literally দশবার বলতে হতো!... কী যে change যে কি বলি ... কী hypocrisy… পুরো দিন কে রাত করে মা ... so I keep looking for proof যে তোমাকে actually ও কী কষ্ট দিতো...

সেদিনকে ওরা দুর্গাপুর যাবে বললো... আমি যাইনি... and I even asked মামনি to give the letter I wrote to her as a last resort… আমি একটা জিনিস ঠিক করেছি মা - তুমিই বলতে না প্রতিবাদ করার অনেক ভাষা আছে ... আমি ওকে divorce-ও করতে পারিনি, ওকে ছেড়ে যেতেও পারিনি ... মেয়েটাকে বড্ডো ভালোবাসি, I can't deprive her of the love of her father… but I will not have anything to do with his family… যতটা সম্ভব ... আমার বাবা, ভাই, বোন, কেউ ছিল না ... all I wanted was to have him be nice to you… সেটাও ও করেনি ...

এই birthday গেল মা ... কোনোদিন তুমি ছাড়া জন্মদিন হবে ভাবিনি ... Cuttack-এর ছবি আর আরো পুরোনো কিছু ছবি album করতে দিয়েছিলাম জানো ... Picture Perfect এ... সেখানে সেই Cuttack এ আমার জন্মদিনের

ছবি দেখছিলাম .... তুমি সেই পাঁচ রকম ভাজা etc সাজিয়ে দিয়েছ like all the other times... আর কতদিন এরম তুমি ছাড়া জন্মদিন হবে?...

আগের বার মনে আছে তুমি যখন অনেক এটা ওটা arrange করছিলে, আমি তোমাকে বলেছিলাম "মা, এত কিছু করার কি দরকার?"... আর সবতাতেই কিরম মনে হত ও বিরক্ত হচ্ছে ... যেন তুমি আমার এত খেয়াল রাখতে বলেই ওর এত বিরক্তি ... না রাখলে যেন ও রাখত... তখন তুমি বলেছিলে "না রে... করি, যদি পরের বার না থাকি..."... আর তুমি না খুব seriously বলেছিলে ... কথার কথা না ... যেন সত্যি বুঝেছিলে আর থাকবে না ...

সেই Apple এ 'live photo' হয় না মা ... একটু ধরে থাকলে কিছুক্ষন video-র মত play করে ... তাতে দেখলাম ... তুমি যেরম usual আমার হাতটা চেপে ধরে আছ আর একটু হাসছো .... একবার চোখের পাতাও পড়ল.... সত্যি মা মনে হয় আবার যদি এমন করে ধরতে একবার ...

11th Jan

মা জানতো, office-এ, sexual harassment নিয়ে program হল নভেম্বর-এ like always... the Ministry had asked us to observe Awareness of Sexual Harassment at Workplaces, and who better represents sexual harassment than Draupadi...

এবারে গায়েত্রী দি phone করে বলল আমার লেখা বা অন্যদের লেখা কয়েকটা কবিতা পড়তে ... আর প্রকৃতি বলল গান করবে ... তাই আমি suggest করলাম একসঙ্গে গান আর কবিতা নিয়ে একটা গীতি আলেখ্য মতো করি ... and everyone requested me to write a script for it... তাই তোমার দ্রৌপদীর সব files কোথায় আছে খুঁজছিলাম জান... I actually sat in your room and dug up all your files and books, including Jagnaseni by Bharati Ray and Nathabati Anathabat by Shaonli Mitra and wrote a script myself...

I know you admire Draupadi a lot... that's why you kept my name Parshati*, which is another name for Draupadi....

(*যজ্ঞসেন বা দ্রুপদের স্ত্রী পৃষতী, তাঁর কন্যা পার্ষতী।)

সিদ্ধার্থকে* জিজ্ঞেস করে, কোথায় তোমার files etc আছে বার করে, যাজ্ঞসেনী, কথা অমৃতসমান, আরো বই সব বার করলাম… সব ঘেঁটে মোটামুটি দু- তিন দিন-এ একটা script লিখলাম… mostly তোমার যাজ্ঞসেনী থেকে… মাঝখানে মাঝখানে আমার দুটো কবিতা, নবনীতা দেবসেন-এর শ্রেষ্ঠ কবিতার বই থেকে (এই বইটা তুমিই আমাকে দিয়েছিলে) দুটো কবিতা … আমাদের Poetry Paradigm-এর প্রেয়শীদির একটা কবিতা… প্রকৃতিদের কয়েকটা গান … সব নিয়ে একটা script লিখলাম…

(*Siddhartha worked at Pursuits, which was an academic organization that Parshati's ma started. It conducted online classes, lectures, etc. It also undertook publishing and editorial works. Siddhartha was employed by Parshati's ma but he kept working even when she was no more.)

Script-টা-এ যেখানে দ্রৌপদী কৃষ্ণকে বলছে, "আমার পতি নেই, পুত্র নেই, ভ্রাতা, পিতা নেই …" তারপর 'চিরসখা' গানটা রেখেছিলাম… প্রকৃতি খুব সুন্দর গেয়েছিল … কী ভালো যে হয়েছিল যে কী বলি … This was one of the poems in the script…

Draupadi

The demands haven't lessened

The demands of love

The demands of work

The demands of duty

Life chafed everywhere

Tightened around the waist

Pulling in all directions

Threatening to dismember

Threatening to detach

Yet actually strengthening

And tightening
Hey Krishna...

And Krishna comes to me
In my verse and songs
In my tears and laughs
In my skilful pretences
And my honest confessions
In the warmth of
My pillow at night
In my dreams
Bringing loved ones near me
And in the unwritten letters
Of love that He writes...

I even wore one of the silks we bought together from Chennai... one of those that you didn't get to wear... সেই Nalli থেকে কেনা যে শাড়িগুলো তোমার পরা হয়নি... তার মধ্যে থেকে একটা পরেছিলাম... rose gold shade... তুমি থাকলে কিছুতেই ওটা পরতে দিতে না ... বলতে ঐসব রঙে আমার complexion চাপা লাগে ... হয়ত তাই লাগছিল কিন্তু তাও পরেছিলাম মা ... তাতে যেন তোমার পরশ ছিল...

Poetry Paradigm* - এ Women's Day program হবে জান... they asked for scripts from their members... সেই office-এর Women's Day program-এর Script-টা জান প্রেয়শীদি বলল Poetry Paradigm এ বলতে... পৃথাদি, অনামিকাদি, executive council etc., ঘুরে সেটা selected

হয়েছে Poetry Paradigm এর Women's Day program এর part হিসেবে... Office এ শুধু বলা/পাঠ ছিল ... এখানে বোধহয় নাচও করব... তাই মা, it's going to be the first time I will dance without you seeing... কোথাও থেকে দেখতে পাও কি?... এই যে লিখছি ... দেখতে পাচ্ছো কি?... আর Poetry Paradigm-এর library space-টায় নাচ করলে দেখা যায় না মোটেই (like last time when I danced Bharat Natyam, remember?)... আমি বলছিলাম auditorium book করতে ... হয়ত আমাকেই টাকা দিয়ে auditorium book করতে হবে ...

(*Poetry Paradigm was a poetry library that Parshati was a member of. Later on due to her differences with the others in the group, she left it.)

ও'র মা (মানে আমার শাশুড়ি) আবার জান একটা নাকি school খুলেছে ... বাচ্চাদের ... ওলিরা যেদিন দুর্গাপুর গেছিল ওদের দেখিয়েছে... তোমার দেখাদেখি surely ... তোমার Pursuits এর কথা মনে আছে কোনোদিন কাউকে বলত না?... তোমার বই বেরোলে কোনোদিন তার কথা বলত না?... তোমার-বাবার কোনো ভালো কথাই infact কোনোদিন কাউকে বলত না...

তুমি থাকতে মা তোমার অগাধ জ্ঞান এমন করে বুঝিনি ... বা বোঝার সময়ই পাইনি... বাবা বলত না মা, যখন আমার পড়াশুনো শেষ করে তোমাদের সঙ্গে থাকার কথা তখন বাবা'র ডাক পড়ল... এখন ওলি একটু বড় হয়েছে, তোমার সঙ্গে কত কী discuss করার থাকতো... আর কেমন করে তোমাকে এখনই চলে যেতে হল মা ... বড্ডো একা লাগে... মনে হয়ে একবার যদি তোমার সঙ্গে কথা বলতে পারতাম ... আবার কখন আমাদের দেখা হবে মা ... যেন তাড়াতাড়ি হয়... তখন অনেক কথা বলব... তুমি আমার সঙ্গে কথা বলতে কী ভালোবাসতে না ... বলতে আমাদের কথার আর শেষ নেই রে... এখন কেউ আমার সঙ্গে কথা বলার জন্য বসে থাকে না ...

নলিনী মাসিকে লিখেছিলাম জান জন্মদিনের দিন ... নলিনী মাসি তো WhatsApp দেখে না ... সেদিন দেখেনি... তারপরের দিন দেখে phone করেছিল .... বলল তোমার স্মৃতিটা যেন থাকে কিন্তু কষ্টটা যেন কমে যায়... কেমন করে সেটা হয় মা ... স্মৃতিতেই তো তুমি, আর, তুমি আর নেই ভাবলেই তো কষ্ট ... কেন এমন করে চলে গেলে মা ...

~

12th Jan

ও পুরো দিন কে রাত করে বলি না ... কালই office-এর Shukla'র নামে কত কথা বলছিল... আজকে সেই Shukla'র কাছেই গিয়ে কমিটিতে থাকতে হবে বলছে... the admission committee that he is chairing this time... বলেছি বলে কী রাগ ...

~

আজকে Oindrila'র দিদিমা'র সঙ্গে দেখা হল জান... school- এ ওলিকে আনতে গেছিলাম তখন ...

ঠিক এটাই বলতে না মা দেখবি আমি চলে গেলে ও তোদের নিয়ে খুব ভালো থাকবে ... ঠিক তাই ... এখন যেন কোন কারণই নেই ঝগড়ার... তোমার সঙ্গে অসভ্যতা করার নেই না ...

ও'র will force strong জানতাম কিন্তু এতটাই strong মা যে তুমি চলে যেতে বাধ্য হলে?... বাড়ি ফেরার ইচ্ছেটাই থাকল না?... যদি খুব চাইতে ফিরতে তাহলে হয়ত ফিরতে, না?... বলতে না তুমি, যে ও তো একবারও বলে না যে তুমি ভালো থাকবে?... সেই সেটাই হল মা ... আমি ওকে ছাড়তে পারিনি, ওলি ছোট বলে পারবও না, কিন্তু তাই বলে আমি ভুলেও যাব না ... আমার লেখাই আমার প্রতিবাদ ... আমার পাহাড়-সম কষ্টের evidence... I will never ever forgive him till the last breath of my life... ও তোমাকে, ওকে, ওলিকে

নিয়ে এক সঙ্গে happily থাকতে দিল না... জীবনটা কেমন করে এমন হয়ে গেল মা ...

~

13th Jan

কাল জানতো Birhan 's Kolkata Literary Fest (BKLF) এ দেখি Poetry Paradigm এর রাজ্য poets-রা আছে... সুমতি দি, পীযূষ, মেহুল গোখলে, থেকে অনিমেষ ভট্টাচার্য, উষা নায়েক, মোটামুটি যতজনকে চিনি ...কিন্তু আমাকে কেউ বলেনি জান... আজকে এত humiliated লাগলো that I withdrew the Draupadi script... পৃথা দি (who's heads the poetry club) দেখছি লিখেছে কেন withdraw করলাম ... এখনও কিছু বলিনি... আজকে গাড়িতে চোখ ফেটে জল আসছিল... and I've decided that I'll leave the library and the WhatsApp group even though I have my subscription for the next one year... সম্মান নেই বলে তুমি তো পৃথিবী ছেড়েই চলে গেলে আর আমি একটা poetry library ছাড়তে পারব না?...

2. Dr Dashorathi

(Parshati got married very early. During college, she had a big crush on a senior boy, but by the time she got married, no one had said anything, and slowly her feelings had faded away. She wasn't even sure that he had similar feelings, though at times she felt that he did. She had another friend, Pratyay, whom we'll meet later, who adored her insanely and which she knew, but somehow she never felt anything as strong and reciprocal. There have been other fleeting brushes with love, but both because she has been very serious with her studies and jobs, and because she got married very early, men usually maintained a decent distance, even when she caused their hearts to flutter. Some of her colleagues, fellow poets, and other acquaintances had visibly mushy feelings for her, but she never met anyone who would cause her heart to melt, till she met Dr Dashorathi, that is.

After they moved back to Calcutta, having stayed abroad and in other parts of India for almost more than a decade, they got acquainted with Dr Dashorathi. He was a senior official in the US embassy and somehow got acquainted with them during some visa issues during one of their travels abroad. Thereafter, he had come to know of Parshati's writings and had been an ardent admirer of her writings.

Usual conversations surrounding writings and books, and poems and life, however carried much deeper meanings for

Parshati. Though Dr Dashorathi was many years older to her, her feelings for him were unrestrained. She found in him a friend, a guide, and a well-wisher. She felt for him like she had never felt for anyone else before. And somehow her mother, as close as they were, perceived her deep feelings for him. He was the first person she wrote to after her ma was no more. These are some of Parshati's messages to Dr Dashorathi, after her mother was no more.

Dr Dashorathi was not a Bengali but because of his professional requirements being posted in Kolkata, he could read Bengali script.)

Dr Dashorathi,

Ma has rendered me completely workless you know… previously at home there was so much to do… recently it's been standing beside ma's bed or outside the ICU ward for long hours… talking to doctors, signing impossible consents and going over an unimaginable sequence of events in my mind, over and over again… and suddenly now, there's no work for me… I've become totally unnecessary and inessential… and the only feeling for these last couple of months has been one of ma and me being thrown into a deep pit and us being whiplashed…I could only hope and pray for mercy to one who has thrown us in there, to take us out of there as well…

অবশ্য আমার চাওয়া বা না চাওয়াতে কিছু যায় আসে না … it's been such a long, difficult and lonely journey… বড়ো কঠিন দীর্ঘ পথ… দুঃখ কষ্ট অত বুঝি না জানেন কিন্তু নিঃশ্বাসটা মনে হয়ে আটকে যাবে… চতুর্দিকে মনে হয় invisible unseen waves রয়েছে… হটাৎ করে ধাক্কা দিয়ে চলে যায়… you know the first part of a baby's body that gets formed in the womb is heart… and it's almost so physically painful to know that the heart that pumped blood into mine, has stopped… the umbilical cord that held me in place has turned to ashes…

A couple of days ago you know I was completely sleepless… till about the wee hours of dawn… but closing my eyes seemed to transport me to a kind of trance… like I was not awake yet fully thinking and perceiving… or the opposite maybe… like I was awake with eyes closed… and wasn't actually thinking or perceiving… whatever it was there was just one image that was with me… yours… it was strange because if possible I really would have wanted to think about baba or ma or the foragers moving through forests*… but no, all I did think about was you…

And whatever had happened would be past… would be memories… whatever is yet to happen would be future… would be imagination… but what if memories and imagination coalesce into something new…

I don't remember what exactly I thought about you… even back then I didn't know… quite like how people perceive Gods I guess… no one knows whether they see God sitting or standing or talking or walking… they just perceive his presence I guess… You were there pretty much the same way…

And you know honestly, ভালো মেয়ে হওয়ার চেষ্টা করেছি…পারিনি… মন্দ মেয়েও হতে পারিনি… and in the middle of the two, I have remained suspended… অত্যন্ত সাধারণ ও সামান্য… and so those hours of the night seemed all the more so extraordinary… like

I was undergoing some extraordinary transformation… it felt so strange…

(*Parshati was reading Sapiens by Yuval Noah Harari, and Dr Dashorathi knew about it. This was an allusion to our foraging ancestors, after Sapiens.)

❧

You know in our first flat… the 430 square feet one… our immediate next door neighbor was a spinster… she worked in ONGC in some high post… and was a Brahma Kumari*… I do not remember much but that she wore long full sleeve white blouses and fully white sarees and sometimes on weekends she had these gatherings where many such women used to come… she wasn't good-looking in the conventional sense but had a way about her that made others feel inferior to her I thought…

And I vaguely remember she once described what life was… first she had ruled out what it wasn't… like it wasn't in the hand or leg etc… if you hypothetically drew an axis from the head to toe, right through the centre of your body vertically and another one right through your ear holes horizontally … where these two lines intersect is exactly the point where life lies… I felt very strange hearing this at that very young age… I still feel strange… well, that was my only brush with Brahma Kumaris… just wanted to tell you what I recalled…

(*On a particular occasion, Dr Dashorathi had mentioned that Brahma Kumaris visited him. This was what Parshati wrote sometimes after that.)

❧

You know meeting you is like Durga Puja… the puja actually is quite short, but think of the days and months that go into thinking about it, preparing for it, dwelling in its happiness and joy…

Meeting you is just like that… it hardly lasts for a few moments (that's what it seems) but thinking about it fills up days and weeks together… in fact meeting you saddens me in a way because I know it's going to end soon… and then it's going to be an arduous uphill wait… just like the coming of the pujas is… when it's here, it ends so soon… so I don't know when and how we'll meet but let me just dwell in the coming of it…

~

আপনাকে সুন্দর দেখতে জানতাম but yesterday* it was like god had painted you in the colours of my heart's desires… and how did you become slightly sunburnt, a bit tanned, a little wheatish, a little dusky?… like you've been out in the sun or on the beach… and that is exactly how you looked so much what I like so much… not that I'd like you any more or less given your appearance… you would have mesmerized me even in a shabby shirt… which you'd never wear because the fact that you're wearing it would make it look so grand… but honestly I am absolutely immersed in you… and don't see any hope coming out soon… I slept and woke up with only you in mind…

In fact maybe that was the reason I was going away to make this and that… so I could turn away from you and my eyes don't give away all my thoughts… and maybe I wanted to go to the terrace too because of that… so I could feel at home perceiving you… in the warmth and shelter that darkness provides… without any of the usual world around… and somehow I feel nearer to dear ones without any obstruction of material surroundings that otherwise bind us… like I can come out of my body and float around… only the infinite sky sees… and guards… and witnesses… this poem's for you…

Red

You dripped red

I dripped red

The night sky dripped red

Your wore my heart

All over you

Dripping with love

Dripping with me

Dripping with stretches

Of lost time

Dripping with yearnings

Of unwritten poetry

Dripping with the warmth

Of a darkness that knows

How to uncover me

How to shed off my body

And let me float out of it

So I could feel you

And touch you

From a distance
And feel the redness
Spread on an infinite sky
Like a carpet spread out
To hold us together
Bodiless and endless
So I could ride its chariot
Like a queen
With you beside me
A king, a god
My king, my god
And we could cruise over time
And space
And destinies
And in our timeless times
And borderless boundaries
Night smiles
Guards and witnesses
And blesses perhaps
The souls
Steeped in red
Racing towards
A hidden moon…

(*Parshati wrote that after Dr Dashorathi had come to visit them one evening.)

I understand that it can be very hard verbalizing thoughts and feelings… even painful at times… so I am especially sorry for insisting about it earlier… it's fine… I understand… I understand that you feel very deeply for me… and honestly there were other aspects in the story* (which you mistakenly thought had us) which could have hurt you (other than what you explicitly spoke about… my daughter)…

Much before you even started speaking to me, I somehow felt that the cold indifference you sometimes showed towards me wasn't actually true… couldn't be true… and then you told about giving up on wearing watches because you lost the watch your grandfather gave you… you know I never needed any proof about you, but nevertheless it spoke so much about the person you really are…

And you feel so deeply for me that you gave up on possibly the most definitive lucrative academic job offer** because it meant you'd be leaving me behind which would make me suffer… and the deeper you felt the lesser you wrote to me or refrained from expressing anything whatsoever… like the ocean being the stillest and calmest where it's the deepest…

And I also know that you feel with me and are with me on all the lines of my poems… surfing waves or plunging oceans… and I am grateful to you for everything you are…

And I also understand that we are social beings... and operate within the constraints of society... I would probably have been with you right now, had it not been so...

Yesterday you know, the whole time I felt like running up to ma, burying my face in her and crying... I couldn't understand why... missing her is like a volcano you know... it's mostly dormant... but sometimes it erupts and there is no holding back then...

And I can't really pinpoint why it would do so right after we talked but it did... you've always been so deeply entrenched in me that I have never been able to speak to her about you... but she always knows everything...

(*Parshati had published a short story which she thought Dr Dashorathi didn't exactly like and approve of.)

(**Dr Dashorathi had an academic job offer from a place abroad which however, he didn't accept.)

⁂

Even if I said I share everything, it wasn't meant to be literal you know... only in essence... but you knew that... that I couldn't share 'you', with ma... and I couldn't share 'you', with you... but it was something that I thought spoke of my composure and restraint, control and painstakingness... something that I have kept myself from expressing even having felt it every moment from the first time I saw you... something that kept me awake nights together... something that made me breathless and soaring... yet I haven't spoken about it... not in clear terms that is... but never vaguely enough for you not to understand... just because no good would ever come of speaking about it… আপনি তো আর পক্ষীরাজ ঘোড়া ছুটিয়ে এসে আমায় উদ্ধার করছেন না… করবেন কি?… তবে বলবো…

So keeping on telling me that I didn't share everything (even if I said so), in spite of knowing, what I didn't share, why I didn't share… and knowing all that I do share, all that happened in the past and all that happens now… was like keeping on pointing to the smallest black speck on an otherwise white paper… like telling the moon that it has scars even if it thinks it's spotless, like telling me I'm dark-skinned even when I want to forget my complexion… and you know how it felt, it felt like I had no right asking you such a question (like what I meant to you) and so you had every right to be cruel and taunting… কেন এতো আঘাত করলেন?…

(This was one of the many rather vague conversations that they often had. Dr Dashorathi was married, so was Parshati, and she was never quite certain as to his feelings for her. He was always most kind, respectful and also perhaps, diplomatic towards her. She tried asking him how he felt towards her. He also asked her whether she's been totally truthful with him and so on, but it was an endless spiral of sweet nothings and no one got anything out of anyone. But Parshati was perfectly happy to have him as her closest friend. She knew love was painful, but she didn't know it could be this painful, the way it would turn out to be.)

(Parshati thought of writing this, but never actually could.)

আপনাকে কী যে ভালোবাসি … অথচ এই কথাটা আজ অবধি বলে উঠতে পারিনি … কিন্তু রবীন্দ্রনাথের শেষের কবিতাতে আছে "উহ্য ছিল কিন্তু গোপন ছিল

না”... আমার মনের কথাটাও উহ্য ছিল হয়ত কিন্তু গোপন ছিল না ... বললে প্রেমের মাধুর্য্য কমে যায় কি?

‘ভালোবাসেন আমায় কিনা’ এ কথাটা কোনোদিন জিজ্ঞেস করতে পারিনি ... যদি ‘না’ বলেন ... সেটা সহ্য করতে পারব না ...

3. The Beginning of the Exit

Parshati was in some admission committee and she had already informed the Chair of the committee, who hasn't been very nice to her on earlier occasions, that she'd be out of station for a while and would grade the admission exam scripts after she got back.

She had been to Chennai the week before to get her ma to see a famous nephrologist in Chennai, and got back on 29th May Sunday. The Chennai trip, as medical consultations here usually are, was extremely taxing, both physically and psychologically. There were unending queues at the doctor's chamber, and the test labs, and not being local, they had to hire cabs or cars and since her mother was not well, and couldn't walk so much, she had to use a wheelchair that Parshati mostly manoeuvred.

After the first day, and after the blood sample was drawn, she didn't want to get the USG and other tests done there, and so she stayed back at the hotel and Parshati went to collect the report and see the doctor. And all the while her ma looked so unwell.

They had booked two interconnected rooms in Marriott, and they kept the door in-between open. Her mother often called her, even during the night, and she really was very unwell lately - she couldn't walk properly because of swollen feet, she couldn't eat properly because nothing would get digested, she couldn't sleep properly because of breathing distress, and so on. After years of fighting diabetes, her kidneys were now dysfunctional and though nephrologists had not prescribed dialysis yet, her ma feared that they might be inevitable.

They came back to Calcutta and she graded her admission exam scripts for the next couple of days. Parshati came back from office on 2nd June having finished her grading work and looking forward to relaxing a bit.

Usually she called up ma when she started from her office. Sometimes ma used to call her and ask her where she was, and sometimes if her ma wanted to sleep for a while, she'd switch off the phone after calling Parshati.

But somehow on that day, her ma was feeling so unwell that she didn't even call Parshati before switching off the phone.

Parshati came back from office, and had some snacks. Usually whenever Parshati returned from office and had something, her ma would sit there at the dining table, even when she was not well, and would talk to her, gossip with her about all that happened during the day, and ask her about what all happened in her office and so on. They loved talking to each other.

Today however, when Parshati returned and had something, her mother was still lying down. Later on her ma said that she didn't have anything herself and had some মুড়ি... then Parshati changed, washed the face as usual, and came down and sat on the sofa downstairs, and her ma also sat on the sofa, in their usual places, with Oli beside Parshati, and they switched on the TV to see some evening serial.

It was then that Parshati noticed that her ma's breathing seemed to be exceptionally laboured. Visibly laboured. Like with every breath her chest and belly seem to be heaving upwards and then downwards with a lot of effort. She somehow felt something really was wrong and checked the oxygen level with the oximeter they had at home. It showed 87.

They immediately called their chauffeur, got a portable oxygen cylinder, and took her to the nearest nursing home. To cut a long story short, they couldn't find any available emergency bed in what they believed was the best hospital, so they took her to what they believed was the second best - AMRI Salt Lake. And by around 1 in the night she was admitted to ICU, and put on HFNC (High Flow Nasal Cannula), which essentially supplies oxygen much forcefully through the nose.

(When her ma was no more, Parshati had written a brief note on her ma's struggles during the final two and a half months of hospitalisation, from which she never returned - mostly for her ma's students, colleagues and friends, whom she wasn't able to update regularly. Here's part of the note. Parshati's ma was a professor of Sanskrit, author and scholar and had a rich academic presence spanning over four decades. Naturally she had a significant presence in her own circles of academia. Moreover she was a very affable woman, easily befriending all who came in touch with her, young and old.)

6th June Monday

The doctors at the hospital never sounded very confident about the diagnosis and her breathing distress kept on increasing. So on 6th June, Monday, after four days of being admitted, when an ICU bed became available in the 'best' hospital (Apollo), we decided to shift her there. Ma, wasn't very keen, but I persuaded her and so on Monday 6th June, we arranged for ICU ambulance and shifted ma to Apollo ICU bed #295.

(Parshati's husband also seems to have some influence. He happens to be somewhat well-known in academic circles because of his scientific contributions, and one of his colleagues' cousin brother was a reputed pulmonologist in Apollo. Parshati probably hoped that this little bit of an acquaintance might bring her ma some more attention and kindness, from the attending doctor(s), who nowadays are notorious for their arrogance and high-handedness. Though, as it later turned out, her hopes were completely dashed, over the next two and a half months, beginning the very next morning.)

While in the ambulance and because of endless delays, once ma, gasping and breathless in spite of full oxygen support, said "এই কি তবে শেষ, মা?..."... The end came. Not there in the ambulance that night, but it was the precursor, alright.

On 7th June, Tuesday, morning, her pulmonologist, while showing me the plate of her CT scan (as if I'd read and understand the plate) said that her kidneys weren't functioning well and because of that there was fluid accumulation inside the body, including in lungs, causing pneumonia. That two-thirds of her lungs were 'consolidated' (means the lungs couldn't 'breathe') and kidneys were shutting down because of the lung infection. He concluded by saying "এই patient আর কতদিন টানবে?"

In a way, the blow was given, the jolt struck. My mother, who walked into the hospital a few days earlier with breathing distress, will probably not be here anymore. And the matter-of-fact manner in which the news was delivered was no less of a jolt - here a doctor, who has been helplessly called upon to cure the disease of an elderly woman, was delivering the death sentence of a mother to a daughter, and there wasn't a trace of kindness and sympathy. And in a way, I am rather sceptical of exactly how grave the situation was, given we had been to Apollo Chennai the week before to consult a renowned nephrologist who we used to video consult earlier. He had examined my mother physically with a stethoscope but said no such thing. Even doctors at the previous hospital never sounded this pessimistic and hopeless.

In the afternoon the next day, they called a 'board meeting' in the room of the Medical Superintendent in the presence of the Medical Superintendent himself, his assistant Superintendent doctor, her treating pulmonologist, his junior assistant, ICU in charge, and nephrologist. All of them surrounded me and like I was someone who would not understand English, I was explained how 'multi' means 'more than one' and since my mother's lungs and kidneys were affected, she is having 'multi-organ' failure and at this age, given her diabetes (which means she is 'immuno-compromised', her immunity is nil) chances of her recovery seems rather bleak. The junior doctor acted more like a note-taker and it was his duty to meticulously write out what his 'Sir' said and get it signed from me which he did.

12:30 am 26th August (midnight)

It's exactly two weeks ma passed away. I had left the hospital around this time like I usually did. Today somehow none of the usual doctors had their duty in the ICU in which ma was admitted. They had sounded exceptionally grave. She was bleeding profusely for the last few days. Something in her gastrointestinal tract was bleeding. At some point they said, it was duodenal cancer. But then they said, it wasn't. They did bedside endoscopy and colonoscopy at least three times but could not detect the source of rupture. Then they took her (in spite of being on ventilation) to the main gastroenterology department which was in another building. And every time I was following her. Then Dr Srivastav, the head of the department, would call me and show me the smooth pulsating tissues on the screen saying how he has very skilfully closed the bleeding parts. But just about after a while she would start bleeding again. Blood instead of stool. So her whole bed sheet would be soaked in deep, red, chocolate-like brown blood. She required some 50 units of blood within a couple of days. And she looked exceptionally sick the last few days.

Like always, I used to keep my mobile right beside my pillow. And after coming back from the hospital at night, I used to write to the nurse on duty to just make sure ma was fine. And then I used to wait for the few hours in the night till I could go back to her bedside again in the morning. In any case nowadays, she wasn't her usual state. It was a strange ma. She neither seemed to be fully here, nor did she seem to be entirely gone. It was like she was vaguely aware of a few things around but mostly unaware of the others, like she didn't know where she was, what was happening to her, who were those people around her, but she somehow knew me. She somehow knew the love we felt for each other. That was possibly too strong to forget and be oblivious of, in spite of extreme physical pain, and even after losing all other mental faculties.

There were two intensive care units in the hospital - RITU (Intensive Respiratory Treatment Unit) 1 and RITU 2. Ma was admitted in bed #295 in RITU 2. Usually the doctors and nurses who were on duty in the RITUs changed but usually, for all these two and a half months that she's been admitted in this hospital, I noticed that broadly the set of doctors and nurses who were on duty in RITU 1 were mostly in RITU 1, similarly for 2. They often strolled in to chat with the doctors and nurses in the other RITU but their duties were mostly in the same place. I thought maybe they had some fixed preferences which were kept in mind while their duties were allocated by the higher authorities.

That night somehow the entire set of people who are usually in RITU 2 was changed. When I left for the night, I usually spoke with the doctor in charge of RITU 2, many of whom I had come to know, I spoke with the nurse on duty whom I also knew usually. This particular night however, everyone on duty was new.

When I approached the doctor, he shook his head very gravely, while writing something, talking to someone else, about some other patient, and said something like, "খুব খারাপ অবস্থা, বুঝতেই তো পারছেন"। Ma always used to feel a lot of nausea. And she suddenly puked out a lot of... what looked like a brownish watery substance... seemed like a lot of old blood that has now turned brown and mixed in some soapy water... It felt horrifying... and I probably literally thought how unbearable ma's situation was becoming. She had the same vacant expression of resignation and hopelessness. I somehow knew the battle couldn't be won by us, by her.

I probably had just dozed off when I got the call in the wee hours of the morning. "Please come", the voice had said. I knew right then that ma was no more. It was kind of a relief maybe. Her suffering was becoming unbearable to see. But still I could not say, it was okay not to have ma here. I desperately wished she would get better, but when I saw that she wasn't getting any better, I still could not wish for her to leave me. Ma often used to say, looking helplessly and pleading with me, "এবার ছেড়ে দে, মা... যেতে দে... আর কষ্ট সহ্য করতে পারছি না..."

Now that I think about it - কষ্ট তো ছিলই... the imminent possibility that ma may no longer be with me... but the fact that she couldn't talk to me for the last two and a half months was possibly the biggest psychological torture (after a few days on ventilation, tracheostomy was performed, which meant she could not speak anymore, even when she regained back her consciousness)... both for her and me...

And unlike in baba's time, with ma firmly beside me when he passed, I wasn't able to say 'মা চলে যাক'... আমার বলাতে কিছু গেল এলো না যদিও... ma did not return...

4. প্রত্যয়

Pratyay was Parshati's classmate during tuition in high school. Thereafter, they hadn't been in touch with each other for nearly two decades. The last time they met was after Parshati's marriage, some twenty years back. Thereafter, he had searched her but couldn't locate her, given she was not on social media etc. Recently he managed to get her contact and called her while Parshati's mother was admitted in ICU. He was based in another city of India, and by the time he finally came to Calcutta, her mother had passed away.

So somehow the timing of Pratyay's return in her life was not propitious, to say the least. Parshati felt lonely and desolate and her mother's absence created a vacuum in her life that wasn't meant to be easily fulfilled. She struggled with an all-pervading depression wherein her only desire seemed to be to be able to shut herself up and to have nothing to do with the outside world. When she woke up in the morning, she felt she didn't have the strength to lift herself up. Even as she laid down, she felt she was so weak, she couldn't even raise her hand. She didn't think grief could physically affect people this way.

She remembered that when her father was no more, she cried her eyes out every night. All her pillows had patches of her tears. This time though, when her ma was no more, she didn't cry that much. Had she become more mature to face grief, she wondered. Or maybe when her father was no more, the thought of how hurt her ma was, actually made her cry that much. The fact that her ma was suffering was just as painful. This time she was alone in her grief. No one felt the kind of pain she did. Last time it was hers and her ma's pains. This time it was her pain alone.

Somehow Pratyay seemed to have matured and grown older in years too. He insisted on meeting and in spite of Parshati's reluctance, they met at a Cafe Coffee Day. At the cafe, Pratyay just couldn't take his eyes off Parshati. He said she looked just like she had been twenty years ago - just as pretty. He described how crest-fallen he was when he heard about Parshati's marriage from a relative. He had come and congratulated her but all the while he was shattered inside. Thereafter he had concentrated on building his career, getting a job and so on.

At some point, after a few years, at the insistence of his parents, Pratyay had married. They have a daughter. But he really has no relation with his wife. The wife also guessed and knows that he really has only one woman in his life - Parshati. He has never really been able to, leave alone, forget her, even love her somewhat less. He was still deeply, madly in love with her - will be so forever.

Parshati felt somewhat guilty at the plight of Pratyay. She wished she could love him back. But too much has changed since in her life. She didn't know whether she loved her husband or not - these things don't matter. They never mattered, at least after twenty years of marriage. But she didn't have the heart to be disloyal to him. She only wished her husband would be nice to her ma. Pratyay definitely would be. Maybe if she married him twenty years ago, ma would still have been here. She shuddered and closed her eyes.

She did not wish to give the space Pratyay wanted in her life - not now. She felt too weak, too lonely, too wrecked after her ma's loss to be involved in this kind of an affair. Pratyay was a very good friend and she knew he always will be. But that's all. Extramarital love was never meant for weak-hearted people like her. She wanted to have Pratyay in her life as a friend, wanted him to come over to her house with his family. But he wanted to be more intimately related to her. Wanted to meet her alone instead of bringing his family over. But she was too engrossed in Oli and her family to want that kind of interaction.

While Parshati was waiting for her car in the basement of the mall, she somehow felt he stood a little closer than he had to. When the bus, on which he'd board, came, he touched her shoulders, a tad bit longer than was probably required to say goodbye. He endlessly messaged on WhatsApp when he went back and sent the lyrics of a popular love song:

A Thousand Years (by Christina Perri)

The day we met,

Frozen I held my breath

Right from the start

I knew that I'd found a home for my heart

Beats fast

Colors and promises
How to be brave?
How can I love when I'm afraid to fall
But watching you stand alone?
All of my doubt suddenly goes away somehow
One step closer
I have died everyday waiting for you
Darling don't be afraid I have loved you
For a thousand years
I'll love you for a thousand more
Time stands still
Beauty in all she is
I will be brave
I will not let anything take away
What's standing in front of me
Every breath
Every hour has come to this
One step closer
I have died everyday waiting for you
Darling don't be afraid I have loved you
For a thousand years
I'll love you for a thousand more
And all along I believed I would find you
Time has brought your heart to me

I have loved you for a thousand years
I'll love you for a thousand more
I'll love you for a thousand more
Ohh
One step closer
I have died everyday waiting for you
Darling don't be afraid I have loved you
For a thousand years
I'll love you for a thousand more
And all along I believed I would find you
Time has brought your heart to me
I have loved you for a thousand years
I'll love you for a thousand more.

Parshati was no Kamala Das. Could never be. That evening she read her favourite poems of Kamala Das again.

Mortal Love (by Kamala Das)

Fidelity in love
is only for the immortals,
the wanton Gods who sport in their
secret heavens and feel
no fatigue. For you
and me, life is too short
for absolute bliss and much too long
alas, for constancy.

A Journey with No Return (Kamala Das)

Desire swims as a dolphin does
In the rivers of my blood tonight,
desire sports as a dolphin does
with sudden leaps and lurches.
My limbs are tense with embarrassment,
I am ashamed to raise my face to yours.
I long to put aside my sacred vows
and long to forget the sweet domestic past.
With an amnesiac's level gaze I shall walk
by this scorching love made new...
There are only two furlongs to reach your home
but it would be a journey with no return,
for the fire that I bear to warm your bed tonight
would burn down the ramparts of my home.

"She confronts and critiques the male figures, the father, the husband and the lover for her 'unloved' self but also desires to fulfil herself through their love. She invokes Krishna her mythical lover, with his infidelities, who is beloved by Radha, an older married woman. ... stranger paradox posed here [in her novella about a child prostitute] is the failure to 'wed' the real love to the mythical in a humdrum life which lacks it.

While Kamala Das's affinities to Meera's love-ethic are apparent, what she felt was lacking in Meera's 'uninhibited' celebration of her sublimated love was,..., 'the body, the physicality', the here and now: 'What happens to a woman, when a man becomes her god, her living god? Has she no right to write about that god?' "

(These lines are in the Introduction to Kamala Das's 'Selected Poems' by Devindra Kohli.)

But somehow they never gave her the strength she needed. Pratyay remained in her life with his promise and unwavering loyalty, friendship and love.

Pratyay wrote again "মনে পড়ে বইমেলাতে তুই শাড়ী পরেছিলি? তোকে শাড়ী পড়লে যে কি ভালো লাগে যে কি বলি..." He sent a deep red-coloured saree for her. He said he had never gone and bought sarees before. And hoped she'd like it. It was printed with rhinoceros. She had never seen a saree printed with rhinoceros but she liked it... she got the blouse made... and wore it (she wore it the day Dr. Dashorathi came).

After few months he even took a transfer and settled in Kolkata. He would WhatsApp her occasionally, saying things like, 'he sees her profile photo on WhatsApp every night and falls asleep'... 'he is alive because of her friendship'... 'often he had thought of ending his life... but just finding her once more... talking to her once more...kept him going'... 'he waited for years and decades just to be able to see his love again'... 'he knows that he will never be able to have her as closely and intimately as he desires, yet she is the reason he wants to be alive - even after twenty years and knowing fully well that she will never be his'...

Pratyay is a kind of emotional wonder - how much can you love someone to be so steadfast for decades?... Parshati had read about such love in books, but had never seen a person like this in her real life or heard of such devotion - yet here he was - as real as he could be, as real as she was. And she perhaps felt a pang of pain deep within that she couldn't return his love the way he wanted her to, even remotely, even a little bit.

But she did not deceive him for one moment - did not play around with his emotions for one moment - did not pretend that she loved him the way he loved her. She knew she was immensely lucky to have such an eternal lover - and she loved him as her friend - always would.

5. Ventilation

10th June Friday

On 10th June morning, Parshati's ma looked a little better to Parshati when she visited her in the ICU, and she was almost hoping that her doctors would say something good too, but as it turned out, they sounded even more grim.

The junior pulmonologist wrote and made Parshati sign this:

"10th June, 10 am

The daughter of the patient has been updated at the bedside that the condition of the patient has worsened and that the oxygenation and renal function/urine output have both deteriorated. She has been counselled to give consent for incubation and ventilation."

The senior doctor then came and dictated this to the younger ones, which Parshati signed again. It was basically what the junior doctor had already said, but now packaged much more professionally, like how lies must be.

"- 10th June 10 am

- Dr Aloke Dasgupta, Pulmo

- The daughter has been clearly explained the requirements for ventilation, and the pros and cons of putting the patient on the ventilator.

- She has also been clearly explained that it is not our intention to put the patient on ventilator only because she is deteriorating.

- Every patient cannot recover from the situation which the patient is in, and in spite of keeping the patient on the ventilator, she may not improve and may deteriorate even further in spite of our best intentions.

- She has been assured that her mother will be sedated so that we can do the incubation in a humane manner and that she will feel no pain.

- Signed (Dr R Dutta)"

Well, no matter how Parshati found her mother, the doctors seemed all ready for putting ma on ventilation. Later on, during the next almost two months, she saw family members of quite a few critically ill patients all of whom, having prior experience themselves or having gathered enough information from others, put their foot down and refused to put their patients on ventilation. The patients remained critical for a while but then gradually improved. But her ma being admitted for only about a week, Parshati could not know this.

During those days, their routine was something like this: Parshati would get Oli ready for school and her husband would go to drop her off. Parshati would then go to the hospital (in their chauffeur-driven car) and be there the entire morning. She'd reach around 8 or so and stand outside in the corridor.

Her ma's treating doctors would come around 9:30/10 or so, and would meet Parshati briefly updating her on her ma's condition. These short meetings literally became a nightmare and a mental torture for Parshati. Because most of the days they would just tell her that her ma would not get better. And that went on for days together, for almost about two and a half months.

On this particular day (the day the doctors got the consent forms for putting her ma on ventilation signed by her), Parshati had just returned home for a few hours in the afternoon (for the quickest possible shower and lunch), when her phone rang and the doctors asked her to come immediately because they would be putting her ma on ventilation.

Her husband drove her. And Parshati thought this was the last time she was seeing ma. Earlier she had asked the junior doctor if there was any chance her ma would recover and come back from ventilation or was it just supposed to mean that she'll not see her again? Dr Dutta, in his characteristic diplomatic way that doctors usually respond in, said something like 'honestly we don't know… my wife was herself on ventilation during Covid… some people do come back from ventilation… but some people don't… given your mother's age, that she has co-morbidities [she was diabetic]… it's difficult… but not impossible… so let's hope for the best…'… typical statements averting all responsibilities for undesirable consequences…

Her ma seemed breathless and gasping, and Parshati clasped her hand as tightly as she could, making space in between channels and tubes, and told her they were going to put her to sleep for a while… "মা তোমার খুব কষ্ট হচ্ছে তো, তাই ডাক্তারবাবুরা তোমাকে একটু ঘুম পাড়িয়ে দেবে…"… Her ma probably believed her and said something like, "আচ্ছা মা… তাই ভালো…"… and both of them had tears rolling down their eyes as a final farewell perhaps.

If you did not belong to the medical profession and if you did not have to worry about your near ones, and if you could still manage to be inside an ICU when someone was being 'incubated' (the medical term for someone being put on ventilation), you would almost think that something celebratory was going on. Almost every doctor and nurse available on the floor would converge around the patient (who would often already be unconscious). They would draw the curtains to enclose that particular bed and after what would seem like a lot of noise and confusion, would emerge jubilant having ventilated the patient (who would more often than not, not come out of it again).

There was a small room right across RITU 2, which was used as an office of Dr Alam, a medical emergency doctor, and who usually met medical representatives in that room, in the afternoon sometimes. They called it a 'counselling room'. It had a small sofa, two chairs and a table.

Parshati, having a little acquaintance of Dr Dasgupta through her husband, was allowed to sit on the sofa of that room, where Dr Dasgupta, after seeing her mother would meet her and update her. To Parshati however, these regular visits, with expected sprinkles of how hopeless the situation was, became quite a mental torture. With no one in the family to share her woes, she almost became paranoid of the room itself.

When they hurried Parshati out of RITU 2 to put her ma on ventilation, she and her husband waited in that small room of Dr Alam's. Dr Alam himself was amongst the little congregation of medical professionals that had gathered around her ma's bed to incubate her. And when the doctors came out satisfied, and Parshati was allowed in, she saw a small tube stuck in her mother's mouth, and she appeared to be sleeping otherwise.

Earlier, Parshati had just kept asking the doctors and pleading with them to ensure that her ma doesn't feel any pain when this whole thing happens. She knew she would probably not see her alive again. At least they should let her leave this world painlessly.

They assured her that they will put her to sleep first and then carry on the procedure. As it happened, against all odds and everything that the doctors predicted, her ma came back to consciousness, and out of ventilation, and even though she could not speak, she could write bits of words that Parshati, often would understand with a great deal of effort. And in fact, one of the things that she said after 'coming back' was "কী নৃশংস অত্যাচার জানিস... মুখের মধ্যে একটা এত্ত বড়ো tube ঢুকিয়ে দিল"... so she wasn't unconscious after all when they ventilated her... and actually it turned out that this was just the beginning of a series of unexpected and unforeseen jolts.

That night, when Parshati was standing beside her mother's bed, and touched her closed eyelids once, a drop of tear rolled down... as if her mother knew she was there... as if she could feel her hand on her face... as if she wanted to come to her, but couldn't... as if that one drop of tear was enough to hold all the pains and sufferings that the doctors had inflicted on her... and on seeing Parshati, her mother was just letting her know of it... conveying the pain that she has borne... that she has suffered just to be with Parshati again... that she still loved her so much that she doesn't want to leave her if she can...

What follows ventilation was just as new as ventilation was to Parshati. What happens after ventilation? A couple of days later, Dr Dasgupta came and announced, that 'as was the protocol' (how is any layman supposed to know what the protocol after ventilation is?), sedatives have been stopped and the patient should come back to consciousness... which her ma didn't. And none of the doctors ever said this before putting ma on ventilation. And this was just one of the shocks that were to follow.

On 13th Monday they said they would drain out fluids from both the lungs of her ma. On 15th Wednesday, in the small counselling room, Dr Dasgupta, and Dr Dutta, along with their retinue of junior doctors once more met Parshati and explained to her about EOL procedures. What they said was along these lines:

EOL stood for End of Life. EOL procedures mean that since her ma was not responding and showing any improvement in spite of 'optimal treatment', they recommended stopping all active treatment and just making sure her end would be 'painless'. So no more aggressive investigations (ventilator support can't be withdrawn because that is illegal in India), and she will just be cleaned, fed by Ryle's tube like now and her body treated with dignity till she is no more. Of course the decision was mine and I had to give my consent before they would start ma on it. I could only manage to ask, "when do you think we ought to start with EOL?" to which the doctor said, "had she been my family member, I would start right now"...

6. How It All Began

(The camaraderie between Parshati and Dr Dashorathi began over a book. After they got acquainted with each other, at some point, Dr Dashorathi gave her Paulo Coelho's The Alchemist. Parshati had not read it before. In fact, she had not been reading avidly for some years now after having become a mother and finding lesser and lesser time and opportunity to read. Neither did she find time to write like she did before. Her husband also was not a general reader and provided no impetus to her reading and writing.

The Alchemist somehow churned the dormant writer in her like never before, and coupled with Dr Dashorathi's kind and encouraging words about her writing skills, Parshati took to writing again. Here are some of the first messages they exchanged with each other.)

Dear Dr Dashorathi,

This is Parshati writing to you... Somehow the book you gave me touched so deep a cord that I am taking the liberty of writing to you - hope you don't mind too much....

In between office, meetings and usual household chores, I managed reading about 120 pages out of about 180 till now... No wonder it's one of your favourite books... Though the writing has a dreamy, fantasy-like flavour, much reminiscent of Rushdie's style, it is at the same time, much more down-to-earth and easily identifiable with the reality around us I guess, and hence the huge appeal... And the life-force that manifests in each one of us beckoning us to find and answer our true calling is definitely undeniable.... Really makes me stop and wonder how to best utilise the rest of my time here... I hadn't read Coelho before so thank you even more.... Just wanted to say that... Thanks so much!

With warmest regards,

Parshati

Dear Mrs Parshati,

Good to know that you find time to read 'general' books. It is hard to find people who like reading books especially in this age of internet and TV.

Do let me know your thoughts, once you are done reading the book. I have read almost all the books of Coelho but this one is the best. So you haven't missed a lot.

Any good book you have read recently? Books which force you to think are the books which make reading so much worthwhile.

Cheers !

Dear Dr Dashorathi,

... And, so you see, it's hard to find people you can talk about books with too...

Yeah, I finished reading it the very next day... You know, I am at an age when a lot of life is gone but a lot of it is still ahead....

and you know the most unsettling thing about this stage is that everything seems so settled.... but the book somehow ruffles a lot of thoughts and emotions that I find hard to settle... really fills me with pining for the impossible, fills me with a desire to live life all over again... somehow the little signs and omens become a little clearer and one wonders about how much courage does it take to leave the beaten track, the comforts of familiarity and the convenience of routine?....

I recently read Manu Pillai's Ivory Throne (chronicles about the princely state of Travancore) and before that Shaharyar Khan's Begums of Bhopal... I happen to be interested in history somewhat... not the facts and figures, but it really transports me to a different world at a different time and I like pondering about what might have gone through the minds of people then... So, for instance, I had this piece in The Statesman a while back which was a hypothetical conversation between Sikandar Begum of Bhopal (who sided with the British) and Rani Lakshmi Bai of Jhansi (who, as we all know, fought against them), on the eve of the Sepoy Mutiny...

It's not often that one gets to talk about thoughts that a book evokes... even rarer that they are heard... thanks so much for listening me out... and I'd love to read more Coelho.... the restlessness is addictive...

With warmest regards,

Parshati

P.S: Please call me 'Parshati'...

Dear Mrs. Parshati,

Good that you liked the message of the book. By your writing style it is not difficult to make out that you have a fiction writer in you which wants to come out of the closet. You must try your hand at writing. Who knows we would not have another J K Rowling! (Am sure you have watched her commencement speech... If not you can check it on YouTube Or easier still can ask me to send the link !)

So I gather you like books like the ones William Dalrymple has written? Is that an accurate description?

You really are an avid reader.. and I have to catch up on my reading so would close this mail here only.

Cheers !

❧

Dear Dr Dashorathi,

... The speech at the 2008 commencement at Harvard?... Just now heard it... Very honest and inspiring really!... But please send me links of other speeches that I might like to hear... I can assure you, I'd love them...

And you really think too highly of my potential... Of course, such magnanimity only befits someone like you (by the way, I shy away from openly praising you but that doesn't mean I don't feel it)... I was merely speaking my heart out - honestly and unabashedly... but if I do end up penning some of my thoughts one day, you will be a big part of the conspiracy of the Universe... somehow the nightly escapades with the Alchemist... with myself (...and with you listening to my thoughts over a few lines of email)... are quite enigmatic... You know, I used to spend long hours at night reading books... But somewhere along the way, the lack of understanding, appreciation and careless agreement to my deliberations have killed the zing... and I've reclined into a cocoon with my books, my music, my writings...

With warmest regards,

Parshati

Dear Mrs. Parshati,

I was referring to the same speech. She started writing at an age - in your words - "when a lot of life has already gone by and a lot of it is still ahead". So don't give up on your dreams, aspirations and desires. An ancient Greek philosopher, Epicurus, argued that the best life is the one that is as pleasant as it can be. Hence pursuing what you desire is great.

There are so many wonderful talks available... Don't know where to start from. One related to your field of education which comes to my mind is by Ken Robinson "do schools kill creativity?" Google it and you would locate it.

And your cocoon seems like a nice place with music, books and writings... But don't let melancholy enter the cocoon !

Cheers!

Dear Dr Dashorathi,

... You probably don't know how much your kind and encouraging words mean to me... Many years back, there used to be another girl named Parshati... she used to sing on radio, have dance performances on stage, have art exhibitions in the Academy of Fine Arts... but gradually she was made to understand that someone else's dreams were a little more important, that his priorities have to be attended to even if that means giving up on hers, that his recognitions were of greater value... like versatility was mediocrity and specialisation was genius... so there she was... alone with her dreams and fantasies... at the receiving end of expectations, responsibilities and duties... which gradually kept burying her deep down... your words somehow reach her...

... And you are as perceptive as you are astute... I try to ward off melancholy as much as I can but you see when conversations are just questions and answers, then the best of reasons - similarity of vocation, years of proximity or even a nice cocoon sometimes fail...

Ken Robinson is amazing!.. and I completely agree about how our yardsticks are miserable... and you see, much of Rowling's contention about job-oriented education (and therefore the discouragement for pursuing other passions) echos in Robinson's concerns as well... and for every ballet dancer and Rowling there are thousands of others (men and women but especially women I would say given our country) whose stories are never heard or written simply because they stopped dancing and writing or wasn't enough successful pursuing their dreams even if they did.... but I wouldn't blame education squarely for it...

I am sorry how my emails keep getting longer...

With warmest regards,

Parshati

ᘓᘐ

Dear Dr Dashorathi,

I had been to a Crossword store over the weekend and out of the books I got, there were a few of Coelho... I just finished reading "By the river Piedra I sat down and wept"... So just thinking aloud...

I am not devout at all... and the questions about whether God has a feminine face (this theme is very central to Dan Brown's The Da Vinci code too!), the conflicts between spiritual and romantic love are quite far from my heart... especially being born into a culture where the face of divinity is overwhelmingly feminine yet women in real life are far from honoured, they're rather esoteric for my taste...

But I did like the idea of letting the child in you flow freely... you know, while spending time with my daughter, her innocent questions and uninhibited stances often shame my adult self... my puerility is a protection, it is a privilege... and I really wish to preserve it... what were your thoughts on reading it?... do you remember?

And I understand that you had been through some pressure at work... it's amazing how you confront the "tiger" elements of the universe (William Blake's poem "The Tyger", misspelt this way, where the tiger represents the violent, ugly aspects of humanity and life) keeping the "lamb" element in your heart intact (all the beautiful and subtle things)... In fact, Blake's question, 'of whether the hand that created the "lamb" create the "tiger"?'... actually find an answer in people like you who can tame the "tiger" not in spite of the "lamb" but because of the "lamb" and using the "lamb" if I might add... you're just amazing!...

Have you read Ruskin Bond? Do you like him?

Warmest regards and cheers in return!

Parshati

Dear Mrs. Parshati,

Good to know that Coelho forced you to visit Crossword ! Which Crossword? The one which has now been renamed Story? Or the one at Salt Lake? We are planning to have a big library/bookstore (not very far from Oxford book store; to be exact at Rippon street) which should start functioning by Mahalaya (hopefully). It would have the same format as that of Oxford book store and other big stores.. books, reading space and a good cafe. Once it is open, and you are visiting Park Street, please do visit it.

Coming back to the book of Coelho... You write - "I am not devout at all'. It is not important to be devout but it is infinitely important to believe in something.

Your description of your 'conversations' with your daughter will put a smile on anyone's face. As they say, a child can be happy without reason, can be busy without business and can love without any expectations. These are the qualities adults need to learn from children.

Another celebrated writer's name crossed my mind when you quoted the famous poem of Blake and asked if it is the same hand which created lamb and tiger; if you have not already read, you can try reading 'The Prophet' by Khalil Gibran. It is an outstanding piece of work by another brilliant author.

And even if you don't like him… we would politely agree to disagree!

Cheers !

Dear Dr Dashorathi,

A very good morning!... I am sorry I may have sounded a little upset yesterday... And absolutely, agreement or disagreement, come what may, I would love to listen to you and talk to you... And nothing is quite fixed in life, and I feel ever ready to learn and evolve... I haven't read Gibran, will surely read the book...

Thanks so much for your invitation - I'll surely keep it in mind... though (other than for my daughter's school) it's quite occasional for us to visit that area... Great initiative and congratulations to your Department for it!...And no, I had only been to the City Centre 1 Crossword store in Salt Lake...

And you're right, my daughter fills up my days and thoughts like nothing before... As Wordsworth has said,

"A child, more than all other gifts,

That earth can offer to declining man,

Brings hope with it, and forward-looking thoughts."

With warmest regards,

Parshati

Dear Mrs Parshati,

....

I am not a fan of Ruskin bond. And copy pasting the poem on children by Khalil Gibran -

Your children are not your children.

They are the sons and daughters of Life's longing for itself.

They come through you but not from you,

And though they are with you yet they belong not to you.

You may give them your love but not your thoughts,

For they have their own thoughts.

You may house their bodies but not their souls,

For their souls dwell in the house of tomorrow, which you cannot visit, not even in your dreams.

You may strive to be like them, but seek not to make them like you.

For life goes not backward nor tarries with yesterday.

You are the bows from which your children as living arrows are sent forth.

The archer sees the mark upon the path of the infinite, and He bends you with His might that His arrows may go swift and far.

Let your bending in the archer's hand be for gladness;

For even as He loves the arrow that flies, so He loves also the bow that is stable.

Cheers !

Dear Dr Dashorathi,

I just finished "Veronika decides to die".... this was extremely close to heart... and I really dwell in this eccentric world of mine.... you know, I am a total misfit among relatives and cousins, my "friend" set is quite null... and I can hardly communicate with women of my age with the kind of things they talk about... just like "the stranger" of Albert Camus... I find everything so "absurd"... but I believe the problem lies with me.... not them....

...the Gibran poem about children is amazing!...

Thanks so much for your kind words... I really am touched and honoured... and I think you write very earnestly and persuasively... have you ever considered writing?

With warmest regards and cheers!

Dear Mrs Parshati,

I was very sorry to hear about the untimely death of your father. May God rest his soul in peace and give you strength to cope with such a huge personal loss.

I understand, such events do shake the foundations of our belief. Don't want to sound pedagogical but would refer you to an article of Arthur Ashe, a tennis legend, when he got infected with a terminal disease - one of his fans asked "why does God have to select you for such a bad disease? Why of all people you?"

He replied - "The world over — 50 million children start playing tennis, 5 million learn to play tennis,

500,000 learn professional tennis, 50,000 come to the circuit, 5000 reach the grand slam,

50 reach Wimbledon, 4 to semi final, 2 to the finals,

when I was holding a cup I never asked GOD 'Why me?'.

And today in pain I should not be asking GOD 'Why me?'"

Happiness keeps you Sweet,

Trials keep you Strong,

Sorrow keeps you Human,

Failure keeps you humble and Success keeps you glowing, but only Faith & Attitude Keeps you going.

Sometimes God tests you and you have to keep your faith even in the toughest of times. I am not sure these words would help you cope up with your loss... But that God smiles on you for sure is evident as He (or She depending upon which form of divinity you believe in) has blessed you with such a wonderful daughter!

How would the universe conspire to make your innermost desires come true if you do not believe in the Universe or believe in it shakily?

Was joking.... on a more serious note, you must go through the journey to rediscover your beliefs and am sure you would !

Dear Dr Dashorathi,

... this (the Arthur Ashe writing) is exactly what we had talked about at some point... you know, about three years before he was diagnosed, I happened to top the state of Orissa in the Higher Secondary examination (my father was posted there at that time and I did my HS from Ravenshaw College Cuttack) with some record marks... when the result came out, amidst the media and newspapers, you know, I had two realisations, first, that success doesn't sink in at all, it doesn't change the person in you one bit, the things you value and are dear are just the same... and second, I was scared... immensely scared,... precisely because (in statistical terms) I knew that the (underlying) "distribution" had a huge "dispersion"... we had just seen a big positive "realisation" but then there could be a big negative "draw" as well... and I repeatedly asked my parents and prayed silently... and you know, I didn't want "the Wimbledon" at all... I would be so much happier just being an ordinary girl... but of course, it wasn't in my hand to rank.... and it wasn't in my hand to let my father leave us....

Dear Mrs Parshati,

I would like to consider myself a science person rather than a literature person, so the idea of writing doesn't excite me. However, reading has its own thrills even for me. Good you liked Khalil Gibran.

And belated congratulations on your success in the HS exam! Which year was it? Coming first requires that special thing which very few of us have. So even by your own logic, one big positive is likely to occur... Hope it happens sooner than later !

Cheers

7. Coming Out of Ventilation… for Goodbye

(This is part of Parshati's note that she wrote venting out her grievances against the medical fraternity of the hospital, after her ma was no more. She continued as follows.)

"I remember, in spite of my grief, I was hit by how icily and easily the doctors could surround a daughter and speak of such things, barely a week after I brought my mother for treatment to get better. Later on, as these daily doses of unkindness were to continue for the next couple of months, I had once gathered the courage to say that they are just talking from a medical perspective while I was listening to all this from the perspective of a daughter about to lose a mother. And the reply was "we are trained to be non-emotional". My mother, being a professor of Sanskrit and having closely worked on Ayurveda and Charaka Samhita, would often talk about the defining characteristics of a good doctor. And compassion and kindness were uppermost amongst them. Strange that we were at the best hospital, under the treatment of the best possible doctors and yet basic human feelings were at such a premium. Somehow I did not sign the EOL consent.

As if to prove them wrong, and as if unable to bear such harshness on her daughter, ma started coming back to consciousness immediately from the day after the day when doctors suggested EOL, around 16th June, Thursday. So the next day doctors said they were putting EOL on hold since she was showing signs of response and would continue with her treatment. On 17th June her pulmonologist said he was going on leave for five days, his junior assistant would be the point of contact and that he will not even be available on phone. Also since it has been a week of being put on ventilation (which meant a tube was inserted through her mouth up to her lungs), this would injure her trachea and so they needed to do tracheostomy, so that she won't be able to talk. But that it wasn't permanent and she could talk again once the tracheostomy was closed. On 18th June they performed tracheostomy on her (which meant she was now breathing through the tube inserted in her throat, and the tube from her mouth was removed). Also she was started on dialysis in the meantime since her kidney function had worsened.

In spite of what the doctors said, ma kept on thoroughly improving. When her doctor returned after five days, she was markedly better than when he had left, but as usual, he only said something like 'there is no improvement from yesterday', not that 'there has been substantial improvement from five days back', not that 'she has proved us wrong, fought back from EOL, and come back to us', not that 'she has fought bravely, done very well, and we want to help her get well'.

Even though she could not speak when she was conscious again, she would try to write. And ma made every possible effort to get well - she would ask about her students, about Pursuits, her colleagues, my cousins and even about our chauffeur.

Later the junior doctors had said things like 'it was a miracle how she came back', 'only a few, if any at all, patients came back from how she was', 'she has travelled a long way from EOL", etc. Yet none of the senior consultants made any sustained effort to keep up this miracle.

They turned off her ventilator support abruptly on 26th June. Initially they said, they'd switch it off for a few hours, then keep increasing the hours till it's completely turned off, giving time to the lungs to breathe on its own again. However, no such thing was followed and I just found the ventilator switched off on Sunday 26th June, while she was requiring about 6 litres of oxygen per minute.

On Wednesday, 29th June, I asked her doctor about at least shifting her to HDU (High Dependency Unit), but he completely turned it down saying, "পাশের ward এ patient দের দেখেছেন - কিরম condition ওদের? আপনার মাকে দেখেছেন?" However, and most surprisingly, the very next day, June 30th, he said, the patient was ready for discharge from their end and we have to talk to the nephrologist about dialysis and other needs.

It was almost a month in ICU and ma and I were overjoyed at the prospect of going home. I arranged for full ICU arrangements at home, and waited to consult her nephrologist regarding dialysis. That afternoon, when her nephrologist came, I literally begged him to tell me of how we might continue her dialysis after discharge - where might we take her in an ambulance with oxygen support etc. All he said was "ধারে কাছে কোনো monitored bed এ নিয়ে যাবেন, কোনো nursing home, hospital এ... dialysis ছাড়া patient সাত দিনও survive করবে না ".

Strange, but why did he think I would keep ma without dialysis for seven days, when I knew she needed dialysis every two to three days? That ma was his patient, that he was responsible for her well-being didn't seem to be his concern at all. That we were discharging her meant she was solely our responsibility and he wouldn't even suggest a place for her dialysis after discharge.

She had her dialysis scheduled for that day, that continued way past midnight, till about 2:30 in the night, and we brought her home in the wee hours of the morning of July 1, Friday, thinking our ordeal would begin to get over, and ma would begin to recover. She used to get dialysis with a gap of every two to three days, so we knew her next dialysis was scheduled by Saturday, 2nd July or Sunday, 3rd July. We made an appointment with the nephrologist in charge of a nearby hospital and took her with oxygen support in the ambulance to see him.

This doctor said he was the classmate of her treating nephrologist during her earlier admission. He checked ma, and said there was no requirement of dialysis (took blood sample for measuring creatinine etc.) and sent us home. That evening I wrote an elaborate WhatsApp message to her treating nephrologist with a copy of the prescription of the nephrologist of the nearby hospital who didn't recommend dialysis, requesting his intervention or at least to have a word with him (his classmate) to assess ma's situation and decide on dialysis. His one-worded curt reply was 'ok' with no indication of whether they would give her dialysis or not and when, if at all. However, the next day, 4th July, Monday by evening, ma's breathing distress which was always there even after discharge, increased manifolds, she began desaturating (oxygen saturation began falling), and we had to rush her to the previous hospital's Emergency ward where she had to be put on ventilator support again.

This whole episode of suddenly being given a discharge by the pulmonologist (who refused to shift her to a less critical ward the day before), the nephrologist totally abstaining from extending any help with dialysis outside and coming back to the folds of the hospital within a couple of days, definitely doesn't speak very highly of the concern and care of the treating physicians.

While in Emergency she was given dialysis overnight and she seemed to be much better. Her scan the next day also showed improvement in her pneumonia patch in the lung. Thursday, 7th July she had her next dialysis. Thereafter, without any intimation, the treating nephrologist went on leave, which we discovered when we saw another senior nephrologist coming to see ma. As it turned out, around Sunday, when her dialysis usually became due, this new nephrologist wouldn't recommend dialysis and ma was visibly becoming restless. Her senses seem to be much worse and I tried to helplessly contact her original nephrologist to try and put in a word for her dialysis. He wouldn't receive calls and his only reply was "talk to the pulmonologist". All that the pulmonologist said was, "we cannot interfere with nephrology".

So it turned out that ma, caught between doctors, in spite of being very much admitted in the 'best' hospital (this time she wasn't discharged and brought home and taken to some other 'nearby' hospital), did not receive dialysis when she needed it and she kept getting worse and the senses deteriorated. They kept doing several other tests for brain etc., and by

Wednesday, which was almost a week after her last dialysis, her pulmonologist confirmed that her brain etc are fine and her distress seem to be related to 'metabolic encephalitis' (toxicity in the blood), and yet they are helpless about giving her dialysis, to which, helpless and desperate as I was, I proposed whether we can consult some other nephrologist, to which they agreed and thankfully the new nephrologist recommended her dialysis and she was given dialysis that same day and she started improving. Caught between nephrology and pulmonology, ma was denied a much-needed dialysis for almost a whole week, in spite of being admitted in the ICU of one of the 'best' hospitals. By whose fault? Someone must have been responsible for ma - who was it?

Ma's health teetered between slight improvement and worsening and her pulmonologist, on the days she would be a little better, would say things like, "আপনাদের রোগী তো ভালোই আছেন, কিন্তু বুঝতেই তো পারছেন there is no light at the end of the tunnel", or things like "দেখছেনই তো এক পা এগোচ্ছেন তো দু পা পেছোচ্ছেন".

During her short stay in the Emergency ward, I happened to hear the kind words of another very prominent doctor and I wished he would see ma once. I gathered up the courage and went to his chamber and my experience with him actually turned out to be the diametrically other end of the spectrum I had with the other physicians till then. An extremely busy doctor, where patients usually had waiting time of 3 to 4 hours for consultation with appointments taken months earlier, showed such kindness so as to talk to me in his chamber - without any prior appointment whatsoever.

He patiently listened to my whole plight and made some suggestions by calling some other physicians. When I thanked him, he politely replied "আপনি আমায় thanks কেন দিচ্ছেন আমি তো আপনার মা'র জন্য এখনো কিছুই করিনি", and on my request even went and saw ma, and suggested treatments. Ma's new nephrologist was also a very kind soul and he spoke of setting up a dialysis unit at home while thinking of discharging ma at some point in future. Both these doctors were like beacons of hope in a sea of hopelessness and unkindness. However, her treating pulmonologist did not take very kindly to advice from them and said things like "এদের উঁকি ঝুঁকি মারতে বারণ করবেন".

Well, to cut a long story short, ma was detected with a blood infection and her health condition steadily deteriorated. During her last few days, she started bleeding massively and in spite of four endoscopies, colonoscopy, CT etc., doctors couldn't identify the source of bleeding or stop it. She required about 50 units of blood within a few days and her haemoglobin had dropped to around 2. Her pulmonologist would say things like "এরম blood দিয়ে prop up করে আর কতদিন চলবে...". And he suggested EOL once more.

I requested him to please help me arrange for whatever ma needed at home - I would very much like to take her home and let her pass with us by her side. To which he replied, "এরম patient নিয়ে যাবেন কি করে, ventilation-এ, blood চলছে...".

The very next day though, he said we should take her home and let her pass peacefully. So I asked him how will I manage her blood requirement etc at home, to which he said something like "blood etc লাগবে না, শুধু নিয়ে গিয়ে বিছানায় ফেলে রাখবেন, চারিদিকে ঘিরে থাকবেন till she passes away". If I did bring her home this way, with none of the support that she needed, I would ensure that she passed away, wouldn't I?… It would be tantamount to killing her. Well, ma did not suffer too long after this and passed away in the wee hours the very next day.

For two months and ten days, she fought the most remarkable battle and for me, performed miraculously well. She could not eat, or speak, or move around, her body was completely covered with painful perforations of tubes and channels and it was hard to see her bear the unimaginable physical suffering. Yet she still managed to smile when she saw me and ask (by indications whenever she could) about her friends, students and colleagues.

Junior doctors, nurses, people in the administration all showed sympathy and kindness. But the person on whom we have all been banking the most did not have the heart to at least once say "আপনি ভালো হয়ে যাবেন". People hear of mental strength, emotional strength doing wonders - who knows whether my mother would have fought her battle better, would have lived for a few more days longer, if the doctors she depended on, whom she would eagerly look forward to meet, would have been a little more positive. Her hope and optimism in the face of utmost physical suffering hung on the response to "হ্যাঁ রে, ডাক্তার কি বললেন?", and the doctors did not have the heart to respond positively to her earnest desire to live.

My mother has been an erudite scholar and people in her domain of research lament of an irreparable loss to the world of oriental studies. There are condolence prayers and meetings in not only the universities she has served as a professor but also various other libraries and academic institutes, even outside the state. Her academic absence only compounds the sense of vacuum that confronts me, and adds fuel to the fire of the suffering that the unkind behaviour of some of the doctors had subjected us to. And possibly their unkindness itself turned out to be the self-fulfilling prophecy of ma being no more - had they been positive from the beginning, maybe ma would have fought better and maybe we would have looked at a brighter future - had they believed that there was light at the end of the tunnel, maybe there would be, who knows.

Ma's journey with us ended. I understand that it is hard taking decisions in life, especially in the medical profession where lives depend on it. But in ma's case, most of the decisions seem to be taken with a lot of false vanity and misplaced ego on the part of the doctors, that prevented them from reaching out to the patients and their close ones. Their behaviour should have been the fountain of hope and strength or at least comfort and solace, even if the outcome which happened ought to have happened, which may not be in the first place, had their attitude been more positive.

I have lost my father to lung cancer thirteen years back but the memory of the loss doesn't jar with this kind of cruel harshness. Ma was of course there with me, but even otherwise, the entire medical fraternity in that hospital seemed to be party to the loss, grieving with us in our loss, standing in solidarity with our feelings and lending us much needed sense of 'having done the best in the best possible way' for baba, so that there was no place for any regrets. In ma's case, we probably got the best possible treatment, medicine and facility-wise, but there's been a yawning distance as far as fulfilment of emotional and psychological support and motivation is concerned, both for the patient and her near ones."

8. Parshati's Pain

My husband hadn't been nice to my mother. In a way, this isn't an issue at all. But that depends, doesn't it? Everything is relative isn't it? To some maybe, this is the least important of all issues that one might have with husbands. To me though it was a big issue. The biggest issue. That mattered to ma and me. For her life and mine. Even if that makes me an outsider. And as Atticus says in To Kill a Mockingbird, one thing that doesn't abide by the democracy rule is a person's conscience. So even if the whole world were to tell me to ignore it, I wouldn't have, I couldn't have. To me, it is a choice between whether I even want to stay in this life of mine or not. Ma is no more and I couldn't avenge her pain in her life, neither can I do so now.

Somehow I have loved peace and dispensed with my own to buy it from others. In a way, I have been extremely selfish. I have avoided getting into nasty quarrels with him lest it hurts my daughter, hurts ma. But there was no one else who could have stood up for her. I could have but didn't. Ma of course would say so… that I shouldn't be quarrelling with him over any issue that concerns her… but even I didn't want to leave the comfort and cosiness of convenience which I was possibly calling 'peace' to appear noble… But I possibly wasn't… maybe all I cared about was myself… otherwise how could I have let ma literally bleed to her end…

Sometimes I think about what have I done to stop this slow torture that ma endured... like our brave doctor* suggested I should have asked him to stop, else... I didn't... I couldn't... usually I felt too tied up with niceties to rupture the artificial semblance of peace that quietude apparently brought. But all quiet is not peace. I was quiet but I wasn't at peace.

(*Parshati and her mother used to consult a doctor, who after many years of seeing both of them, had sympathetically understood Parshati's pain. She herself was a very bold woman, and told Parshati how she had divorced when she was fifty, and her son was in college. She tried to embolden Parshati into taking a decision regarding her husband, rather than mutely suffering the pain that he inflicts on both of them by his behaviour. But Parshati was much softer and delicate and emotionally attached to their daughter, and possibly even unconsciously, to him.

The only person she could open up to about such personal matters was Dr Dashorathi. Here are excerpts of her messages to him.)

... And what did I do about it?... literally nothing... I talked endlessly about it to ma... talked to you about it whenever I could... sometimes with great effort I could splutter something like "তুমি মাকে বললে না?" etc., that was only met with defiant arrogance and a turned-away look... something that was too unimportant to be answered...

Just once I could muster up the courage to write a letter to my mother-in-law* hoping but not expecting her to give some sane advice to my husband... but nothing came forth...

(*This letter is produced in Chapter 20 later.)

Usually when someone hits or injures or kills someone visibly, we call it a crime… how do we see hitting or injuring or killing someone with words or actions?… that doesn't leave any visible trace at all?…. no blood, no swelling, no cuts, nothing… but yet the person is just as much in pain and suffering… every time he didn't respond when ma spoke, every time he looked away when she spoke… every time he wouldn't offer to help when I am not around and ma is possibly making tea (and for her taking the cup, the tea bag, the water etc, putting in microwave etc. meant a great deal of effort… but that was very little effort for us…)… every time he just ignored her, he put a little bit of pain in her eyes… and all these little bits of pain after a point clouded all her vision and emotion… and filled up the sky of her mind… and where once there was only love for him, all I could perceive was pain… layers and layers of pain, accumulated from all his humiliations…

I couldn't even want him punished given he's my daughter's father and I couldn't wish any harm befall my daughter's parent… can I ever get any peace in this life?… probably not… simply because I couldn't give any peace to ma… even if I didn't actively do anything, actively not doing anything maybe is just as worse… just being a passive onlooker to the insults that he kept heaping on ma, not only bit and nibbled and ate her spirit away but also mine…so in a way I am equally to be blamed and punished for my utterly selfish behaviour of not doing anything at all… "অন্যায় যে করে আর অন্যায় যে সহে, তব ঘৃণা তারে যেন তৃণসম দহে"…

If I did, for example, ask for a divorce, would he have behaved better?… under the threat of divorce?… like the ultimatum our Dr asked me to serve him?… ma may have still been here…

Dr Dashorathi,

I am writing to you because there is no one else I'd rather write to. আমার ঝগড়া করার, অশান্তি করার শক্তি বা মানসিকতা, কোনোটাই নেই … আর আমি ক্লান্ত … নিজের সঙ্গে বোঝাপড়া করে ক্লান্ত … যে মা চলে যাওয়ার দশ দিনের মধ্যে আমার সঙ্গে ঝগড়া করতে পারে, তাকে কিছু বলার প্রবৃত্তি আমার নেই… তার অনবরত অভিনয়ে আমি ক্লান্ত … আগেও করত, এখনও করে … আমাকে ভালো রাখার অভিনয় … মা non-existent এই অভিনয় … আমাকেও অভিনয় করতে বাধ্য করে … যেন কিছুই হয়নি … এই অভিনয়ে আমি ক্লান্ত … আপনাকে বললে আপনি কষ্ট পাবেন জানি, yet I have to tell you…

You know crime দেখা গেলে তার punishment হয় … শুধু অপমান করা, খারাপ লাগানো, সেরম tangible crime নয় না তাই তার punishment ও হয় না … আমার দুটো classmate এর কথা মনে পড়ছে জানেন প্রিয়দর্শিনী aar চঞ্চলিনী…

You know out of all my classmates, only the two of them, Priyodorshini and Chanchalini are no more… On the surface, there were immediate physical causes, of course… but you know, if you were to tell me to guess which if any of my classmates, I thought, were to be the first ones to leave us, I would probably name Priyodorshini and Chanchalini…

Priyodorshini, rather ironically, was anything but pretty in the conventional sense. She was obese and dark, and being the only child of her parents, was also very pampered and rude in disposition. I was not in touch with any of them after I left school. Then after coming back to Kolkata, I learned that both her parents were no more and she herself was diabetic. She was married and had a son. However, soon I learned that she was very sick… her diabetes was uncontrolled… her husband has left her and she stays with her minor son... and then one day, she was no more...

Unlike Priyodorshini, Chanchalini was a close friend in school. She was about fourteen years younger to her elder sister who was already married and with a son, when Chanchalini was in school. Her parents were quite elderly, and she used to adore my mother. Whenever ma used to go to school to pick me up (which happened very occasionally), she used to come and snuggle her and say, "ইশ! কাকিমা যদি আমার মা হত!"...

Chanchalini wasn't pretty in the conventional sense, but her hair was very long and beautiful and she had very large and expressive eyes. I wasn't in touch with her regularly, but once when I came to India during my studies abroad, she said that she was in love with a teacher of hers in college, but he said he wouldn't marry her because "she was too thin"... her father was no more, and her mother was very worried and anxious to get her married...

Many years later I heard that she was married but was childless... and the next thing I heard was that she was no more...

In a way, apparently it was hugely shocking that two of my classmates were no more with us... how untimely, it seemed... what a waste of life, it seemed... but in a way, you know, it was not shocking at all... in a way, this would have been most expected... Priyodorshini and Chanchalini were perhaps two of my classmates, who were in some sense, the most neglected of all, the most unwanted, the most unloved, the most uncared for... especially the way their lives unfolded, who would have wanted them to live?...

So I really think people live, not because they want to, or maybe in small part because they want to… but for a large part because others want them to… because they feel loved and wanted and important and respected by near and dear ones… Priyodorshini and Chanchalini left us because they didn't feel loved and wanted enough by the others who surrounded them…

And I believe that is what happened with ma too…

আগে, জানেন, ওর মা কলকাতা এলে maybe একবার এই বাড়িতে আসত… এবারে already একদিন অনেকক্ষণের জন্য এসেছে, আবার কালকে আসবে for lunch and dinner… like suddenly our home has become much more accessible… there's no inhibition for coming here anymore… যেন মা থাকাটাই কাঁটা ছিল … এখন পথের কাঁটা কেউ নেই - মা-ছেলে তাই একসঙ্গে থাকতে পারবে … কেমন মনে হয় যেন মা-ছেলে, ওরা সবাই মিলে আমার মাকে শেষ করে দিল… আর তার কোন প্রতিকার নেই… কোন প্রতিকার করতে পারলাম না…

But I still don't want to accept anything and everything as a mute spectator…. তবু মা'র কাছে, বাবা'র কাছে গিয়ে বলতে তো পারব যে আমি সব মুখ বুজে মেনে নিইনি … I did what I could without hurting Oli or hurting her as little as possible… ওরা আমার দুর্বলতার সুযোগ নিল জানেন… আমার মা'র দুর্বলতার সুযোগ নিল…

It was a crime to be attached too much… Text bookish ছিলাম না কোনদিন… and having an extremely liberal and progressive upbringing, it never occurred to me that my mother (or his mother, for that matter) could be unwelcome in our place… মেয়ের মা বলে আমাদের সঙ্গে থাকতে পারবে না?… মা was so very eager to be together… she was so ecstatic that we were moving back to Kolkata, you know… but it actually turned out to be just the opposite in some sense… her dreams and hopes about staying close to us, staying with us… and happily so… were so rudely crushed… from afar, she did stay with us, especially for the last few years… but I couldn't keep her happily so… not as much as I wished I could, for sure… Kolkata ফিরেই যেন we hastened her end…

At first when we decided to move back to Kolkata, to ma and me, it seemed obvious that we were going to stay with her… where else can I stay in Kolkata (given my husband's ancestral home was in the suburbs, not in Kolkata)?… তখন আমরা Bombay-তে… and I alone could see his reluctance… নানা ভাবে he used to say things like অনেক furniture etc.,… used to say things like, 'that's impossible… where will our furniture etc. fit in her apartment?'…

One of her main concerns was will I get maids, and chauffeur etc. to run my house (Oli was much smaller then)… মা'র তখন খুব ভালো দুটো কাজের লোক … তারা আমাদেরও কাজ করবে, that's what she thought… কিন্তু ও (my husband) যে দূরে যাওয়ার চেষ্টা করছে সেটা তো মা ভাবতেই পারছেনা … so when my husband quite blatantly ruled out staying with ma, she began to search for apartments in her own complex, maybe adjacent to the one she had… but she didn't get any apartment available… so then she began looking for apartments near her complex…

মা, in fact, probably understood something, because ma খালি বলত যে let her give some amount and we can buy some apartment together, so she can stay with us more freely… আমার না for a very long time আমার টাকা, ওর টাকা, বাবা-মা'র টাকা, এই distinction গুলো মাথাতেই আসত না … so finally দেখে ও যে flat টা choose করল in Gladioli… something that was so interior that it was far enough from ma… not that we could meet everyday… and her maids couldn't work here… for a long time I tried to keep it from ma that he actually didn't want to stay with her or have to do anything with her… but she did find out later on… when her life was about to end… or maybe it ended when she found out… because she found out…

I don't know exactly how many years my life got curtailed because of my marriage… I am sure they will have their own reasons and justifications… I am obviously writing the way it came to us… গুমরে গুমরে মা চলে গেল … I wish I don't carry on with this unpardonable burden of not being able to do anything for too long… and then show this to him… tell him that there was no one else I could turn to but you… I had no sibling no parent who'd speak on my behalf… my parents gave me up completely to him and he did not respect my well being… only to the extent of exactly what he thought and did… which unfortunately didn't coincide with mine… even his mother did not do anything to help me when I wrote to her…

When my end will be near, show it to him and tell him that I have suffered a lot because of him… and no matter how many counter arguments and justifications he can think of in his defence I am beyond hearing all of them…

Kolkata ফিরলাম বলেই, ওর coldness-এর জন্যই, মা আরও অনেক আগে চলে গেলেন … আগে আমাদের সঙ্গে থাকবে বলেই কত আনন্দে থাকত… বাড়ি করাটাও তাই জন্য … কিন্তু বাড়ি করার সময় একদিনও দেখতে আসত না জানেন তো … বলত না, 'এটা হলে ভালো, ওটা হলে ভালো …'… usually people who get homes built, almost sit the whole time supervising, asking questions, giving suggestions, making sure everything is happening according to contracts etc…ma actually thought, building our own house would be that kind of a family engagement and exercise… I did give my suggestions for the interior etc., but often when workers were working it's hard for a woman to come and oversee everything… it's usually done by the male members of the household… but he was so reluctant in doing anything… only after innumerable requests maybe he would agree to come to the site once… even if he did, it was never on his won… পুরোটাই একটা futile effort… 'কেন করছ'… 'না করলেই হয়'… এরমি attitude for the whole thing….

মা Life-এ* ঘরও ওই জন্যই নিয়েছিলেন so she didn't have to stay with us… because after her stroke when I said I couldn't leave her alone, his audacity to be disrespectful to ma became quite open and obvious… 2019-এ stroke হওয়ার পরই, ওর অসভ্যতাটা চূড়ান্ত হয়….

When we were in ma's apartment, I had an acceptance for a conference in Israel… but he wouldn't help me with my visa etc.,… he would not help me with anything… ওলি আরও ছোট… and it was impossible for me to manage everything… আর আমার যাওয়া হল না …

(*'Life' was a serviced apartment for senior citizens.)

Ma was so upset… and she realised that the only reason he was doing this to me was because I was staying with her… ইদানিং, এই গত দু বছর before ma left us forever, day in and day out, he has subjected us to this indifference, this coldness… it's so unbearable at times…

রাত্তির বেলা she would often voice message her near friends and colleagues talking about people who've been disrespectful towards her… but the biggest disrespect was shown to her by her nearest one… but who could speak about one's own family to others?... and I feel that all her bitterness towards others actually stemmed from the humiliations that staying with him filled her with...

মা আমাকে বলত আমি হাসতে ভুলে গেছি... actually both of us had forgotten to smile... আমি doctors-দের ওপর এত কিছু বললাম কারণ বলতে পারলাম (referring to the note she wrote after her ma was no more, about the unkind attitude of the medical fraternity)... যে 'কারণটা' আরও অনেক near, আরও অনেক true, 'তাকে' তো কিছু বলার উপায় নেই... তাই বলা হয়নি ... বলা যায়নি ... মাও পারেনি... আমিও পারিনি ... শুধু মনে মনে শেষ হয়ে গেছি ... মাও কষ্ট পেয়ে গেছে... আমিও যাচ্ছি...

আগে ভাবতাম জানেন কিছু হবে না ... কষ্ট হলে আর কি হবে ... but মা'র চলে যাওয়াটা was a big eye opener... I now know that কষ্ট পেতে পেতে চলে যাওয়াও যায়... that's exactly what happened to her... এই last দুবছরেই he has hastened her departure... হয়ত মানুষটাকে ভালো রাখলে আরো কদিন সুস্থ থাকত ... শরীরটা আর ভালো থাকতে চাইলোই না .... in spite of me... and ওলি ...

I will definitely leave him and go one day... I know I've made you very sad, but this is all for later, many years from now, till my daughter's adult and settled, but I had to write it now lest I don't feel like writing anymore...

I know you will tell me, have I done anything that was not solely well-intentioned?... No... but I haven't protested either... not doing anything is also crime...ধরুন nationalist-দের যখন British অত্যাচার করছে, তখন রুখে না দাঁড়ানোটাই অপরাধ ... 'অন্যায় যে করে আর অন্যায় যে সহে', দুজনেই অপরাধী ... আমার বর অপরাধ করেছে, কিন্তু আমি সহ্যও তো করেছি... আমিও equally অপরাধী নই কি?... সেই অপরাধের সাজা আমায় মা দিল ... চলে গিয়ে ...

ওর তো কিছু যায় আসে না, না... যত ভাব করে কিছুই যায় আসে না, ততই ভালো... this is exactly what he wanted … how he wanted… যেন কিছুই হয়নি… if I could forget everything and pretend like he does, that nothing happened, he'd be the happiest … but I can't … এই compromise-টা আমার basic honesty-র সাথে compromise…that hurts a lot…

ঝগড়ার মধ্যে থালি বলবে 'আমি তাই ভাবলে (that he is responsible for ma's end), লোককে তাই বলব… লোকে কি ভাববে!'… সেটাই ওর headache! What I will say and what people will think!… not what actually happened!… not that ma is no more… and his role in it, is not unblemished…

'Last দু মাস পাশে থাকিনি?!'…he'd say… মানে? আর কে থাকবে?… last দুবছর যে অপমানটা করল তার কে হিসেবে নেবে?… লোককে নিয়ে তার এত মাথাব্যথা… মা কি ভাবলো, আমি কি ভাবলাম … তার চিন্তা গেল তল … লোকে কি ভাববে!…

Within seven years of moving back to Kolkata, ma ceased to be around us… you know, once I was talking to a senior colleague of mine and told him that ma was no more… and I also told him that she was so happy when we moved back… somehow he smiled and said something like 'but that isn't commensurate with what happened…'… ma সত্যিই আনন্দে থাকলে আমাদের ছেড়ে যেত না কি?

I am so sorry for this rather pensive missive… here's a poem for you…

Everything smells

Even the mind

And even when I could not see you

Just the thought of your face

Filled me with a sweetness
That felt warm and enduring
Like your hugs and strokes
Would come invisibly
In the odour of the evening
And settle on me
Like an unknown smell
Of love and kindness.

The darker it gets… the lonelier it gets… All I see are you eyes… in front of me… inside of me… seeing all and knowing all… ড্যাব ড্যাব করে তাকিয়ে আছেন জগন্নাথদেবের মতন …

9. "পেয়েছি ছুটি, বিদায় দেহ ভাই"

"সেই মায়ের জন্য আয়া রেখে দিলি!", she had said complainingly while coming out of the bathroom in the morning. Parshati usually adjusted her class timings etc., in a way so that she didn't have to be in her office any more than she had to be. She used to give ma all her medicines, breakfast etc. in the morning and then leave for office on the days she had to go, and then try to come back by evening. But even during those hours when she wouldn't be around, it was difficult for her ma to go up to the kitchen and get something if she needed it, warm her lunch etc., and she didn't want to ask her son-in-law at all. So Parshati finally decided to keep a help exclusively for ma, which her ma didn't like at all. And which she was complaining about, when Parshati came to say bye to her mom before leaving for office that day.

Given her dysfunctional kidneys, there were innumerable dietary restrictions that had to be followed. Doctors asked her to not consume more than 1.5/2 litres of water per day including tea, dal etc., which was near impossible to stick to. She needed to consume around twenty tablets daily (split in three phases - after breakfast, lunch and at bedtime), other than take around ninety units of insulin. Consuming so many tablets, itself required a lot of water.

Doctors advised Parshati to "leach" her vegetables, which means cutting them and immersing them in lukewarm water for a few hours before cooking them. There was strict restrictions on calories for her intake (though given her worsening kidney conditions she usually felt nausea and couldn't eat much), usage of oil in her food, amount of salt and sugar in her diet etc., which were there even for her diabetes, but which became immensely important after creatinine levels in her blood started exceeding normal range.

She was allowed about three tablespoons of oil for her cooking and about three grams of salt (which were like three small sachets of salt that they gave you with packed omelette on a flight for example). And the biggest challenge for Parshati was how to keep these measurements when food was getting cooked together along with those for the rest of the family members? So, for some time now, Parshati had been thinking of having a separate cook for ma... just to be able to stick to her stringent dietary constraints...

For example, her ma was not supposed to consume potassium-rich food... and it turns out that whatever we usually consider to be healthy and nutritious are potassium-rich... tomato, coconut, green leafy vegetables, for example... so Parshati, every morning, used to be quite lost deciding what to have for meals.

In any case, Oli was a small kid and had her own preferences... moreover she needed to have all the items that her mother was prohibited to have... and her cook (who kept changing because she hadn't found a good stable one) wasn't the most helpful in accommodating their various mutually exclusive needs... and Parshati had a hard time managing the household to the best of her abilities, even when she had a cook… leave alone when she didn't have one… (imagine what a hard time she must have had during the pandemic!)…

Parshati's mother had been diabetic for the last two decades, ever since her father was diagnosed with lung cancer. Her father had diabetes too. But then her ma used to take care of him. They say diabetics need to have small portions of food every couple of hours or so - should not have too much food at once. So her mother used to give him small tiffins for him to have during his office - she'd pack about two or three small snacks and a meal for him.

But when her mother was diagnosed with diabetes, her father was already diagnosed with lung cancer, so that diabetes seemed nothing at all compared to it. The attention of the whole family, including her mother, was with his father's ailment.

Even when her father was no more, it wasn't that her ma started taking a whole lot of care of herself… how many Indian women would consider making three or four small tiffins for herself? And she was a professor in a leading university but they did not have separate rooms for faculty, and there would be continuous streams of students, and she would hardly get time to have the tiffin she did manage to carry. So her mother surely did not give the attention and care to herself, the way she did to her father. And Parshati was away studying and with her jobs, all this while before returning to Calcutta. Even after she returned, she was busy with her daughter, Oli, and her job, and her ma was an independent-minded woman staying alone and being academically very active and involved…

Now, after years of diabetes, her blood creatinine level had finally started going above the upper limit of the normal range. General doctors asked her to see nephrologists or kidney specialists and no one gave her any good news. Parshati went with her to every doctor she could. One of them told them that creatinine level, whatever level it reached, became a floor… so that it could never come down below it… but could only go upwards… so blood tests became days filled with unbearable anxiety… and Parshati spent sleepless nights when reports used to be due… she feared, as did her ma, that she was inching towards dialysis… but none of them possibly thought that she was inching towards the end of life itself…

Normal creatinine levels were supposed to be 0.6 to 1.1 mg. Around the time when Parshati's mother's blood creatinine level exceeded 1.1, her feet had also begun to swell whenever she sat, so all her academic endeavours - reading, writing - even just sitting had become problematic. And maybe because of the swelling of her feet, her movements - walking - had become very imbalanced - and she needed support to walk around. She even fell twice - and terribly hurt her tailbone once and her wrist also got fractured once.

Moreover, because of kidney dysfunction, her haemoglobin levels had also started falling… it was around 9 when one nephrologist prescribed taking injections - once every fortnight… and there was this continuous nausea so that she mostly couldn't have any kind of food properly.

One nephrologist told them that when creatinine levels reach around 6 or 7 dialysis has to be started, thrice a week.

Parshati's mother was horrified - she was extremely soft-hearted and very scared of such medical procedures.

In fact, visiting doctors, that invariably involved long waiting had become extremely inconvenient for them since Parshati's mother had to use the restroom frequently (given her diabetes) and also had to eat intermittently, both of which became a problem for long hours of waiting. So once Parshati went to the nephrologist with her mother's reports and regretted it soon after… the doctor sort of sounded very negative and told her when the creatinine levels start to rise, 75-80% of the kidneys are already damaged… and she should prepare herself for what's coming… she didn't want to hear more…

So finally Parshati arranged for a visit to Chennai to see a famous nephrologist on hearing about him from a colleague… and after coming back from Chennai decided to keep a maid specifically for her mother… when she complained… the day she was to get admitted to the ICU… never to return home again…

During the first few days, when her mother was in ICU, and she could still talk in between her oxygen mask… she always tried to prepare Parshati for facing times ahead without her…

পেয়েছি ছুটি, বিদায় দেহ ভাই--

সবারে আমি প্রণাম করে যাই॥

Parshati knew this was from a Tagore's song… and, as if to start preparing her for what was coming, she had also said,

"ভালো মন্দ যাহাই আসুক

সত্যেরে লও সহজে।"

And she also said, "Que Sera, Sera"... (which means "what will be, will be")... it was the name of Parshati's latest poetry collection... "পরিণত বয়েসে মা যাচ্ছে, কোন আফসোস করিস না"... "I have seen you well settled in life, with a happy family... what else can I want...", she would say... "ঈশ্বরের কাছে আমার কোন অভিযোগ নেই... শুধু নিঃশ্বাসের কষ্টটা বড় কষ্ট... আর সহ্য করতে পারছি না..."…. She would gasp through her oxygen...

Parshati was not that well-versed in Tagore as her mother who was remarkably erudite and very well-versed in Tagore. Later on when she was no more, Parshati had looked up the lines she told her. Here's the song and next is the poem from which she quoted when she possibly felt that her end was nearing... and she was trying to prepare Parshati to move on in life without her...

পেয়েছি ছুটি, বিদায় দেহ ভাই--

সবারে আমি প্রণাম করে যাই॥

ফিরায়ে দিনু দ্বারের চাবি রাখি না আর ঘরের দাবি,

সবার আজি প্রসাদবাণী চাই॥

অনেক দিন ছিলাম প্রতিবেশী,

দিয়েছি যত নিয়েছি তার বেশি।

প্রভাত হয়ে এসেছে রাতি, নিবিয়া গেল কোণের বাতি--

পড়েছে ডাক চলেছি আমি তাই॥

বোঝাপড়া

রবীন্দ্রনাথ ঠাকুর

মনেরে আজ কহ যে,
ভালো মন্দ যাহাই আসুক
সত্যেরে লও সহজে।
কেউ বা তোমায় ভালোবাসে
কেউ বা বাসতে পারে না যে,
কেউ বিকিয়ে আছে, কেউ বা
সিকি পয়সা ধারে না যে,
কতকটা যে স্বভাব তাদের
কতকটা বা তোমারো ভাই,
কতকটা এ ভবের গতিক –
সবার তরে নহে সবাই।
তোমায় কতক ফাঁকি দেবে
তুমিও কতক দেবে ফাঁকি,
তোমার ভোগে কতক পড়বে
পরের ভোগে থাকবে বাকি,
মান্ধাতারই আমল থেকে
চলে আসছে এমনি রকম –

তোমারি কি এমন ভাগ্য
বাঁচিয়ে যাবে সকল জখম!
মনেরে আজ কহ যে,
ভালো মন্দ যাহাই আসুক
সত্যেরে লও সহজে।

অনেক ঝঞ্ঝা কাটিয়ে বুঝি
এলে সুখের বন্দরেতে,
জলের তলে পাহাড় ছিল
লাগল বুকের অন্দরেতে,
মুহূর্তেকে পাঁজরগুলো
উঠল কেঁপে আর্তরবে –
তাই নিয়ে কি সবার সঙ্গে
ঝগড়া করে মরতে হবে?
ভেসে থাকতে পার যদি
সেইটে সবার চেয়ে শ্রেয়,
না পার তো বিনা বাক্যে
টুপ করিয়া ডুবে যেয়ো।
এটা কিছু অপূর্ব নয়,
ঘটনা সামান্য খুবই –
শঙ্কা যেথায় করে না কেউ

সেইখানে হয় জাহাজ-ডুবি।

মনেরে তাই কহ যে,

ভালো মন্দ যাহাই আসুক

সত্যেরে লও সহজে।

তোমার মাপে হয় নি সবাই

তুমিও হও নি সবার মাপে,

তুমি মর কারো ঠেলায়

কেউ বা মরে তোমার চাপে –

তবু ভেবে দেখতে গেলে

এমনি কিসের টানাটানি?

তেমন করে হাত বাড়ালে

সুখ পাওয়া যায় অনেকখানি।

আকাশ তবু সুনীল থাকে,

মধুর ঠেকে ভোরের আলো,

মরণ এলে হঠাৎ দেখি

মরার চেয়ে বাঁচাই ভালো।

যাহার লাগি চক্ষু বুজে

বহিয়ে দিলাম অশ্রুসাগর

তাহারে বাদ দিয়েও দেখি

বিশ্বভুবন মস্ত ডাগর।

মনেরে তাই কহ যে,
ভালো মন্দ যাহাই আসুক
সত্যেরে লও সহজে।

নিজের ছায়া মস্ত করে
অস্তাচলে বসে বসে
আঁধার করে তোল যদি
জীবনখানা নিজের দোষে,
বিধির সঙ্গে বিবাদ করে
নিজের পায়েই কুড়ুল মার,
দোহাই তবে এ কার্যটা
যত শীঘ্র পার সারো।
খুব খানিকটে কেঁদে কেটে
অশ্রু ঢেলে ঘড়া ঘড়া
মনের সঙ্গে এক রকমে
করে নে ভাই, বোঝাপড়া।
তাহার পরে আঁধার ঘরে
প্রদীপখানি জ্বালিয়ে তোলো –
ভুলে যা ভাই, কাহার সঙ্গে
কতটুকুন তফাত হল।
মনেরে তাই কহ যে,
ভালো মন্দ যাহাই আসুক
সত্যেরে লও সহজে।

She was very concerned about Parshati not giving up on her passions and hobbies. She knew Parshati loved writing so she told her, "এগুলো নিয়ে লিখবি তো?"... "Ma, can you see this ma?... ma, can you see that I am writing like you asked me to?", Parshati thought as she wrote...

10. Conversations

Over the years, emails to Dr Dashorathi had become less informal and there were frequent conversations over WhatsApp - often during late hours of the night. Parshati was ecstatic conversing with him for completely unknown reasons and looked forward to sharing her writings with him. He would read them and often comment on their content and style. Their distance and formality had gradually withered down and the tone and tenor of their conversations had become a lot more intimate, though Parshati realised there really was no future for this. But nothing ever was explicitly told by anyone. Parshati didn't even know what, if at all, were his feelings for her. Other than the fact that he seemed to like talking to her just as much as she liked talking to him - she really had no clue what went on in his heart and mind. But then why would someone talk with someone else throughout the night?

The first time they talked on WhatsApp was when Parshati had an Italian professor visiting her. She had felt so special that the conversation has literally been etched in Parshati's mind and she could recall it almost verbatim even after years. It went something like this (as written below).

(At around 12:30/1 in the night, Parshati had finished all her household chores and retired to bed to sleep. Dr Dashorathi had asked her earlier whether she or her husband would like to go see a soccer match that was being held in the city (given his diplomatic passes). Parshati wasn't that interested in sports and her husband was also busy, so she had asked her visitor Prof Occhino, but he didn't want to go either. So at night, she thought of informing Dr Dashorathi that they won't be needing the match tickets.)

Parshati:... Hello, I asked Prof Occhino but he said he is perhaps the only Italian who is not interested in football!:-)... so thanks, but I don't think we need any tickets...

Dr Dashorathi:... O good, so you don't need to chaperone him around:-)...

Parshati: O no, I wouldn't have to anyway... you know, he's more independent than the most independent of Kolkatans... he's been visiting around the city entirely on his own... availing the metro!:-)...

Dr Dashorathi: O that's very good!...

Parshati: And you know, he in fact was so surprised to see that we don't drive ourselves... we ride chauffeur-driven cars!:-)... he said that in Italy, it was supposed to be quite snobbish and only the elites rode chauffeur-driven cars... and I felt so ashamed...

Dr Dashorathi: O every system has its pros and cons...

And my son seems to be calling from the US...

Parshati: Oh okay bye then...

Dr Dashorathi: Oh no no... it's okay... he's gone... for some soccer match there...

Parshati: What's your son's name?

Dr Dashorathi: Shiva

Parshati: After Lord Shiva?

Dr Dashorathi: Yes

Parshati: Are you his devotee?

Dr Dashorathi: Yes...

Parshati: What is he studying there?

Dr Dashorathi: Undergraduate in Computer Science

Parshati: Why did you send him abroad so early?... he's just a kid?:-)

Dr Dashorathi: Oh it's Maktub you know... Know what it is?

Parshati: Yes, after Coelho...

Dr Dashorathi: Something like "it's written"...

Parshati: Oh I thought you were a scientific man... why do you sound so fatalistic?

Dr Dashorathi: :-)... Well... you have to say something interesting to keep me from falling asleep?

Parshati: I think you're great...

Dr Dashorathi: Well, if there's nothing else that you want to say, then let's say bye...

Parshati: You're the Mecca I never want to visit...

Dr Dashorathi: What does that mean?...

Parshati: Can I please explain later?

Dr Dashorathi: Now… please… but later if you're sleepy?…

Parshati: Remember, in Alchemist, there was a character who worked very hard and saved money just to be able to visit Mecca one day… but he never would visit… because if he did, his urge, his passion for visiting Mecca would be gone… I absolutely loved this idea…

Dr Dashorathi: Yes?… and so?…

Parshati: :-) I don't speak much you know…

Dr Dashorathi: And you should only speak when you can improve upon silence…

Parshati: You can speak in silence too, you know…

They talked till about 2:30 or so in the night. Dr Dashorathi did not write till the next day again… and he wrote something like, 'he did not want to disrupt her speech in silence…'… and many such conversations happened over the course of quite a few years. Here are some more of Parshati's messages (some written while her mother was still with her):

Just wanted to talk to you… it's hard to summarise even a moment's thoughts and I'm looking back at about two decades… so pardon my haphazardness… I know you don't know my father but you can probably guess how cordial, friendly and liberal he was… and so is my mother… and I was their world… so when I got married it was like having another person who'd become their world… you can probably imagine their efforts at trying to come close to him…

But somehow he'd never let go of the distance... it was always a completely one-sided effort from my parents... he would never be cordial to them or talk to them normally... but that wasn't entirely attributable to his nature... because he seemed to be talking and interacting quite cordially with people in his own family... the distance was just with my parents... and I found this hypocrisy unbearable but there was nothing I could do... it hurt me a lot... I couldn't imagine spending my life with someone who wouldn't be nice to my parents...

Initially I used to protest and talk to him and tried to make him understand how painful this is for me... but I realised he wasn't one to change... the temperamental gulf between the families was huge... years of acquaintance didn't help things and even when my father was no more, things didn't improve with my mother... but my mother kept up her efforts, talking to him and trying to discuss things with him even when he chose to be arrogantly absorbed in his own world... he couldn't care less...

Recently though, after my mother's stroke, when we were all staying at my mother's place, his churlishness increased many times... he never came forward to help my mother with anything... never had any interest in the house getting built.... in a male-dominated society, you will understand that it is hard for my mother and me to negotiate and deal with people of all kinds... he has never been of any help whatsoever in the practical front....

My mother all along used to look upon him as her son... but she has now realised there is no reciprocation at all from his end… to cut a long story short, my mother and my husband have completely stopped talking to each other… well not really, my mother has stopped talking to him (he never used to talk to my mother on his own anyway)… my mother feels completely unwanted with him and totally exhausted with continued efforts at trying to talk to him and get him interested in things around her (in spite of all that my mother does for us)…

I see couples around me, and see the husbands appreciative of their wives' efforts, and I see couples around me with husbands so encouraging about their wives' talents, and I see couples around me with husbands talking normally to their mothers-in-law, and I wonder about the big fallacy of my parents… my mother laments over it and so do I….

Everyone somehow expected our marriage not to last… yet it did… Had it not been for my daughter, I think I would have parted ways with him and walked out of his life way back… Or maybe not, maybe it is just my wishful thinking… because you know, 'middle- classiness' has a kind of resilience… like coconut trees amidst a storm… they will keep bending to the extent that you will think it is on the brink of getting uprooted… but eventually, when the storm stops, you will find it upright and quite in its place (this metaphor is borrowed from Ashapurna Devi's Subarnalata)…

That they are not on speaking terms, is a kind of a respite to my mother from strained expectations that weren't to be fulfilled, from an artificial sense of normalcy that was never meant to last and from relentless efforts at winning over a lackadaisical indifference…

I was going through the Alchemist and in the introduction Coelho writes, "Intense, unexpected suffering passes more quickly than suffering that is apparently bearable; the latter goes on for years and, without our noticing, eats away at our soul, until, one day, we are no longer able to free ourselves from the bitterness and it stays with us for the rest of our lives." … and I think this is so true for me…

Every time I come back from office you know, it's like entering a nightmare… where there is no conversation between my mother and my husband… and though I go about the usual chores, the pain gnaws away at me, I lie awake and sleepless and helpless at night thinking about it, and inwardly it kills me…

This email is really like talking to God, without any expectation of reprieve or complaint against destiny… sometimes suffering just wants to shed its weight on sympathetic ears… but please don't worry about me… I am sure things will brighten up… and I really know what you'd say and what I've come to believe in… Maktub*…

*This is a term Parshati borrowed from Coelho's Alchemist, meaning something like "what's written" or "what's destined".

Let me share this wonderful quote with you (from Great Gatsby)... "It faced - or seemed to face - the whole external world for an instant, and then concentrated on you with an irresistible prejudice in your favour. It understood you just so far as you wanted to be understood, believed in you as you would like to believe in yourself, and assured you that it has precisely the impression of you that, at your best, you hoped to convey."

Somehow it describes the way I perceive you at times... somehow it makes me feel so warm and cosy amidst the chill...

And do take care...

❦

I just finished reading The Great Gatsby (I hadn't read it or seen the movie before)... Just wanted to share some beautiful lines at the end of the novel which, irrespective of the context, you will be able to follow... and they'll definitely make you think!...

"... for a transitory enchanted moment man must have held his breath in the presence of this continent, compelled into an aesthetic contemplation he neither understood nor desired, face to face for the last time in history with something commensurate to his capacity for wonder.

And as I sat there brooding on the old, unknown world, I thought of Gatsby's wonder when he first picked out the green light at the end of Daisy's dock. He had come a long way to this blue lawn, and his dream must have seemed so close that he could hardly fail to grasp it. He did not know that it was already behind him, somewhere back in that vast obscurity beyond the city, where the dark fields of the republic rolled on under the night.

Gatsby believed in the green light, the orgastic future that year by year recedes before us. It eluded us then, but that's no matter—tomorrow we will run faster, stretch out our arms farther... And one So we beat on, boats against the current, borne back ceaselessly into the past."

I wanted to share it with you since somehow, philosophically, it is just the opposite to what Coelho wants us to believe in - chasing one's dreams... Here, it's the futility of doing so... I know that life is seldom about binaries like black or white, chasing a dream or not, being successful or not, being right or not... it's all about the grey shades in between that make life so much more complicated and enchanting…

this is the recipe of life

said my mother

as she held me in her arms as i wept

think of those flowers you plant

in the garden each year

they will teach you

that people too

must wilt

fall

root

rise

in order to bloom

-rupi kaur

Beautiful, isn't it?... And as you had once said, it is beautiful because it is true... but sometimes, truth hurts...

After Parshati's ma was no more, Parshati had written to the only other friend she really thought she had - Dr Dashorathi. He got back to her very kindly and understandingly, and interacted with her with even more intimacy - or so she thought. He asked her to express herself freely, and promised her of not stopping to speak with her (often with pressure of work etc., he would not write for many days, and Parshati would make him do such promises).

They often exchanged books and this was after Parshati had read one such book that Dr Dashorathi gave her.

Dr Dashorathi,

Please don't think that tears after seeing you has anything to do with feeling sad after meeting you… we know of tears when we're sad… we also know of happy tears… tears when we're happy… I don't know whether you read the Fieldnotes book that you gave me far enough to have read the anecdote about Bibhutibhushan that he writes?… remember he writes about Apu and Pather Panchali and Bibhutibhushan quite a bit in the book?… on one occasion he writes that once Bibhutibhushan was reading something in his literature class in the school he used to teach at… and was crying profusely… later on a student recalled that the passage had neither pain or sadness and yet he was crying while reading it… and he realised that sometimes just beauty evokes tears… whatever he was reading was so beautiful that he was crying while reading it… ma used to tell me you know that I used to cry while listening to a particular sitar recital of Nikhil Banerjee… so good music being a piece of beauty also evoked tears I believe… well I guess that's closest to how I feel meeting you… you are so beautiful… so is your kindness… and your caring about me… and your understanding… everything is so beautiful… yet just that word doesn't nearly begin to describe all that happens within me… it's like oceans keep swelling and swelling and I keep dissolving and disintegrating till all I have left is you… and borrowing words of Wordsworth you just evoke feelings that do often lie too deep for tears… and from what deepest ocean bed you stir my tears I don't know…

(And she wrote this poem for him.)

One day

One day I will liberate myself

From the confines of this brown body

And then I'll never leave you

I'll somehow mix myself with the rain water

And shyly wait for you in the muddy puddles

That you will surely step on

When you walk in the balmy evening

On your quaint little hilly road

That takes you on your inward journey

Towards me

I'll splash myself with the tiny specks of mud

That stick to your feet when you walk by

And walk with you
In your every step and every turn
Every pause and every shuffle…
I'll float around in the smell
Of the wild bushes that waft
From the not-so-distant mountain
Bringing the promise of rains and peace
And you'll know that maybe
I was able to make peace with myself after all
It is possible that all the expectation
All the desire and all the complications
Just arose in this very brown body
In its efforts trying to understand truth
In its machinations trying to understand others
But beyond it, it stands relieved of all of that
No failed attempts again
And then I shall not leave you
In the air that you breathe
I'll mingle with the freshness of hope
And be in your heart forever
And I'll stare at you
From the pages of your book
Intently devouring knowledge
And be the feel of the joy
That touching the pages brings you

I'll find myself in cosy sunshine

That bathes your skin in winter

To give you all the warmth you need

I'll be the calmness in your lake

And fill up your senses

Till you can no longer do mine apart from yours

And then I'll never leave you…

11. The Trance

About six months back, probably in January sometimes, just when this year began, on a cold winter morning, Parshati woke up and heard her mother say, very seriously, that something extraordinary had happened during the night. This is what her mother said:

It could be the wee hours of the morning but it was winter and it was pretty dark still, and her mother was sleeping in her usual place, when she woke up. Just where the door was, she saw a kind of bright white light. She wasn't afraid or in pain, but she somehow knew that it had come to take her away. Ma suddenly felt very sorry that she had to leave without even saying goodbye to Parshati and Oli, and so requested 'the light' if it could please spare her this time, for a little while. It did. But she somehow realised that she wouldn't have a lot of time with her daughter and her granddaughter. Maybe she won't even live till morning and see them again. So she got up.

And in spite of her problems walking (she initially had problems walking after her stroke in 2019... recently, with her feet swollen, she had a lot of problem balancing while walking... plus she had slipped and fell twice, in spite of grab bars etc. placed on the walls for her to hold while walking for support... in short, it was really hard for her to walk alone nowadays), she took her phone, got up and almost as if she was walking in a trance, she went out of the room, out of the living space and to the corridor outside. She called for the lift, took it, and went downstairs to the library-cum-office room of Pursuits - all alone and in the darkness of a cold winter night. And she could barely walk a couple of steps properly, and it was quite some distance between her room and the lift. And from the lift again to the room downstairs.

Once there though, she sat in her chair and opened WhatsApp to the chat of an acquaintance who was a lawyer. Not a friend, not a colleague, not a relative, not even her daughter - a lawyer. She voice messaged her (she could not type in the phone anymore because of deteriorating eyesight) along the lines of ... that she was fully in her senses and speaking of her wishes, that in case she is no more, this message should be considered as her "will", that she would probably not be around for very long, so everything that she has will be her daughter's, thereafter her granddaughter's. She spoke about Pursuits and that she wants to formalise the organisation, forming a trust if required and so on.

Thereafter she had visited him (the lawyer) with Parshati, though the lawyer assured her that no legal formalities were required since Parshati was the only child, and everything that was hers, would automatically be Parshati's, when she'd be no more.

Had anyone else told Parshati what her mother said about the phenomenon she experienced in the wee hours, she would probably not have believed, or have a hard time believing. But the fact that her ma told her, almost vividly describing the light that came, that wasn't scary but rather inviting, that she asked it to wait, that she almost stumbled out of bed on a cold winter morning, walked over in the darkness, took the lift, went downstairs to the office, voice messaged a lawyer to secure her daughter's future, made questioning her ma, impossible. She believed her. She had to believe her. But she realised that something strange, something from out-of-this-world, had truly come to call her mother.

As the "light" would have it, she was spared for about six more months. But she couldn't see the next year.

ᘓᘔ

Parshati woke up and it took a while to sink in that she didn't have to rush downstairs to see how ma was doing. Give her a warm glass of Horlicks and let her sleep for another hour or so, later giving her চিঁড়ে দই for breakfast. It took a while for her to realise that ma was no more downstairs, no more in RITU bed #295, no more in any part of the world. She was just gone.

ᘓᘔ

When Parshati's mother did come back from ventilation the first time, it seemed almost like she had visited some other world and come back to her, just to tell her that it's okay to be on the other side… and somehow Parshati felt, that the fact that her ma could not speak to her, almost killed her fighting instincts… talking to Parshati and Parshati talking to her… mother and daughter, just talking to each other… were like the ultimate good things in their lives… when that itself was taken from her, life itself was rendered meaningless… she didn't want to live anymore if she couldn't speak to Parshati anymore…

Since she could not speak, for many days, Parshati used to take writing pads and some pencil or pen, and insert it between her fingers, so she could scribble something and she could try to read it… she did in fact, try to write a lot of things whenever she felt strong enough to hold something in her fingers… and they were extremely hard to decipher… and Parshati even when her ma was no more would go through those last writings…

One of the things that she described partly and what Parshati could understand partly was this: that she was lying somewhere near water… there were lots of dead bodies lined one after another covered in white… "dead body-র মেলা… পর পর dead body শুয়ে রয়েছে"… and she was one of them… she heard Parshati scream "ma" just once… and there were flowers strewn all over…

For many days after Parshati's ma regained back her consciousness, she kept asking her whenever she could convey it through her lip movements, "বেঁচে আছি?"… "তুই sure বেঁচে আছি? "… she did not seem very convinced that Parshati was telling the truth that she was alive… it was like her ma literally had gone off to someplace so far away, that it was really hard for her to come back to this world again… in a way it was almost painful that she had to… she seemed to have travelled such a great distance that literally there would be no return from there… she had that distant lost look in her eyes that seemed to suggest she was finding it really hard to acclimatise herself to this world again…

You know like newborn infants seem to be completely in some different worlds of their own… no physical rule of this world seems to apply to them… Parshati's mother gave her the same kind of feeling… like they had dragged her mother back from a completely different world… a world totally unknown to them… and though Parshati was never very devout, she was overcome by a deep sense of mystery and intrigue for what lies beyond… like she could neither disprove nor prove anything, but she was filled with a strange sense of not knowing a different world… where her mother would be… and from where her mother had come back just because she couldn't leave her that suddenly…

12. Rains

(Dr Dashorathi was Parshati's ultimate succour, ultimate respite from daily chores, ultimate bed of love that she snuggled and slept in. Here are some excerpts of her emails, messages and poems that she sent him from time to time.)

Please don't worry... Just wanted to talk to you... You know just from 10pm onwards I did these... Made dinner for my daughter (she had chicken sandwich and an egg poach today), then for my mother (she had a potato preparation with roti), then I heated our food (that's been cooked in the morning by the cook who comes after my mother fell down) and had dinner... Then I cleaned the kitchen, made tea and also some snacks for my mother to have during the night, made her bed, gave her medicines... Listed things needed from the market tomorrow... Then my daughter and I came up, read a bedtime story, and I put her to sleep... Then I went down again to check on ma and see if she needs anything... And most of the days, by then, it's about 4/4:30... And I am probably sitting and thinking alone for a while... Like now...

You know there was a squall in the evening today... Like a mini Nor'wester... Not torrential rain like the rush and the roar of the mighty... Just a little splash to quench and drench the dried and the parched... The rough and the rude... To bring the much needed assurance and comfort of peace and politeness... I wish I could rain healings on ailments, peace on the perturbed, tranquillity on the troubled, absolutions on the guilty and mercy on the mistaken...

And you know I can still smell the scent of the newly wet earth in the air... Like the rain just wants to let us know that it's not representing the victor and the virtuous... But rather it's coming for the lonely and the forgotten... Those left behind and trodden over like the fractured earth and the shrunken leaves... Like it wants to let us know that every grain and every bit and every speck of everything everywhere is important in its own way and for its own ones and it loves all of them... And it's here to let them realise this truth...

You know I didn't write one poem but kind of a series... see...

Of soil and rains

1

And then you turn me into soil

And all I see in you are rains

Rains that rush down in eager drops

Rains that drip down in coy showers

Rains that plant deep kisses in tiny specks

Rains that play with tiny particles

Binding them into loose lumps

Of wet love

And there are wild flowers springing up

In maddening mirth you know
From all pores and valleys
Like they've never been roused before
And scent of rains mixed in soil
Mixed with the scent of wilderness
Mixed with the scent of the limitless sky
Mixed with unbounded joy
Just smells of wet love

2

My soil melts into your sweat
And absorbs the salt and water
And forms beads of soothing care
And sticks onto your soft skin
Just where your chest begins
Snuggled cosily but ever scared
Of slipping down
Without restraint…

3

I am brown
All outside and deep inside

Rain, pelt down on me forever
And cleanse me
Of all my weaknesses
So I might rise
In the deepest shades of
Me.

4

My brownness
Dissolves into you
Like the last remnant of me
Rest are all you
Elegant and pure
Pouring down in
Incessant showers of
Forgiveness and understanding
I am small
I am not even there
Yet you descend with
All your grace
And embrace my last bit
So that right where

The rains touch the ground

Soil and rain are into each other

And it's hard to know

Whether the wet soil

Chooses to rise to heaven

Or the raindrops

Choose the abode of earthy puddles

And all brownness

And all wetness

Mould into a fresh new beginning

That smells of only a wet earth

5

Suppose I could melt into the rains

And then I could pour all over you

And drench you

And seep in you

And enter through pores in your skin

And if you saw your skin browner

That'd be me

All over you

6

Seen the immense distance
Between land and sky
That's the distance
Between you and me
Seen how the rains stay way beyond
The reach of the land
How the land breaks up
Parched and dried
Looking up eagerly
Braving the scorching heat
And standing the unbearable rage
Of the unforgiving sun
And then Gods decided to have mercy
To let my thirst be quenched
Let my soul be calmed

And so they made the rains
They let the rains rush towards me
Uninhibited and unhindered
Let all fetters around you get loosened
So every drop can freely
Coil around the smallest of pores

And meander in the smallest of streams

To deeper and deeper me

In bosoms of unexplored feelings

Lying in untouched depths

To soften and stir

And moisten and love

And leave the Gods happy and satisfied…

7

There I was

All coarse and rough

And all brown and dry

And then you rained within me

Every moment of the day

And amidst the dreary hot unending day

You filled me with

Loving softness

And calmed my soul

And moistened my lips

And moistened my eyes

And moistened my heart

And everything that was hard in me

Melted with your touch

And you turned me into water

To dissolve in you

And float away with you

To unexplored destinies

And unfulfilled dreams.

8

Write an unwritten story…

Like the pristine rains write stories

On the bosom of unspoilt soil

Both untouched by the impurities of the world

Unleash the captured streams in my soul

Paint forests in the tapestry of my emotions

Let flowers blossom from impossibilities

Let sunshines fill all forgotten dreams

Let the dreams of shared lives

Be woven together

Let destinies converge

On the edge of dusk

And let the waters hold our memory

Clearly and lovingly…

(And here is another poem Parshati sent him.)

If they could speak…

I just want to close my eyes

When you're nearest

I just want to close my eyes

And inhale the ocean

That is suddenly born all around me

That submerges me

And resurfaces me

The storm that sucks me into its vortex

Every hair on my body suddenly

Become magnets

To your presence

Every speck of invisible dust

Stretches like strands of mind

That assumes lighting speed

But then you're lightyears away

I dare not move

I dare not breathe

I dare not exist

I am just suspended

In time and space

And in your thoughts

And in your smell

And in your nearness

And in the oceans and lightyears

That suddenly creep up

In the narrow space between us

In the air that touches you

And then changes its mind

And touches me

And then suddenly become still

Holding us so near

And yet so far

And in that unending stillness

The treacherous moon

Beams down like a balm

On my clammy skin

Like a strength

So I can open my eyes again

And the oceans and storms

And air and moon

All brew up a tumult

That's hard to understand

That only causes a sharp pain
So sharp that I stand wounded
And bleeding
And my tears would tell you
All that happened
If they could speak...

Like the ruins of an ancient temple
Scattered amidst a savage forest
Your smell sprinkles holiness
Sprinkles restraint in all the wilderness
All the savageness, all the restlessness
That creep mysteriously into me
Like the severity of the meditation of
Silent formidable mountains
From time immemorial
From unfathomable abyss
Stretching into infinity
Holding roots digging deep into time
Covered in smooth green moss
That covers the wrinkles of time
Your presence fills me with

Inexplicable timelessness
Like all that's ever been
All that's ever going to be
All that's ever dreamt of
And all that's ever imagined
Come rushing to me
In invisible waves of solitude
And invisible waves of togetherness
And all that happens are
Warm tears flowing down
My cheeks that I can no longer feel
And my tears could tell you
All that happens
If they could speak…

In the depths and ravines of wants
I sink like a lost soul
Your skin's all love
Mine's below yours
And then everything else
Just falls through
The sieve of uncharted desires

Like dews and drops
That make up formless moving clouds
That drift across the unknown abyss
Of you and me
Of when you began and where you'd go
Of when I appeared
And disappeared maybe
And all the touches and forms
And smells and smiles
Mix and mingle
And melt and moisten
And all that remains
Are salty remnants
Of streams that trickle down
And my tears could tell you
All that happens
If they could speak…

In the ramparts of pain
You hold me like sunshine
Like light coming through darkness
Like the fragrance of morrow

And the stillness of peace
Like the hope of love
And the promise of understanding
You become the mountain
Whose might caresses the
Breast of the soft earth
The protector of
All that's delicate and beautiful
The guardian of all from which
Spring passion and joy
And rays of days to come
And songs of beliefs
And all I am aware of
Are ripples of endlessness
That all seem to converge
In softest tears that
Slowly start rolling onto
The slopes of love
That you smooth out for them
And they would tell you
All that happens
If they could speak...

All the crimson of my sunsets
That seep into my blood
And all the oranges of golden sunrise
That drip down molten from the sky
On the cold mountain snow caps
All the first dewdrops
Sparkling on the forgotten leaf
Born alone in the distant mountain crevice
All the sounds and smells
Of loneliness
That shroud me
All somehow get ruffled
And dispelled when your look
Comes snuggling by
And your gestures
Make me float away
On golden chariots
To crimson dusks and orange sunrises
And lets me float in infinite peaks
Of sunbathed sky
And all I can feel then
Is you

In me

And everything gives way

To streams that flow as tears

And they'd tell you

All that happens

If they could speak…

13. On the Sofa

In the first hospital where Parshati's ma was admitted for a few days, outside the ICU, there was a sofa on which visitors of the patients admitted in ICU could wait. As one waited on the sofa, one was bound to feel a kind of hopelessness as every other day someone or the other would pass away. Sometimes even more than one person would pass away on a single day.

On one of the beds of the ICU, was an old unconscious woman. Everyday day her daughter would come during the visiting hours, stand by her bedside and call, "মা... ও মা...."... A few days later, the mother passed away... On the sofa, while the daughter was on the phone, intimating her relatives presumably, she said something like, "এই তো কাল রাত্তিরে ventilation-এ দিল, আজ সকালে চলে গেল"...

On another instance, a mother and her two daughters sat on the sofa, all crying... The mother was crying and saying something like, "Board meeting এ ডেকেছে..." ...and a few days later, the mother saw Parshati and cried out loud, "তোমার কাকু আর নেই...".

Every time Parshati felt a chill down her spine... what if one day the doctors tell her the same thing?... So Parshati, during the first few days had acquired a feeling that 'ventilation', 'board meetings' were things that almost surely meant declaring the end of people in there.

Once they shifted her ma to the other hospital, Parshati once more had to witness several people passing away, before her mother did. Like the "light" was preparing her for what was coming.

Parshati's mother had her seventieth birthday while she was admitted in ICU. Parshati had ordered and taken a 1.5 kg chocolate truffle cake for her mother that had a "get well soon" message written from Oli. Her mother she knew, will not be able to eat, so it was mainly for the doctors and nurses and for them to celebrate her birthday… it turned out that there were two deaths in the ICU that day, and everyone was very busy till late in the afternoon…

When some doctors and nurses did converge around her mother's bed, they had taken some photos in the mobiles of some of them and Parshati had given her phone too for someone to click a photo… these photos were treasures to Parshati later on… they were "live" photos in her Apple phone, which meant that if you touched the photo for a while, it plays like a very short video for a few seconds… so one can hear the sounds and see the movements slightly before and after the moment that's captured in the live photo frame…

Parshati saw these live photos over and over again, hearing the beeping sounds of the ICU monitors, the voice of a nurse calling another nurse, the doctor asking some other doctor to come, and most importantly her mother straining and staring with a kind of look that borders on very little understanding, yet patience with all that's happening around her… her mother really had ceased to be with them consciously sometime before that itself… but Parshati never could accept that she would really be leaving her… how could she… and so she kept hoping against hope… that maybe something miraculous will happen and her mother will recover and come back home with them…

And most of the times, Parshati saw these photos as a reminder of the horror of her ma's physical pain… in her mind, she would list the tubes/channels that could be seen… there was one tracheostomy tube (about 7 mm in diameter) through a hole in her throat (to which two other tubes was connected to the ventilation machine)… there was one channel in her left or right jugular vein for her dialysis (it is the vein in the area of the side of the throat, between the chin and the ear in some sense)… left or right because after a few days, they had to change the channel because there was chance of infection in case of multiple use of a single channel…

There was a central channel on one of her hands… that was regularly used for drawing blood, administering medicines, monitoring blood pressure etc… but again the channel would get blocked, her hand would get swollen and so they would alternate the hands for the channels… they also inserted a catheter to monitor her urine…

She had also developed bed sores…and doctors also warned Parshati of blood infections that often happen due to such insertions of tubes and channels that invariably happen during prolonged ICU admission…

In general her condition was abysmal… and then her bleeding started, that doctors couldn't stop after multiple endoscopies and colonoscopies… and the procedures themselves were invasive and painful…

It was ironical that this same person who shuddered to think of dialysis at one point and did not want to visit the nephrologist thereafter, had been subjected to so much medical torture… or maybe it wasn't…

Parshati remembered that every time doctors would say something like the central channel had to be done or the dialysis channel has to be changed etc., her mother would put up a huge denial and protest (even when she couldn't talk) and would refuse to get it done till Parshati came…

When they talked about a central channel and catheter for the urine the first time she was admitted to the second hospital, Parshati remembers the helpless look she had seen on her face… "তুই ওদের বোঝা, মা…", she had pleaded with Parshati… she remembers how the doctors called Parshati to the doctor's desk at one end of the ICU and told her threateningly, coldly and almost rudely, "patient-কে বোঝান… এরম করলে কিন্তু চিকিৎসা করা যাবে না…"…

Parshati had walked back, held back her tears, held her ma's hands, and still thinking probably they did have her ma's best interests in mind, had persuaded her ma to please let them do what they wanted… her ma had agreed, never disobeying her daughter, and believing perhaps that enduring some pain might actually help her recover…

Often after her tracheostomy, when she couldn't talk anymore, she would ask a sympathetic nurse to call Parshati when she returned home for a few hours in the afternoon… like she knew her moments with her daughter were really numbered… and the nurse would call and then hold the phone to her mother's ears… Parshati would only hear the myriad beeping sounds of the ICU and a blank silence of her mother's voice... not able to express anything with her voice anymore... but pregnant with all the love in the world... just listening to Parshati's endearing voice, "মা... মা... আমি এক্ষুনি যাবো মা তোমার কাছে ..."...

Parshati prayed that either God help ma to recover... or let Him take her away... she prayed to Him to stop this inhuman torture on her... it was such a psychological torture for Parshati as well... and almost a relief when her ma ceased to be... like God just made her mother undergo this level of pain to help Parshati accept more readily when she'd no longer be around... to feel relieved that she was no longer in that pain... to make Parshati almost want her mother to go...

Was that the reason God sent her back from wherever He had taken her when she was put on ventilation?... so Parshati couldn't think forever that she couldn't try enough to keep her mother with her?... so Parshati could see the limits that medical torture could stretch to and wish herself that ma be freed from these?...

14. Opening Up

(Over the years, Parshati became more and more open with Dr Dashorathi. He was the only one she wanted to talk to. She could never say or express openly how much she loved him, but there really was no one but him. Here are some of her earlier messages to him… from the times when her mother was there.)

I really would like to have a separate identity as a writer, rather than have people evaluate my writings with the knowledge or conjectures about my personal life... Tagore may or may not have been in a relation with his sister-in-law (Kadambari Devi), Ashapurna Devi may or may not have seen in-laws like those of Subarnalata, Kamala Das may or may not have had a Carlos in her life, but we should never judge Noshto Neer or Subarnalata or My Story through their personal lives, should we?...

All great storytellers like Maugham and O'Henry drew on real life experiences from their surroundings to write their stories… All writers draw from their experiences but it is rather embarrassing and undesirable if readers start identifying their personal lives with their creations... Writers become great because their creations ultimately transcend the immediate and become universal, throughout time and space...

It is in fact very embarrassing and undesirable for a writer to get identified with her personal life... You know someone once read one of my writings and said it sounded autobiographical... I have never again shown him any writing of mine... There have been others who've tried to discuss my thoughts behind my writing... And I've cautiously moved away from them... I wish I could hide the writer in me in an invisibility cloak (like in Harry Potter:-))...

That's why it is so comforting talking to you... You've never talked to the wife me, to the daughter me, or to the mother me... You've always talked to the person me, to the woman me, to the writer me, to the me who has a passion and searches for a true calling... And you've talked to that me without judgement, without evaluation, without expectation and without reprimand.... With support and sympathy but measured and not unconditional... And without intimacy and with distance...

Yet that's precisely what makes me feel so secure writing to you... You're like the guiding star that guides from afar... I know you will understand even if I don't express too well, I know you'll forgive me even if I transcend a limit, and I know you'll never turn away from me... You're the most treasured companion a writer can ever have!...

O and you know because I was apprehensive of some such similar situation down the lane, I even explored the option of using a pen name for my first book... but apparently nowadays copyright laws and norms are much stricter than before and my publisher said that couldn't be done... I wish I could grant my writer soul 'creative immunity'... From questions and analysis... And keep her unanswerable to mindless inquisitiveness of casual readers prying into the source of creativity... Or of close ones who think it is within their right to impose restrictions on what essentially survives on freedom…

You know the first time I saw you, when you had come to our apartment, you were wearing a white half-sleeve shirt, not milk white, just a bit off, a little bluish greying white and my husband, rather half-heartedly I thought, introduced me to you… It seemed you didn't even want to look at me… You frowned and looked in my direction but I thought your eyes didn't even rest on me for a fraction of a second… It just swept over me in the smallest possible furtive look… It seemed like exactly at that moment, something had fallen in your eyes and you quickly turned away distracted by it…

And you kept yourself busy discussing physics with him… I remember I offered you some non-vegetarian snacks which you refused (now I know why) and only had some water… I even remember what I wore… I wore a sleeveless salwar (white-red printed)… And sat for a while with you guys listening to your academic discussion, but then felt too ignored…

My daughter was with my mom, so after a while I said I would go and pick her up and so I excused myself and left… Later on though when I said I liked you a lot, my mom asked me whether you liked me too… noticed me… I shook my head and said that you didn't even look at me when we met and my mom said that my father also hadn't looked at her when he met her for the first time… Often, we ignore the things we love the most…

❧

... You know, all the strands of genes that keep me awake at night, seemed to have passed on to my daughter:-)... She becomes hyperactive the nearer her bedtime is and nowadays doesn't go to sleep before 3/3:30... It's slightly better on weekdays but way more later than is usual for her age... You know Kamala Das had written somewhere how she wrote in the wee hours when the milkman gave milk... I remember when I was in Bangalore, I used to write my lecture notes in the early hours for the next day's class... I guess that's why they call it Brahma muhurto (you said that, remember)... Because Brahma himself gave strength to all mothers... nursing mothers, working mothers, creative mothers... To write and follow their passions at that time...:-)...

ꟷ

Noticed the slight chill in the air?... Around early morn and evenings... And the air having a strangeness... A sudden awareness of an upcoming situation... A pregnant silence... Like that which descends on a family when an unwanted visitor suddenly strolls in... Sometimes you know, you just want to lay back and keep the uppermost, burning, life-changing, issues at rest... And talk about the most obvious, truly inevitable, thoroughly inessential and utterly uncontrollable things in life, like the weather... Like how the seasons change... And no matter how much it's expected, every farewell brings sadness with it... Even a season... Because after all, what the sights and sounds and smells of a season evoke are feelings... Memories... That linger way after the season has made way for the new one...

I just now received a rejection for one of my papers... It's strange how we spend our lives seeking and craving acceptance from all quarters... for our honest toil and sweat from some less than scrupulous academician disbursing decisions with less than honest considerations; from our spouses who may be temperamentally way different and far inferior as human beings than ourselves; from our relatives whose only contributions in our lives may have been to engage us in unproductive activities; from our colleagues who we know would stab us from behind in the first possible opportunity; from our friends who are more there out of familiarity than out of feelings... Strange how we try to be civil and nice and be accepted when deep down all we want to do is revolt and rebel and be done with all of this!...

... you're still on medication then I believe... I thought you must've been a lot better when you were doing physics etc... do take care please... are you weak?... I know chicken stew, eggs etc to be very helpful to get rid of weakness, but given you're vegetarian, I don't know what to say... mosambi (sweet lime/lemon) is also very good... I know you're having the best of advice from all quarters so let me not bother you with that... I remember you liked mushroom sandwiches, so maybe someone can make you some mushroom soup etc?...

And I hopefully won't give up, on all quarters... you know, when my mother used to single-handedly look after my father (when he was sick and I was in the US), everyone used to exclaim and say how my mother could do and manage everything!... and my mother used to smile and say, anybody thrown into the river would try to swim - nothing remarkable about it... in a way that's true... when you do have an ailing husband, what do you do but look after him, even by expending your last bit?...

because if she chose not to, my father would just be left to his Fate... so she really had no choice...

It's possibly a bad analogy, but it's somewhat similar to keep trying (for anything for that matter)... because the alternative is not to try... to leave everything to Fate... to adapt to inaction, inactivity... to stagnate and rot and age... without a fight... without the bitterness of failure maybe, but also without the flicker of hope... that alternative seems to be much more horrible than that which comes with failure... so I'd probably keep trying even if I know I'd fail with probability 0.99... and that's what you always say and do too... how do you manage to keep your spirit so indomitable... and face all adversaries and adversities with such extraordinary resilience... you're such a remarkable person!..

❧

With the recently concluded US elections, I had been meaning to share an old paper of mine with you (but didn't since you weren't well)... Thought you might be interested in the electorate (and its expansion)... It's about women's suffrage in the states of the US... Even though it's the first world, women were universally enfranchised only as late as 1920... However prior to that states could extend suffrage to women and the paper's about that... Ironically (and sadly maybe) though there were a lot of apprehension as to how women voters would vote, it turned out that they voted almost on similar lines as their male counterparts (I guess they've never been able to come out of the influence of fathers and husbands and sons...)... Please have a look at your convenience and let me know what you think of it...

It is one of my dissertation chapters and the only one in which I have used empirics!... I remember I used to spend hours in the library actually looking up American Census reports of the 1860s or so... And I used Stata for the analysis... Sometimes at the end of the day, I found I had run the software some 800 times!... But I am sure I am not an empirical person per se and didn't have enough enthusiasm to do such exercises again...:-)...

On another but related note, I have a new phd student who wants to work on gender issues... commonly known as feminism... though I hate to call it so since the word feminist conjures up images of loud voices, protests and resistance to any and everything that has any 'male' perspective which I don't always find very acceptable...

I guess I feel too much of a scientist to think of myself only as a woman and again, too much of a woman to think of myself only as a scientist... and it's a little problematic to feel both...

I remember I had presented this women's suffrage paper of mine at a feminism conference in Italy which neither my advisor approved of... nor the feminist audience approve of... my advisor didn't want me to be identified with the feminists (you're a mainstream scientist!, he'd say and he wanted me to distance myself from them)... and the feminists didn't like the rational political explanation to women gaining suffrage (they'd rather be happy with the 'hard-fought-hard-won' right story)...

So you'd either be a mainstream scientist with mostly no sympathy for gender perspectives at all... or you could be a feminist where your narratives are mostly coloured and gendered... somehow both extremes seem unsuitable for me... and I wander here in between... most of the feminists actually belong to gender studies kind of departments, not 'science' departments... no wonder, I'm the only woman in our department and in our university, and the only faculty member interested in such issues... but the questions themselves that concern gender are very close to my heart... and the nuanced perspective of studying these issues with sympathy and understanding, away from the accepted and the standard techniques and outlooks...

❧

You mentioned the other day that ma will be better soon, especially because I take good care of her... I was so touched that I didn't know how to respond... you don't even know what I do (and what I don't), yet you know I take good care…

I give medicines to her from time to time as per doctor's prescription, given her high doses of insulin, I also try to give her snacks and meals frequently (which means I have to keep the ingredients ready and make them as required)… Given her poor eyesight, I help her with most of her academic commitments (like typing her recommendation letters for her students, helping her with proof reading etc.)… sometimes when she doesn't feel well, I am usually awake most of the night trying to comfort her… it feels awkward even thinking about things that are perhaps obvious and any considerate daughter would do, yet they take entire days (and nights) and are bounded by physical ability and limitations... Maybe I could have done more...

And there's been colleagues and friends you know who've wanted to have coffee with me... sometimes ones who've been visiting from abroad even... but honestly I haven't been able to spare that one hour for coffee... not just now... even before, it's always been either work or family for me and I couldn't manage to take out an hour from either...

Now when I think of it, it seems perhaps I didn't want to... they wanted to have coffee with me but not I with them... but with you it's different... it's probably the other way round... you probably don't want to have coffee with me but then I'd like to have a cup with you...

⁂

Very occasionally, Parshati wrote letters to him (on paper).

A letter... again... in lieu of inhaling aromatic coffee... in lieu of feeling your penetrating gaze... in lieu of seeing the pattern (or its absence) on the shirt you're wearing... in lieu of your stiff upper lip letting a smile slip by... in lieu of your head smartly jerking with a chuckle... in lieu of your curly hair crowning your very handsome physique and all of it housing an even more handsome soul... in lieu of the light and shade of the cafe and the muffled out din of the street outside... and in lieu of an interminable and often unbearable wait end... the wait continues and so does conjuring up all the excuses in the world to meet you and let it end...

In a way, that we don't meet is good... I often think it would be nice if I could meet you invisibly... And if we probably did,

I think I could never say all that I think I would over all the days and nights that I keep imagining this absolutely ethereal bliss… of meeting you… In a way writing gives you the space and the time to put down your haphazard and piled up thoughts of years together in a somewhat sane manner…

I think here I will leave you. It has come to seem

there is no perfect ending.

Indeed, there are infinite endings.

Or perhaps, once one begins,

there are only endings. (Louise Gluck)

So let me not begin my letter… let me just pen a few scattered thoughts and take you along with me through my words… and the golden dusk… and the tired day… and the vibrant night… and the blushing cherry blossoms and the coy city whispering to her enslaved girl…

Well, as I said, a letter that hasn't begun cannot end… or maybe it can … in words and pages and punctuations… but let the feeling and the thoughts linger and melt in you long after you're done with physically reading it…

Well, happy to indefinitely smile and wait on you… I will remain yours patiently forever…

P.S.: Sorry if I went overboard in expressing a torrent of emotions… writing with the abandon and confidence of a child* includes writing to you as well, doesn't it?:-)

(*Once when Parshati had expressed her anguish over how she got torn between the writer in her and the woman in her, Dr Dashorathi had laid all her vexations to rest and said that she should write with the "abandon and confidence of a child".)

15. বড় দীর্ঘ কঠিন পথ...

When I used to stand in the lobby area outside the RITU for long hours during the day, and watch the hospital stir into activities in the morning and then lull into rest at night, somehow there were a few lines that kept coming to mind... খালি মনে হত, মা... "বড় দীর্ঘ কঠিন পথ..."... মনে হত "we've been thrown in a pit and we're being whiplashed"... কিরম যেন visualise করতাম... অন্ধকার একটা গর্তের মধ্যে ফেলে দিয়ে আমাদের দুজনকে, কে বা কারা যেন চাবুক দিয়ে মারছে... কোন নিস্তার নেই... আর আমি তোমাকে বাঁচাতে চেষ্টা করছি...

আর যখন বুকের মধ্যে জল জমেছে বলত না মা ডাক্তাররা, খালি মনে হত তোমার মনের মধ্যেকার কষ্টগুলো জল হয়ে জমে আছে... একবার ওগুলো বার করে দিলে আর কোনদিন কোন কষ্ট তোমার মনের মধ্যে জমতে দেব না... সে সুযোগ তো আমাকে দিলে না মা...

আমি অনেকদিন ভাবতাম জান মা, যে অন্য লোকেরা কি pray করে... অনেক বছর আগে বাবার জন্য pray করতাম... তুমি সেই বাবার বুকের কাছে একটা হাড় একটু ওঠা ছিল বলে হাত বুলিয়ে বলতে না "হ্যাঁগো, কিছু না তো... হ্যাঁগো কিছু না তো?"... আর কটকে যখন ছিলাম, ওই quarters -এর সামনে তিনটে গাছ ছিল না... somehow ওগুলোকে ভগবান ভাবতে বড় ভালো লাগত... আর HS -এ যখন stand করলাম তখন আরও মনে হত তোমরা যেন সুস্থ থাকো, যেন ঠিক থাকো... খুব ভালো কিছু হওয়া মানে, খুব unexpected খারাপ কিছুও তো হওয়ার probability বেশি, না...

So I wondered what might be a foolproof prayer... so God might not let any harm descend on my parents?... I distinctly remember when I prayed for my father, I used to mention all the organs... something like "বাবার যেন ব্রেন ভালো থাকে, হার্ট ভালো থাকে,... etc"... but I was around 16/17 and to err is human and somehow God made me err on an organ He would later choose to take my father away through… somehow I had suddenly realised that I did not mention "lungs" in the long list that I tried to say in my prayers every night… but why had God made me forget "lungs" specifically?… because He was planning on giving him lung cancer later on?… I started mentioning lungs when I remembered but after a while… but I guess it was too late and he passed away from it when he was only 57…

We never get to see other people's minds… so we never really know the thoughts and prayers that people have… so ma, remember, I often used to ask you "মা… তুমি কি pray করো?"… and you used to say something like, "ঠাকুর, আমাকে কোন বড় দুঃখ দিও না" or "give me what I deserve"…

So ma, I really didn't know what to pray this time, after baba was no more… what should I pray to have you with me for a long time?… আবার যদি ভগবান আমার ভুলের সুযোগ নেন… this time I did not want to take any chances… so I used to say something like "মা যেন সুস্থ থাকে, মা'র sugar, pressure যেন ঠিক থাকে, মা'র অন্য কোন বড় অসুখ যেমন cancer যেন না হয় …"… but I guess God has his way of finding loopholes no matter how foolproof your prayers are… or you think they are…

মা, তুমি চলে যাবার পর, তখনও তুমি শুয়ে আছো বিছানায়, সবাই আমার সঙ্গে কথা বলছে শুধু তুমি ছাড়া… কী যে অদ্ভুত লাগছে যে কি বলি… সবার কিরম অদ্ভুত কথা জান… মাসীমণি বলছে 5 years থাকলে না নতুন বাড়িতে… মানেটা কি?… What is so sacrosanct about 5 years?… 3 years তো ছিলে… সেটা বড় কথা নয়?… How did she even come up with the threshold of 5 years?…

আর বলল, মুখটা কালো লাগছে ... which was probably true... I think, there was some kind of bleeding inside you and all the blood had gushed towards your face... বাবা কেওড়াতলায় গেছিল বলে তুমি ওখানেই যাবে বলেছিলে না... on the way, তোমাকে পেছনে শোয়ানো ছিল তো... নাকে তুলো দেওয়া ছিল... তবু মনে হল deep brown colour-এর watery liquid নাকের পাশে জমা হয়েছিল... I believe it was some kind of blood oozing out... old brown blood... the blood that didn't let you be... আর ভাবো, সায়ন মামা প্রথম জিজ্ঞেস করল কত খরচ হয়েছে ... imagine...

তুমি চলে যাওয়ার পর কিরম physically কষ্ট হত জান... মনে হত, নিঃশ্বাস নিতে পারছি না ঠিক করে... মনে হত, invisible ঢেউরা চতুর্দিকে আছে... এমনি কিছু করে না, শুধু হঠাৎ করে এসে ধাক্কা দিয়ে যায়... মনে হত, শুয়ে থেকে আর উঠতে পারছি না... আমি তোমার থেকেই তো এসেছি... I mean literally, physically... বাবা চলে যেতে একরকম কষ্ট হত... তোমার চলে যাওয়াটা কিরম যেন অন্যরকম কষ্ট দেয়... সত্যি নাড়ির বন্ধন ছিন্ন হল যেন...

ওলি হওয়ার সময় internet-এ দেখতাম না কি করে বাচ্চা বড় হয় মায়ের ভেতরে... how the first part of the body that gets formed inside the mother's womb is the heart... imagine a small heart beating... that was how I was inside you... your heart pumped blood into mine... a lot of motherhood is emotional of course... but a lot of it is purely physical, isn't it...

I wrote this a few days after you left us ma...

The heart that pumped blood into mine has stopped
The umbilical cord that held me firmly inside the womb
Was now just ashes...

I had taken her in the car a couple of months back
To the nearby hospital
Sat beside her
Held her tight
She panted and gasped for air
I had pumped oxygen in her mask
From the portable cylinder
Till we reached the hospital…

A couple of months later
I once again sat beside her in the car
This time she was not panting
Or gasping for air
She looked happy and peaceful
The man in the photo shop held an umbrella over her
While they helped her in the car
This time also I held her tight
She sat framed in a photograph beside me…

ICU-তে বাইরে যখন দাঁড়িয়ে থাকতাম, কত লোকের কত রকম কথা শুনতাম জান মা… দুজন ছেলে ছিল রাঁচি থেকে… তাদের বাবা ভর্তি ছিল ICU-তে… ওই তোমার মতো…অনেকদিন… তাদের ও লাখ লাখ টাকা bill হয়েছিল… তারা তাদের জমি বিক্রি করে এখানে হোটেলে থেকে বাবার চিকিৎসা করাচ্ছিল… এখানে চিকিৎসা ঠিক করে হচ্ছে না বলে ওরা air ambulance-এর ব্যবস্থা করে অন্য কোথাও (probably Haryana) ওদের বাবাকে নিয়ে গেল… কিন্তু তুমি চলে যাওয়ার কয়েকদিন আগে শুনলাম ওদের বাবা-ও নেই…

মালদহ থেকে একজন ভাই-বোন তাদের মা'র চিকিৎসা করাতো... ওদের Dr-ও বলল ওদের মা'কে ventilation-এ দিতে হবে... আগে একবার ওনার ventilation হয়েছিল few years back...but she was well after that... this time their family refused... I don't know how she was after that but they got her discharged and took her home with oxygen masks etc...

There was another woman, on the bed next to you, who had lung cancer and doctors had all given up hope... but her husband also got her discharged and took her home... with a lot of faith in some ayurvedic medicine that he was getting from somewhere else...

Another woman (a junior doctor used to call her 'auntie' আবার জানত!) really had no one around her... distant relative/ friend type-এর দুজন আসত... হয়ত ছেলে মেয়েরা বিদেশে থাকে... she was put on ventilation and dialysis, just like you... just within a few days, একদিন সকালে গিয়ে দেখি she is no more... আগের দিন dialysis চলার সময় নাকি কিছু হয়েছিল...

But you know why I remember her... because just the previous night when I was there to see you, since she was just on the adjacent bed, I could see her... and I especially saw her feet... they were pedicured with bright red nail polish on it... হয়ত বাড়িতে কোন function ছিল... হয়ত এমনি সাজতেগুজতে ভালোবাসতো... সে কি আর জানতো যে কয়েকদিন পরে আর এ পৃথিবীতে থাকবেই না... কিরম অদ্ভুত irony না...

Blood cancer-এর আরও দুজন patient ছিল... আর এই আড়াই মাসের মধ্যে যে কতজন চলেও গেল মা... and I just wished you wouldn't be one of them... but you were...

আর যেরম nurse-দের গাফিলতি তো ছিলই...তোমার dialysis চলার সময় potassium injection দেওয়ার কথা ছিল... সেটা আমি গিয়ে বললাম... তবে দিল...

কেমন করে patient-দের রাখে মা... কেমন করে লোকে ভালো হবে?...আমার বলার কথা?... nurse-গুলো দেখবে না?... বিন্দুমাত্র কোন coordination নেই জান... একবার তোমার pressure 60/30 হয়ে গেল... আমি তো হাঁ করে চেয়ে থাকতাম তোমার monitor -এর দিকে ... আমি বললাম তবে ওরা ওষুধ দিল... dialysis -এর সময় continuously pressure fluctuate করে বলে someone has to continuously monitor and take steps... so I mostly insisted that dialysis be done when I would be there...

একবার জানো তোমার Albumin injection 2 units যাওয়ার কথা... আমি দেখলাম 1 unit গেছে...when I asked them they had all kinds of excuses like রাত্তিরে pharmacy -তে indent হয়নি, etc... and they confessed 1 unit গেছে... had I not pointed out, it would have been 1 unit... বাকিদের বাড়ির লোক তো আর দেখছে না ... আর আমিও তো সব সময় তোমার কাছে থাকতে পারিনা ...

একবার dialysis রাত্তিরে schedule করল ... সেই সময় cardiac arrest হল তোমার ... ওরা ওই electric shock না কি দেয় না... সেবার ভালো হয়ে গেছিলে but it was signalling the end you know... তারপর আর রাত্তিরে dialysis schedule করতে দিতাম না ... সেটাও commercial reason - so the dialysis machines would be available for OPD during the day... in-patient-দের রাত-বিরেতে দিত... when there were fewer people around and monitoring was much less and no one's family members could be around... যা ইচ্ছে তখনই তো করা যায়, না?!...

সত্যি মা এই আড়াই মাস তোমার তো একরকম কষ্ট গেছে ... এই সবের মধ্যে দিয়ে যাওয়াটা যে আমার কী কষ্টকর হয়েছে যে কী বলি ... I know you'd understand... I know that you know...

And you know the other day our ex-CM was rushed to the hospital with oxygen level 70 (much worse than yours) and was put on ventilation... and he is a COPD patient... and about ten years older to you... but then he came out of ventilation after two days and came back home after about ten days… and they said in the news that there was a dedicated team of doctors looking after him round the clock… তোমাকেও এতটা attention দিলে, এতটা যত্নে রাখলে হয়ত তুমিও ভালো হতে মা… বাড়ি আসতে আমার কাছে… হয়ত আরও অনেক patient-ই ভালো হত… best হাসপাতালের ICU-এর এই অবস্থা হলে, বাকিদের কি অবস্থা… কোথায় যাবে সবাই…

শরীরটা তো হাতের বাইরে… মা'র diabetes, kidney dysfunction, এগুলো তো হাতের বাইরে… কিন্তু মনের মধ্যে কষ্ট নিয়ে চলে গেল মা?… মনের মধ্যে কষ্ট নিয়েই চলে গেল… কেমন যেন মনে হত ওই কষ্টগুলোই pneumonia হয়ে ছিল lungs এর মধ্যে … যখন মা'র scans দেখাতো না ডাক্তার, তখন খালি মনে হত lungs এর ওই patches গুলো কষ্ট থেকেই হয়েছে…

ইদানিং তিনটে জিনিস ঠাকুরের কাছে চাইতাম… একটাও কথা শুনলে না ঠাকুর… প্রথমত চেয়েছিলাম মা ভালো হোক, যখন বুঝলাম, মা হয়ত ভালো হয়ে আর বাড়ি আসবে না তখন চেয়েছিলাম at least আমাদের কাছে থেকে চলে যাক বাড়ি থেকে, তাও না হলে at least hospital এ দেখি চলে যেতে… সেই তুমি চলে গেলে হাসপাতাল থেকে আমার চোখের আড়ালে… শেষ সময়টুকু তোমার কাছে থাকতে পারলাম না…

একটাও কথা ঠাকুর শুনলে না … ঠিক ভোররাতে হাসপাতাল থেকে ফোন এলো মা আর নেই বলে… গিয়ে দেখতেও পেলাম না… কেমন যেন মুখ ঘুরিয়ে শুয়ে ছিল আর দেখবে না বলে…

বাবার সময় যেরম হয়েছিল… বাবা যখন চলে গেল, আমি, মা, পাশে দাঁড়িয়ে… baba's eyes were so dilated… he had lung cancer and was counting moments of his life… it was dusk… and in that fourth floor room of the nursing home, ma and I were right beside him… he looked at ma, and then looked at me, and with a questioning look seemed to say, 'what the hell is going on?… do you have any clue?'… and not getting any answer from us, he had closed his eyes forever… but somehow the end was beautiful… beautiful in that we could be with him right till we couldn't follow him any longer… ma and I could think of this last moment forever…

But with ma it was different… she was in this ICU for about two and a half months… with the most hard-hearted bevy of medical professionals that I have ever seen… it was like she was surrounded by hostile, unfriendly faces and couldn't even see me when she had to leave…

কেমন মেয়ে হলে তাদের বাবা-মা অনেকদিন থাকে?… I used to ask God… why did you take both my parents away so early… would you not have, had I been a better daughter?… outwardly I appear very heartless, haven't shed a drop of tear in front of anyone, even when they were crying… the only person I've cried in front of is ma… I sometimes couldn't control myself standing beside ma's bed… it hurt when doctors said all kinds of things… it hurt even more to think how hurt ma would be to know they were hurting me… it hurt because I couldn't share everything with ma when she asked Dr কি বলল? … it hurt to lie to ma…

এরম concerned আর কেউ কোনদিন হবে না মা… কে এত ভাবত আমার কথা?…তুমি বলতে মনে আছে guard রা তোকে উঁচু-নিচু কথা বলবে আমার সহ্য হবে না, তুই যা … and used to send me away…

16. Lost in You

(Parshati had written a letter of recommendation for Dr Dashorathi when he applied for some academic program abroad. He however, did not accept it citing some financial reasons. But later on when they met once in his office, Parshati had a feeling that financial constraints were there but he could have gotten around them - the real reason he did not go was because he didn't want to leave Parshati behind.

Parshati did not know the full import of Dr Dashorathi leaving when she had agreed to write for him. But once he got accepted, she felt devastated. Just at the thought of Dr Dashorathi going far away, something wrenched deep within her, and the night he sent her his acceptance letter, she couldn't stop her tears from flowing. Though, even when both of them were in Kolkata, they hardly met. They had possibly met about three or four times in almost a decade. Yet Parshati had never felt so closer to anyone else.

She had met him once after he received his acceptance letter. And she wrote this to him after getting back.)

When you asked me to write for you, you know, it was like doing something together... like talking about your essays together, thinking about your childhood... I agreed mostly because it involved 'you' every moment of it... and that was so tempting... much longed for... much desired... much like taking the Artificial Intelligence* course... I honestly took it not for the sake of AI as such, but more because it was something you were learning with so much interest... just to be doing what you had been doing… just like spending some time with you without actually having spent it… like when I was doing something that you had done, it was like bringing a whiff of you to me... in all the abstract senses that an admiring mind conjures up... so when you asked me to write for you it was like a dream coming true... but maybe I wasn't really matured enough to anticipate how I'd feel if you actually got through… often we don't know our feelings, till they are tested isn't it… everything was so uncontrollable when I thought you'd leave… everything got so blurry and teary whenever I thought of you being far away…

And it's been so hard writing to you since the last time I visited you… wasn't like other times at all… I think it will never be the same again… it's been hard thinking about it… it's been hard writing to you about it… in fact that's the reason I didn't write to you about it at all… what I felt was somehow too deep for words, too deep for expression, too deep for poems even… I don't know if I'll ever feel the same again… that hour with you was so blessed... was like a lifetime... I could never imagine that someone other than my parents would care so much about me… ma had cancelled her tickets to Malaysia on the day she was supposed to travel because I had cried… and you... I am sure if you wanted enough you could have managed something on the financial front… you didn't because you didn't want to hurt me… no one has given me so much importance… has valued my emotions so much… has cared for my feelings so much after my parents, the way you have… the way you do... and I honestly am lost for words… because I really don't know how I feel… it's way too deep for any expression whatsoever…

whenever I wrote anything after the Saturday I visited you, it sounded so jumbled and confused... but here's something... it's not a poem like the others... I won't share it with anyone... read it with having a totally-lost woman in mind... totally lost in you and your kindness...

My blessed hour
My lifetime in an hour
And all I felt were gardens and oceans
And storms and sunsets
All together and all at once
That spread in acres and acres
Within me...

Have you seen
The you-me space that you built
Has a little village
With inviting gardens
Where time rolled into us
And we rolled into timelessness
And all the time you kept playing with my soils
Digging your strong hands in them at times
Loosely gathering the lumps at times
Crumpling them with your strong fingers at times
And letting them fall all over at times

And strands of grass
And the tiniest of green leaves that were mine
Would cling on to your muddy hands
And everything that smelled of moist grass
And moist soil and moist sun
And moist air and moist love
Now unmistakably smelled of you…
And you'd plant the softest sapling
In my soils and water them with your smiles
And they'd nod their heads
Like they want to grow...

Somehow you made me float
In the waters that made waves
Yet stayed still like a lake
Water that made unseen deep marks
And created beautiful patterns
Like rain criss-crossing on the pane of my mind
Water, that kept me afloat and drowned me
Water that slipped off me like your furtive look
Water that clung to me like your deep affection
Water that washed away all that I tried to cover
And laid me completely bare before you

And water that hid me behind
Oceans of impossibility and dreams…

In that fraction of a second
When my eyelids descended to cover my eyes
And stop me from seeing you for the last time
I felt you right beside me
In the deepest forest
And the loneliest night
Just where my skin ended
And everything that wasn't mine began
You kept vigil lest an erratic wind touched me
Alert lest an unwanted thought crept up
Cautious lest an unloving whiff made way
Attentive lest a hopelessness brushed past me
And you smothered my being in a you-ish cloak…

Life's such a big sieve
Lets everything fall through
In the abyss of time
While you are the strands of hope
And belief and trust
Leading me on through darkness
Lending me your chest

To rest my head on

While I slip into a peaceful sleep

In the calmest sunset

Forever and forever…

*Artificial Intelligence was an online course from Coursera that Dr Dashorathi, given his academic inclination, had taken. And Parshati too had taken it later on.

17. They

The first time doctors said ma could be put on ventilation, I stayed in the hospital at night. (Though she wasn't put on ventilation that day.) This was the first time I had left Oli overnight. The rule in the hospital was for the patient parties to wait in the lobby on the ground floor. But I didn't want to go far away from ma. We couldn't stay in the ICU, so I stayed outside in the corridor, sitting on the stairs, leaning against the wall.

Ma was extremely opposed to my staying overnight in the hospital. She was fully conscious then, and in spite of the oxygen cannula in her nose, she could speak, even if indistinctly. She kept saying how, when my father was ill and hospitalised (he passed away around twelve years back, succumbing to lung cancer, that he fought with, for six long years, during which he often had to be hospitalised), she used to stay with him, but hospital during the day time was vastly different from hospital during the night. She made me promise that I won't stay during the night again. And our chauffeur also came much later than when I asked him to the next day. So, I kept my promise to ma. I did not stay in the hospital overnight again.

It was a daily ritual for me to put some cream etc. on ma, when I left for the night, while she was in the hospital. I kept these in the small bedside drawers that they provided for every patient - Body Shop's vitamin E enriched lip balm for the lips, vitamin E enriched cream for the face (which ma actually indicated earlier was even sometimes used by the nurses) and Nivea 24 hours moisture protection lotion for her legs and hands. Recently the hands seemed skeletal, once there were deep black patches which they called 'hematoma'. Often there was an arterial line in the hand so I could not find enough space on the hand to put cream on.

At some point towards the end, they said there was 'footdrop', that is, neurologically her control of feet was gone for one of the feet. Nowadays anything that didn't sound life threatening made no impact. Actually we've been warned so many times that even anything life threatening seemed to have little impact. That afternoon, when my husband and daughter came to pick me up, it was almost the end of ma.

Nowadays she used to open her eyes but not look at anything specifically. There didn't seem to be any focus. When I went to talk to her that afternoon, everything in her face seemed to be drooping and ending and I called out to the nurse who was taking a blood sample from the central line on the neck. Swati di called out to Jayram dada (who was the head nurse) and the doctor in charge, Dr Satya. When all of them had come, I came away thinking probably this was the end of ma. Turned out that the next day was. That afternoon they stabilised her BP, once more did the arterial line for monitoring of BP because it was fluctuating.

Since we went back late, my husband didn't come back and I came alone for the evening. I remember I told my husband that I don't want to leave ma, but he said my daughter loved having me wake her up, that she was growing a bit silent and wouldn't talk in the car. So I came back. When I went in the night, somehow all the nurses and doctors who usually had duty in RITU 2 were not there and other doctors who usually had duty in RITU 1 were on duty. When I left for the night, they said her haemoglobin was 7 and at that moment her BP was stable.

I called up Palashi di the nurse in charge, and she said ma was sleeping… was okay. But in the wee hours of the morning around 5, when I had probably dozed off a bit, my mobile, that I usually kept right beside my pillow, began ringing. I really didn't have to receive it to know what would be said. There was someone calling from Apollo. "আপনি 295 patient-এর বাড়ির লোক বলছেন তো?… cardiac arrest… আমরা খুব চেষ্টা করছি … আপনারা please আসুন…"…

I almost knew what I'd expect when I reached the hospital… everybody else was busy doing other stuff… ma's bed had curtains drawn around it… that is how things were when someone passed away… I saw it for other patients in the ward who had their time come… and earlier I earnestly prayed, it wouldn't be ma's…

The dr came and explained that she really was no more and what seemed like her breathing was really the ventilator support… সেই ma was no more…finally, she was no more… she had left me… forever… where I could not follow her…

They said it'll be some time before the bills are cleared, the body is prepared, whether we'd like to bring her clothes from our home (to which I said no)… to check the name of the spelling of her name, address etc., somehow only her mother's name and my father's name were required, both late.

While we waited in the small room opposite the RITU ward, Subhrajyoti, a kind, junior doctor, who didn't see ma directly, but knew me from my waiting outside for days together, came to say sorry, Rakesh Gupta the security supervisor came to talk to us. Then visiting hours started but I didn't have anyone to visit inside.

They took her out face covered, everything covered in white and took us out through a different exit and ma came out of Apollo forever. At the burning ghat I put ghee on her forehead and chin and cheeks just like I used to put vitamin E enriched face cream. Usually she used to move her face and chin and lips around a bit to help me put the cream. This time she didn't do anything of the sort…

I wrote this after I began writing again, which would be about a couple of months after ma was no more…

They

Usually phone calls in the wee hours of the morning

Bring lurking fears right into your bedroom

The phone rang and even before I received it

I almost knew the news

They called from the hospital…

Strange I didn't want to look at ma

She looked so white

So bloated

So disproportionate

And her head was turned away from me
Like she didn't have the heart to talk to me…

They wrapped her in white
And led her out from a different exit
One that we hadn't seen before
One that didn't have visitors jostling in the lifts
Or the ardent ones
Offering prayers to the idol
That religiously guarded the entry
To the path that could
Either lead you back to earth
Or take you to some unknown land…

Ma who was scared
Even of getting into an MRI machine
Was hurriedly carried away
Like some ominous secret
Like a child born out of wedlock
Whose existence they want to
Wash their hands off from
Like wiping off the last blood stain
After a heinous murder
And she didn't even protest…

They had it all decorated with white flowers
The ones she loved the most
And they kept her on the road
In the blistering sun
No one cared that she might get scorched
But they led us in the shade
To get things signed
And have the papers in order…

Instead of cream on her face and forehead
And vaseline on her lips
Like I usually used to apply,
They asked me to apply
Ghee, from a big bottle
Even on her toes and legs
Like greasing the wheels of the vehicle
That will take her to some unknown land…

18. Night

Dr Dashorathi,

You know I just happened to stumble upon the boy on whom I had a huge crush in college... At some point I may have cried because I couldn't reach him, I cry now because I did...

At some point he said he wanted to trek in a desert, and believed in leftist ideals and used to sing songs... I was in fact surprised to learn that he admired me a lot too (remembered vividly small things about the times we did get to spend time together in college like what I was wearing etc.)... And that he found me very pretty and attractive and that he was a fan of my "obscenely gigantic brain"... though none of us ever said anything along those lines...

Now he doesn't sing anymore, and is a corporate slave... talks about back to back calls and meetings and clients from the US and Europe in the evenings... dinner at 8 and bed at 11... a bit of cooking during the weekend... and doesn't have kids since he doesn't have that kind of commitment... This time, I found it hard to even talk to him... Strange, how, at times, conversations just wouldn't end, and now they just wouldn't begin... I realised that it's impossible to recreate spaces and times... and that the person I adored was lost, possibly trekking in the deserts of time... but I still let him live in my memories...

You know I am thoroughly city-bred and totally urban in tastes and preferences... Yet I guess nature has its way of finding inlets through unlikeliest of chinks... Like an occasional dove nesting on my window sill... :-)... And you know I hardly know the names of trees and plants... So I can't tell you the name of the pink flowers that coyly colour the sky and remind me of the spring cherry blossoms of Washington... But I do know the red Krishnachura, Shimul and Palash or the yellow Radhachura... But just the names... I don't think I have the ear to hear their beats or the heart to feel their rhythms... Or the eyes to read the hidden messages in the riotous inviting colours... Pity I haven't been close enough to flowers and birds to write about them the way Tagore or Jibanananda did... Pity I don't hear their songs the way Wordsworth did... Pity I don't see and paint their stories the way Van Gogh did...

Yet there are unmistakable streaks of spring strewn here and there that capture the thought of even someone like me... I don't know whether you're near or away from Nature and how the landscape around you looks... But since you've been away for a while... Just wanted to wish you the unexplained ecstasy and the freshness in the scent of our beloved city during the onset of spring... :-)...

❦

Ma's (possibly) 27th book just got published you know... it's a monograph on Roma Chaudhuri - a stalwart oriental scholar... she was a student of Radhakrishnan in Oxford... and had extensively worked on Vedanta etc.... Ma even organised a webinar on her and it was a huge success...

But everything has become increasingly harder for ma... she is now having to make great efforts to read... newspapers are completely illegible to her and even for books, she needs about three very powerful lamps and magnifying glass... nowadays, even sitting for a while, has become problematic... her feet become incredibly swollen...

And yet she sits for long hours writing... in a way, that's what keeps her absorbed and distracted... how much can you harp on one's ailments... and she says it takes her mind off distressing thoughts... her review is due in a few days, you know, and I feel so weak and nervous...

I know whatever is the truth has to be faced and dealt with... her creatinine was already above upper limits and doctors say diabetic nephropathy is progressive... I try everything possible to be done physically but still I am afraid her symptoms don't seem better...

And I do want to tell you again that I understand how incredibly busy you are and that writing to you and sending you my writings now and then, surely disturb you and amount to being annoying elements perhaps... but honestly, even when you don't respond, I have this feeling that if and when you do get some time, maybe you will have a look... and I'd wait till eternity for that moment... And sharing about ma and my daughter, I really have no greater friend... no one evokes greater feelings of blessedness and security the way your presence does... no one instills greater sense of indispensability and benevolence of my presence for my family, the way you do...

Let me share this poem of mine with you.

Night

Night's a shawl
That squeezes distance
Into tears
And brings the freshness of spring
Into hot dreary summer stillness
And speaks to me
In unheard whispers
Carrying your scent
Across perpetual oceans
And drenching me
In your purest dreams...

Night's a relief
Because others can't see
The lump that seems to choke
My throat and mouth
That melts through tears that
Somehow can't stop
Wetting my cheeks,
And the night that stays awake
In my eyes

Feel smothered and released
All together and all at once
In one seamless trail
And one unending streak
Of a void that's so sharp
It numbs all pain…

Night's a traveller
That finds its ways
Through my veins
And in my heart
Exploring the treasures
You might have
Carelessly strewn
When you walked by
The sunshine that your look
Has gifted me
That I had carefully
Preserved for light
When you leave
And my road's all dark…

Night's all nests and love
The other day when

The storm left the nest
All lying scattered
Across the window
The eggs shattered and
The home destroyed
I somehow knew
You could smell the disarray
Within me and in the air
And see the vacant empty
Look that my eyes had
And the helplessness
That my dove felt…

Night's a story
The spring that the air held
Couldn't travel too far
But it brought you to me
In splashes of pink blossoms
And fiery red drops
And vibrant shades of green
And unashamed yellows
That torn away all inhibitions
From my trembling heart
And laid it bare for you

To write on
It's another matter that
You left it quite blank...

Night's a storm
The scorching heat
That turned the salt in my skin
To sweet sweat
Somehow found freshness
In the thought of your look
That seemed to slowly
Weaken all resolve
And disintegrate
All determination that I
Had gathered up
All through the long winter
And the unannounced nor'westers
Finally blew off
All that I thought was mine
And left me with all that was 'you'...

Night's a desire
The golden dusks
Seemed to spread your smile

All over me, unabashed
And unhindered and it
Sometimes carried
You in chariots of gold
To reign unrestrained
Over all I ever had
Over all I ever want
Over all of me
Spreading like a burning desire
That burns itself
Like a god who doesn't know
His own whims and wishes
And that he sometimes kills…

Night's a lake
The lake that held our gazes
The lake that heard
My confessions
The lake that sent
Across calmness
To soothe my restless soul
The lake that knew much more
Than both you and me
The lake that cried with me

And waited with me

And longed with me

For one who had promised

A ride with me…

Night's a pillow

That doesn't speak

That doesn't smile

That doesn't turn away

That doesn't cheer you up

It just absorbs

And sends you its silence

In peace and reconciliation

In truth and destiny

In understanding and sympathy

In resignation and hope

In love and fortitude

In friendship and company

In promise and certitude…

(Parshati wrote this after one of the few times she met Dr Dashorathi.)

Strange night

It was a strange night yesterday
You sat as a dew drop on my cheek
The whole night
Sentinel to the chaos in my heart
And the unseen storms within
And you slid along my eyelashes
And tiptoed and balanced
And just settled on the tips
To catch a glimpse of
All that it was hiding inside
As if you needed to…
The smudged kohl lining my lids
Was a remnant of the landscape
That painted our dreams
And bordered our ignorance…

April, they say, is the cruellest month
It is also the kindest
Somehow entwining your life with mine
Letting the roots hold each other
And dig deep

To search for comfort and company
And letting your memories
Share a season of longing
And build a castle of belonging
In the vast aridity of loneliness
And fill it with a you-ness
That smelled of love…

19. A Dream

Dr Dashorathi,

So this is what I dreamt... I had gone somewhere with my parents... I was an adult girl but not married or anything... I woke up in the morning but couldn't find my parents... so I went out and there was this small lobby kind of a place with single sofas, upholstery in wooden structures... so I sat there and was wondering, when I felt someone walk in.... My back was turned so I turned to see... and I saw you...

I thought I knew you were in the same place but didn't think you'd be there, so then I was delighted and said let me just wash up and then we can talk for a while, would you please be there?... and you said you'd leave at 11 and I saw the wall clock it was around 10:10 then, so I said 'great' and started walking back to the room and you followed...

Then I saw you in the sort of living space near the bedroom and you were talking on the phone and I went inside the bathroom... and bolted it... there were two bolts, one on top and the other below... the bathroom was pretty big and I was washing my face... but I could hear you talk on the phone...

Then at some point I found you talking on the phone still but you were walking inside the bathroom... but I wasn't aware and was still turned away from you at the basin, so you held me slightly from behind and just indicated that you'd be going outside and waiting for me (because you still couldn't talk to me as you were on the phone)… and I acknowledged and said just give me two minutes, I'll be with you…

And then you just went out… then I wiped my face and unbolted the two bolts and opened the door and came out… and you stood there, slightly leaning on the backrest of the sofa that was turned away…

And I was wide-eyed with wonder and said 'How'd you do it?…'… 'Do what?…', you asked… 'How'd you come out through the door?…'… And you laughed and said something like "You know, I have a few powers and I can sometimes do a few things here and there…"… and shrugged the whole thing away…

I woke up at this point… I saw it was 3:42am… and I vividly remembered every detail… I am fully convinced that you are indeed some kind of God you know… I couldn't sleep for a while after that… when I saw you in the lobby outside you were wearing a deep green kind of half shirt… back in the room, you were wearing a white half shirt…

Dr Dashorathi,

Read this amazing book, Mrs Dalloway by Virginia Woolf… want to know what it's about?…

So Mrs Clarissa Dalloway is fifty something upper class English woman… with an eighteen year old daughter… and the whole story revolves around a single day in her life while she's planning for a party in her place in the evening… and there are simultaneous sub plots… how someone becomes mad having lost a friend in the war… and the plight of his wife… many others of her friends… like one lady who invites her husband Richard (who's very well established) but not her, to lunch etc…and the whole narrative is in thoughts… the biggest plot though is someone (Peter) she was in love with some thirty years back who suddenly show up confessing his love for some other married woman to Clarissa… turns out Peter and Clarissa had both been loving each other but Peter was this wayward intellectual type while Richard was very established well to do and finally Clarissa marries him… but somehow her thoughts wander off to Peter… and a particularly nice line goes… they "keep on loving, keep on quarrelling, keep on making up"… Richard too loves her but can't express it and there's this beautiful line "it's a thousand pities one can't say what one feels"… and even at fifty three Peter is irritated when Elizabeth Clarissa's teenage daughter comes in just when he was talking to Clarissa and she says "here comes my Elizabeth"… why did she say "my Elizabeth" thought Peter… she could have said "here comes Elizabeth"… why "my"… etc

And the narrative is one of a stream of consciousness and most of it is in thoughts rather than in dialogues… jumping from thoughts of Clarissa, to thoughts of Peter, to thoughts of Richard…

I mean the story reads so natural… so inevitable in some sense… in about ten years I will exactly be Clarissa's age… and the details aren't important but this sense of longing… of being past one's age for making decisions… of not being able to say what one feels irrespective of age… of not being able to go back... feels so authentic... so real... this sense of lack of fulfilment....

And there was a painting of a woman on the cover of Mrs Dalloway... it was lovely... I wrote this poem on seeing it...

The wind waited
To caress your soft brown curls
And help them carelessly
Roll on the nape of your neck...
Those words waited
Just behind your
Almost invisibly parted soft lips
With just a hint of a suppressed sigh
While your look
Felt
Those lucid eyes
Wrote stories over
The wrinkles of time
And the deserts of space
They felt the eyes of a lone woman
Black eyes set within a dark skin
Centuries later
And across distant lands
Feel the hint of warmth in

Your soft ruddy cheeks

Your eyes spoke of kindness

Of a pensive understanding

Of all that womanhood meant

Of all that lay hidden within

Skin and paints

And youth and beauty

That stretches across

The infinity of uncollected verses

Of unacknowledged sacrifices

Of dreams that were born

And buried in eyes themselves

In the nothingness of evolution

What fathomless oceans

Flow from your deep look

That sweep me over

Unexpressed truths

And unfelt love…

Natasha is my daughter's friend… she had come to our place for my daughter's birthday party with her mother, Naina, and her grandmother (Naina's mother)… so they had been talking to ma and knew about my husband a bit… I met

Naina yesterday again… she knew about ma not being there anymore… she has a strange life too (which she told us last time)… or maybe that's not strange at all… she and Natasha stays with her parents, and her husband with his parents… and from what I gathered it's because Naina couldn't adjust with her in-laws and her husband was too attached to them to leave them etc… so they are not legally divorced or separated but they don't stay together either… and it's been years… without any chance of getting together again… yesterday she told me that she was actually going around with a person who's about fourteen years younger to her (just graduated about a couple of years back… still studying something)… he knows everything - that she's married with a daughter and she was never going to get married again, etc… he's based in Siliguri and Naina got to know him from FaceBook… nothing much but they hang out together for movies, lunch etc when he visits Kolkata… she said she has another friend who's also in an affair with a boy around his age, so around fourteen years younger to her… I felt very strange, thinking about these affairs…

(And Parshati shared some of her poems on the futility of marriage, with Dr Dashorathi.)

She sometimes sees her old Benarasi

Red, and exquisitely embroidered

In golden and orange zari,

And then from nowhere

The smell of crackling golden fire
Wafts across decades
And she remembers the picture
Of crimson sindur sprinkled
On her forehead, and on her nose
She remembers her putting
White innocent khoi somewhere
And her hand all sweaty on another
Loaded with flowers and leaves
And all the while unintelligible mantras
Weaving a kaleidoscope
For her next phase of life…

She wasn't looking through a kaleidoscope
She was in it…
Suddenly she was supposed to call
Baba, someone else, ma someone else
Suddenly someone else will have
Unrestricted rights to her body
Suddenly someone else will even
Start growing in her…
She often buried her face
In her old Benarasi, and tried to see

Where exactly the beautiful
Symmetrical patterns of the
Kaleidoscope they promised
Lay hidden…

Several discontinuities
Eventually seem like a continuity
From afar it seems like
A wonderful piece of cloth
A sari, a dress, a skirt,
But if you look closer
You'll see thousands
And millions of smallest gaps
Squares and checks
Amongst the threads
That bind and stretch to infinity
And some of them
Have marks of burns
And spills
And cuts
And tears
And pulls
And stitches…

But from afar, as I said,

Everything just makes up

One integrated whole

Undivided continuous piece of…

20. Parshati's Letter to Her Mother-in-Law

(Below is a hand-written letter that Parshati wrote to her mother-in-law, few months before her ma was no more, in the winter of last year.)

27th December

Dear Mamoni,

ভেবেছিলাম তোমার সঙ্গে দেখা করে কথাগুলো বলব, কিন্তু গুছিয়ে বলতে পারব না বলে ভাবলাম লিখি - হয়তো গুছিয়ে লিখতেও পারব না, তবুও বলার থেকে হয়তো better লিখব, তাই এই চিঠি। এখন রাত সাড়ে তিনটে বেজে গেছে, তাও আমি জেগেছিলাম এটা লিখব বলে - hope you will understand how aggrieved I must be. এখন রাত সাড়ে তিনটে বেজে গেছে, তাও আমি জেগেছিলাম এটা লিখব বলে - ঠিক কোথা থেকে start করব জানি না but I'll try.

এমনিতেই he was never that cordial to ma. সেই যখন Bangalore-এ আমরা প্রথম এলাম, তখন মা পুজোতে যখন গেছিল, তখন ও বলেছিলো ও নাকি বিজয়ায়ে আর প্রণাম করে না। পরে, ধরো বিদেশ থেকে ফিরল - তখন ওলি, আমার জন্য অনেক জিনিস আনলেও, মা'র নাম করে একটা chocolate-ও দিত না। এগুলো মা একদম উড়িয়েই দিত - বরং আমি ওকে কিছু বললে, মা সবসময় ওর হয়ে আমাকে বকতো - বলত normal yardstick -এ ওকে বিচার না করতে। এখানে আসার পরও ছোটো খাটো নানা ব্যাপারে মা'কে এরম neglect করার ঘটনা ঘটে। যেমন ধরো, মা'র কাছে গেলেই, কাগজ নিয়ে বসে পড়ে, বা TV খুলে দেখতে থাকে - এতটুকু hi / hello না করেই।

মা'র stroke -এর পর, dr যখন মা'কে একা না রাখতে advice দেয় and when I asked her to stay with us, তখন থেকে এই ignore করা ব্যাপারটা অনেক বেশ প্রকট হয়ে উঠতে থাকে। মা ধরো চা করছে বা অন্য কিছু দরকার রান্নাঘরে, ও হয়ত পাশেই আছে (আমি নেই হয়ত বা দূরে আছি) এতটুকু help করতে offer করত না। আর প্রত্যেকটা জিনিস বলে আদায় করতে কার ভালো লাগে - no human being wants to be a beggar, especially সেটা যদি something as abstract as respect হয়। এই ধরো Spencer's - এ order দিচ্ছে - আমাকে, ওলিকে জিজ্ঞেস করবে - পাশে হয়ত মা রয়েছে কিন্তু মা'কে জিজ্ঞেস করবে না। ইদানিং ওলি বড় হওয়ার পর, ও-ই আমাকে বলে - আমি যখন office ছিলাম - papa, emamma একটাও কথা বলেনি। চান করতে গেলে বা অন্য কোথাও গেলে, ওলিকে বলে যায় - ওলি আমি আসছি - তবু মা'কে বলে না (আমি যখন নেই এমন সময়)। মানে ছোটো থাটো সব কিছুতেই মা'কে totally ignore করে - as if she doesn't exist.

অনেকদিন ধরে আমি ওকে বলেছি - রাগ করে, ভালো করে - আজকাল তো কত ছেলে মেয়েরাই বাবা-মা-দের কাছে নিয়ে থাকে - office এই কতজনকে আমরা চিনি যারা এরম থাকে - তবে ও কেন এরম করে - আর আমার মা tried her level best to talk to him, get along with him - তবুও ও'র কিসে এত অসুবিধে আমি কোনদিন বুঝিনি। Usually কারুর সঙ্গে তো কথা হয়না, তাও একটু একটু রাহি* যখন এসেছিল, ওকে বলেছিলাম - ও'র বন্ধু উল্লাসকে কয়েকবার বলেছি - so this has been gnawing at me for as long as I can remember. আমার কোন siblings, কোন relatives, কেউ নেই, বাবা'ও নেই - all I wanted was for him to be a bit normal, bit cordial to ma - সেটাও ও হবে না।

আর honestly প্রত্যেকবার যখন দাদারা আসত, বা ধরো তুমি এলে, I tried to be nice thinking ও হয়ত reciprocate করবে, মা'র সঙ্গে একটু ভালো ব্যবহার করে - but he hasn't. In fact, তোমার হয়ত মনে নেই, Durgapur-এ গিয়েও আমি ঠিক ও যেরম আমার মা'র সঙ্গে করত, আমি সেরম করার চেষ্টা করতাম (গিয়েই phone দেখা etc.) just to make him understand how much it hurts. কাউকে প্রণাম করব না-টাও ওকে বলার চেষ্টা that it's not right to do it. And I know that I have gradually distanced myself from all of you - but a large part of it is because I couldn't stand to be nice to all of you when he repeatedly and continuously had been hurting ma. যে মানুষটা ওর against এ একটা কোথাও বলত না বা ভাবত না, ধীরে ধীরে এতটাই গুটিয়ে নিয়েছে নিজেকে যে তুমি কল্পনাও করতে পারবে না।

এখন মা'র শরীরটা খুবই খারাপ - আর আমার মা'র পাশে থাকাটা আরও দরকার, তাই মা এত mentally কষ্টে আছে দেখে I thought of writing to you as a last resort - I know it's hard for you to believe me - যে না এটা দেখেছে for years together সে perceive করতে পারবে না - বাইরের কেউ তো নয়ই। তুমি কিছু করতে পারবে কি না, বা করবে কি না আমি জানি না - but I felt I had to tell you - and I hope you don't doubt my honesty - so maybe you will believe me. মা in fact এখন ভাবছে আবার মা'র flat -এ shift করে যাবে, কিন্তু মা'র শরীরে it's hard for me to let her stay alone. And I totally get torn inside - as if I have to choose between staying with him happily or with ma happily.

As the only child of my parents, when my father is not there, আমাকে তো মা'কে দেখতেই হবে, কিন্তু তাতে যে ওকে পাশে পাব না, সেটা আমার কাছে totally unthinkable. ইদানিং ও'র আর মা'র মধ্যে এক-আধবার অশান্তিও হয়েছে - কিন্তু প্রতিবারই মা নিচু হয়ে sorry হয়ে ও'র কাছে গেছে - তাতেও though things haven't improved. পৃথিবীতে সবার সাথে ভালো করে কথা বলে - আমার মা ছাড়া - এখন ওলি পর্যন্ত gets to understand this.

এই চিঠিটা হয়ত ও'র সামনেই আমাকে দিতে হবে তোমায় but I will hope that you will not discuss it with him. যদি আমার কথা বিশ্বাস করে, মা'র সঙ্গে কথা বলতে চাও, please বোলো but please don't tell her about this letter too - রাত জেগে কেউ যাতে না জানে, তাই জন্য লিখছি। ছোট ছোট আঘাত অপমান জমে এখন অনেক বড় হয়ে উঠেছে।

আমার প্রণাম নিও,

Parshati

(*Rahi is Parshati's sister-in-law, her husband's brother's wife.)

She wrote this letter to her mother-in-law in the winter before her mother passed away. She arranged to give it to her in person while she went to office the next day. (Her mother-in-law was staying in their vacant apartment in Kolkata at that time.) She had come in the evening to their house, but there was no visible change and Parshati knew nothing was going to change. It was like she had never written anything and her mother-in-law never read anything, as blind as mothers-in-law usually are towards their sons.

Later on when her mother was no more, Parshati had requested her mother-in-law to give the letter she had written to her. She did not give it to her but took photos of the pages and sent them via WhatsApp to Parshati. She saved the photos and often came back to read them - as a reminder that this actually happened.

Parshati was reading Orwell's 1984, and the particular part on how history can be changed made her feel very uncomfortable. The way her husband behaved now, like he did nothing, and nothing happened, made her very uncomfortable. On page 200 of the edition that she read, it said, "The mutability of the past is the central tenet of Ingsoc. Past events, it is argued, have no objective existence, but survive only in written records and in human memories. The past is whatever the records and the memories agree upon. And since the Party is in full control of all records and in equally full control of the minds of its members, it follows that the past is whatever the Party chooses to make it."

Her husband clearly has chosen the path to believe that he was very nice to Parshati's ma, and that's what will be written in history, she shuddered to think. So she clung to the photos of her letter - not for anything else, just to remind herself of the truth that he was gradually trying to erase away.

There wasn't any obvious and perceptible respite from the continuous, slow, but certain scars that his silent humiliations heaped on both of them - ma left this world with the burden, and she has to bear the bitterness for the rest of her life.

21. Conversations with Dr. Dashorathi…

(It was one of the strangest conversations Parshati had. She usually didn't have any record but this was so strange, she had come home and recalled some parts of it and wrote it down before time laid sand on it and it lost its freshness and strangeness.)

Dr Dashorathi,

I said something like "May I ask you something?… why am I not worth your liking?… honestly?… because I am not as great a physicist as my husband?… because I am not as powerful a woman as our Principal Secretary?… and as sometimes preferences and likings are… "just like that"?… (in your own words)…"

And you said, "Come on, what is the leading question?"

And I said (and I honestly didn't understand), "Didn't get you… what is a leading question?"

And you said something like "You are asking a leading question to get a response"

And then I said something like "Oh I see what you mean:-)" "Want to tell me what a leading question should be?"

And you said "You shouldn't be asking such questions :-)"

And I said "Why?... because it does not have an answer?... because it should not have an answer?... and you know even if you don't speak out aloud, questions do come to mind... whether you like them or not... how can you stop them"

And you said something like "Will explain on FT (FaceTime)"

And I said something like "What will you explain?... question?... answer?... why I shouldn't be asking such questions?"

And you said, "All of the above :-)"

And I said "Tell me when we meet?" (I meant that you will explain to me when we meet, but you possibly took it to mean I was asking you when we are meeting...)

So you said, "Whenever it's convenient for you"

And I said, "Then you'll explain all of that to me?"

And you said, "Yes"

And I said, "Promise?"

And you said, "I see no reason why I should not"

And I said, "আমি অত খারাপ মেয়ে নই না?"

And you said something like "Why should you have such self doubt?"

And I said "এমন প্রশ্ন যা করাই যায় না..."

And you said, quoting (আমি অত খারাপ মেয়ে নই না) "Yes, you shouldn't be asking questions like this..." "You want to hear praise"

And I said something like “No no, no praise from you” “Not praise…”

And you said something like “Validation”

And I said “Nah not even that:-)… can’t believe that you can’t guess what else I might want from you… but you don’t have to say… anything…”

And you responded saying “So that settles it” and then quote (What will you explain?… question?… answer?… why I shouldn’t be asking such questions?) and said “All your questions have been answered”

At this point I reach home and I don’t write back anything (I was writing to you while travelling back from office in my car)…

A couple of hours later I write “Hi, I reached home so I couldn’t write back…”

And you write “What do you want”

And I said “কিচ্ছু না :-)…”

And you said “মানে…?”

And I said “If you want to say anything please go ahead but I won’t ask for anything…”

And you quote this and said “So I take this as your final reply…”

And I said (because I was genuinely confused) “Oh but you didn’t ask me anything did you? কিসের reply?”

And you said “What do you want?”

So I take a while and write "Whatever you want to give me Dr Dashorathi… I never ask for anything… আপনি যা দিতে চান, আমি তাই চাই"

And you said something like "How will I say what you want…"

And I said "Is there anything you want to tell me… leave my question alone"

And you said "Now you're changing tracks"

And I said "No please…"

And you said, quoting (Is there anything you want to tell me… leave my question alone) "Of course I will tell you once you tell me what you want" "Otherwise, how will I say yes or no…"

And I said ":-) how do you know that the answer to my question will be in binary yes or no?"

And you said "I presumed… so you see I don't know what your question is"

And I said something like "প্রশ্ন নাই বা করলাম … please say what you want to say"

And you say "Question ছাড়া answer কি দেব"

And I said "Because you just want to say it without being asked about it?" "Really want to say it?" "Won't you say?"

But you keep quiet… and I wait for a while and write "I have a feeling that you want me to tell you what I want so that you can say what you want to say… as an answer… rather than an expression of your feelings… তাই কি?" "আপনাকে কষ্ট দিতে বড্ড

কষ্ট হয় ... it's okay if you don't want to tell me..."... "But I feel আপনি যা বলতে চান, না বলতে পেরেও কষ্ট পাচ্ছেন... so please tell me... I just can't stand you suffering... and I feel you are..."

But you still don't say anything and then I write "এতো আত্মাভিমান আপনার?:-).... আর আমার একটুও থাকতে নেই?... না চাইলে, কিচ্ছু দেবেন না তো?:-)"

And you write "Will talk on ft or face to face"

And I don't write anything else...

In a way, সব আত্মাভিমান ভুলে if I could tell you what I wanted, what would I want, I asked myself?... what would the right question be "ভালোবাসেন আমায়?" নাকি "কতটা ভালোবাসেন আমায়?" নাকি "এত্তটা ভালোবাসেন আমায়?" I sometimes think... rationally speaking none of it makes sense... irrationally speaking everything does... sometimes I have this feeling you know, that you love me so much it is possibly beyond all measure... and that you took your office close by so you can come see me sometimes... that you didn't go abroad because you couldn't bear to hurt me... that you're having an apartment in Rajarhat because it'd be close to my home...

But I did give you a letter finally (because I couldn't resist your insistence after a while.)

The letter I gave you was something like this:

I'll leave this unaddressed because I'm not sure I should address it and honestly am a little scared to do so. But you know I'm writing... to you. And I hope this letter makes no difference, you surely knew everything. I wish you could just read it and forget about it.

You have killed me a thousand times and resurrected me a thousand more... You have let me taste untasted feelings, savour unfelt desires and explore untouched emotions, and I am thankful to you for all of these. And it's possibly been rather late but it was like being reborn again. So here I am - my dykes all broken, and I am flooded, and burnt, and scorched and devastated. Marital oaths and vows peep like relics out of ancient ruins. If God didn't want me to write this, He shouldn't have made me feel this either. How much worse can expressing one's feelings be... I want to hold you in the deepest possible embrace till the last moment of my life... and I think I'll turn into a lunatic in my love... this is it... and that's all...

Why do you ask what I want from you... I don't want anything from you... I want... you... wholly entirely fully... every bit of your mind, every bit of your soul, every bit of your body, every bit of your love, every bit of your life, every bit of your everything... every bit of you...and I want to hold them and love them and caress them and be in them forever and forever... এমন করে কি বলা যায় আমি কি চাই?... আপনি যে নিদারুন বেদনা দেন তাই চাই... আপনি যে গভীর আনন্দ দেন তাই চাই... আপনি যে আন্তরিক আশ্বাস দেন তাই চাই ... আপনার সবটুকু... শেষ বিন্দু অবধি চাই ...

But she didn't write this to him... instead she just talked about other things till she realised he wasn't talking to her...

And I said:

I know I've hurt you... and honestly I've tried to write what I want from you... but I'm a writer you know... so maybe they're my feelings themselves ... maybe it's the expression of my feelings... but what transpired looked so outrageous I was scared to share with you... I will still if you want me to and promise you won't think ill of me one bit… and I don't want any of my wants fulfilled… do you still want to know?…

And he said: Please do… no issues

And I said:

You know it's one thing writing a poem or a story… quite another writing to you… my hands, thoughts, tongue, everything seem so tied when it's you on the other end…

I think you're too kind and patient with me to let me express myself so freely… like I did in my letter… but I really don't expect any return or favour from you… just knowing that you're there… that I can reach out to you makes life worth living for me… so honestly I'm on top of the world with your messages and your visits… tell me what more can I want…

আপনার কথা ভাবলে, আপনার সঙ্গে কথা বললে, কোথায় ভেতরে না খুব কষ্ট হয় … অথচ বার বার সেই কষ্টই পেতে চাই … I know I sound totally contradictory… but that's how you make me feel… I'm so sorry I sound so pained and helpless…

And he writes once again quoting (I know I've hurt you… and honestly I've tried to write what I want from you… but I'm a writer you know… so maybe they're my feelings themselves … maybe it's the expression of my feelings… but what transpired looked so outrageous I was scared to share with you… I will still if you want me to and promise you won't think ill of me one bit… and I don't want any of my wants fulfilled… do you still want to know?…) yes

And I write, 'you want to know how much I want you?'

And he doesn't write anything… and she keeps writing this and that like "আর যা জানেন already আবার শুনে কি হবে?" Silence "Why don't you say something that I don't know?""Because everything started after I asked why am I not worth your liking" Silence and then I quote "আর যা জানেন already আবার শুনে কি হবে?" And ask "But if you still want to know I will tell you… validation in your own words:-)… let me know and I will tell you as many times as you want…" Silence "Please Dr Dashorathi … আপনার কি হয়েছে?… why are you being so strange?" Silence "You're in your Delhi office?" Silence… so then I write: "So you're not talking… well, here's what I wrote and I sent the earlier letter…adding, you promised this won't matter, Now please talk to me?"

⁂

She cried quite a bit having sent it… and didn't even check her WhatsApp to see whether he had seen it… she thought perhaps he would get back but he didn't… she didn't quite understand what he wanted… why did he insist so much on knowing how she felt for him which obviously he must have known all along?…. why was he being so cruel… why was he causing so much pain to her making her confess when she didn't want to?… not because she didn't feel it that way but because she didn't want to say it aloud… as if saying things would reduce the depth of her feelings, the purity of her love, the endlessness of her devotion… yet he made her say it… somehow she felt so undressed… so bare… like the cover of her sanctity and morality has been ripped apart and she was being paraded naked in front of him… why couldn't he just let her be… her love be… something that she thought was supposed to be cooed in his ear… in some intimate moment…

perhaps whispering while lying on his bare chest… why did he make her say it in the most unromantic way over WhatsApp?… Everything doesn't need to be said… in fact a lot of things are better left unsaid… just hinted…. Just understood… just felt… just perceived… it was like, just saying about her love, killed it… no one spares her like her mother… she's sure if ma knew she wasn't too keen on saying something, she would have let her be… why didn't he… just making her say about her love belittled it…

No one understood her like her mother… and she wrote this…

Split me sideways

And this way

And that way

And inwards

Split me your way

With your looks and words

And spread me in sheets

To cover you

Have me rolled into warmth

To keep you warm

In the wintry solitude

Of unsaid words

I am yours

In the cells of the mind

That grow like small lips

Planting thousand kisses

On the song of your mind

That descend like

An ardent dream

On heavy eyes

Drooping with memories

Getting filled with

The scent of the night

And the tears of the moon

The sighs of the stars

Because everyone knows

I have lost today

Lost myself and my love.

Mistake

Imagine you make a mistake

And fall in love with me

Imagine…

Love will suddenly give you

New eyes you know

New senses

New feelings

And maybe you'll become

A new citizen

In the land of dreams

Where I am a permanent resident

You'll find yourself

Holding me at dawn

Burying your face in my soft hair

The smell of the coy sun

Filling you like an

Unfinished dream

In the land of poems

You'll discover

It's very easy to hurt a poet

And you'll see me bruised

And bleeding and

Not even looking at you

All because you looked away?…

I know I am very difficult

Very different

A citizen in a castle of promises

(What promise?… By whom?

To whom?…

Never mind...) a castle that's way
Up in the air
Where the clouds and gods
Wait for us
To shower rains and blessings
And mistakes perhaps
Like arrows that dart from
My look into your heart...
But I know
You never make mistakes.

I could never ask you
Whether you love me
In my imagination
I could never stand the pain
Of you saying no you don't
Every time I have
Embraced you in my mind
I have cooed something
In your ears
Just barely having my lips

Almost touch your ears
And kiss them lightly
Just a hint of a kiss maybe
And have whispered
Unintelligible something
That even I haven't heard
In my imagination…

Every time I have felt pain
All I wanted was to get buried in you
And never wake up
Hoping your strength and resolve
Will somehow take my pains
Away from me
And blow them away to distant lands
And in the mellow dusk
I have closed my eyes
And stood still feeling the wind
Filling me up with your scent
That they've carried from
Faraway blue mountains
And long winding roads
But I could never face the wind
And ask it whether you felt

Love for me

Lest they whisper something

That sound like no

And I get crushed

In the evening silence

And get lost forever…

তার আগে না আপনাকে দুটো প্রশ্ন করেছিলাম…আমাকে কি ভাবেন other than physicist's wife?… and what do you want for Christmas and New Year… for all the days with occasions, and all the days without any… usual days in between of longing and waiting… and you said I had to think about it… and then there was this message that you deleted… and when I asked you, you said you wished Happy new year… and I asked you is that what you wrote in the deleted message, and you smiled,… and I said yes? Tell me? Please?… and at night there was this one word "Friend"…

ওটা কিসের উত্তর? আমি already বন্ধু, না আমাকে বন্ধু করতে চান?… আপনি যখন বন্ধু বললেন না, তখন there were two conflicting thoughts… বন্ধু could mean so much you know… very close friends, bosom friends… and those that are just acquaintances… আমি কোন category তে পড়ি?… আপনাকে জড়িয়ে ধরে আপনার বুকের মধ্যে মুখ গুঁজে কাঁদতে পারি এমন বন্ধু?… দ্রৌপদী -কৃষ্ণের মধ্যেও তো বন্ধুত্বই ছিল … বন্যা-মিতার (শেষের কবিতা) মধ্যেও তাই ছিল … the border between বন্ধুত্ব and ভালোবাসা is very ill-defined জানেন তো …

সেই শব্দটা দেখার পর থেকে জানেন নিঝুম গহন রাত্তির কেমন যেন স্পন্দনহীন হয়ে গেল… all I could do was lay down weightless and limp close my eyes and see the word friend float around me…

reverberate in my heart with its beats… like you were literally the blanket that covered me… the warmth, the peace, the rest was all yours and god just wanted me to live in the moment… and I honestly wouldn't have minded it as my last moment in this world… তারপর থেকে প্রত্যেক মুহূর্তে আপনার ছোঁয়া যেন সর্বত্র … like you've suddenly touched every nerve in my body and I've felt your life touch mine… like I've suddenly become a sieve just for you and you've percolated through all of me… till there is none of me left behind… and right at the peak of happiness I could call it my day…

You do feel a lot more than a friend for me don't you?… it does hurt you to think of me in someone else's arms doesn't it?… মাঝে মাঝে মনে হয় আমি আপনার সারাটা মন-প্রাণ জুড়ে আছি… আমার জন্যই আপনি বিদেশ-যাওয়া থেকে আরম্ভ করে সবকিছু ছেড়ে দিতে পারেন … আমার জন্যই আপনি Salt Lake এ office আর New Town এ বাড়ি নেবেন … আমার জন্যই আপনি অন্য রাজ্য থেকে ছুটে ছুটে আসেন Diwali-র পর দেখা করবেন বলে … লাল পাঞ্জাবি পরে শুধু আমার জন্যই এসেছিলেন … আমার হৃদয় রাঙাবেন বলে … আবার মাঝে মাঝে মনে হয় আমাকে বুঝি আদৌ মনে পরেই না … কোনটা সত্যি?… ভালোবাসেন আমায়?… এমনি যেরম আর পাঁচজনকে বাসেন সেরম? নাকি অনেক অনেক গভীরে?… অতল সমুদ্রের মতো?… কোনটা সত্যি?…

Here's a poem for you…

The Moon

Will you know me

If I were the moon

And would rise

In your soul like

An obscure whiteness

That absorbs all your dark sweat
And rounds out
All your rough edges
Filling them with honest love
And the white silken cover
That drowns out the din
Of the restless city
That stirs up in you
Calling you names
And shaming your honour
Would you know
That I am the mild warmth
That instils life
In your city
On its coldest day
And even in the darkest deepest
Forest in your heart
I'd kiss a tree or two
And let them drop their shadows
On broken forlorn windows
And abandoned floors
Of forgotten fortresses
And I'd stay behind
When most have gone
Just like the day

And you've turned away
From the rest
Like bokeh patterns
Adorning your loneliness
Like a long-known tune
That's hard to remember
And even harder to forget.

22. Nothing Would Matter

(Parshati wrote these poems after her ma was no more.)

If I didn't write anymore
It would not matter
Nothing that does not happen, matters
Just like people who are not there
Don't matter
Like their presence itself weighed down
And everything suddenly feels
Lighter and less burdened
Like raindrops in the air
No matter how natural they seem
They are but a burden
To the lighter purer holier maybe, air
So once the rain stops
We relish the freshness
The sparkles and clarity
The fragrance and the crispness
Yet the rains are gone
Just as naturally as it had come…

Every morning
I still draw the curtains apart
Religiously, avoiding the bedside table
Lest I topple something
I let the warm sunshine trickle in
On the bed that's not slept in anymore
I let cobwebs not accumulate
In the corners and the window grills
And every evening at dusk
And switch on the lights
And draw the curtains back on
Lest people outside can see
Though what can one possibly see
In an empty room, I don't know
And for all I know
Nothing would matter…
Wasn't that the first lesson we got
From the first days of our lives
The sun disappearing every evening
Naturally and beautifully
Just leaving the hint of the day behind
The memories
The longings
The sweetness in mind

The peace of it all…
The moon gradually leaving us
Every morning
Just spreading its calmness
And serenity in our souls
And giving us the depth to
Hold ourselves in our hopes
And dreams and beliefs…
Yet they know
Nothing would matter…
****

Nowadays no one reminds me
Of putting ma's phone to charge
Yet I never forget putting it for charging
I keep it beside my pillow at night
Alongside my own mobile
As if touching it
Would bring back her touch to me…
I believe it was very early,
Maybe when I was 8 or so
When ma used to recite Sanskrit shlokas
And I was happy to learn them
Like Pita swarga pita dharma

Or Janani janmabhoomischa

Or Vasamsi jirnani

Or even ashadhasya prathama divase

But I didn't know Sanskrit

I couldn't understand them

And I would recite them like mantras

Now I have enrolled myself in

An online course that teaches Sanskrit

As if ma dwells in the language

And learning it will bring me

Nearer to her

It does…

Or so I hope…

23. So, That's It Then?

22nd Jan

কতদিন মা জান Dr Dashorathi ঠিক করে কথা বলেননি... আগের week এ লিখলাম class-এর পর office থেকে phone করব... he said he was in some conference somewhere else... বললাম "আমি কিছু শুনতে চাই না ব্যাস!... আমার সঙ্গে কথা বলবেন ব্যাস!"... তাতে লিখলেন "Okay..."...

আজ ওরা বাড়ি নেই and he insisted that we talk... so we video-called... মা আজ বুঝলাম উনি কেন দূরে চলে গেছেন... এতো ভালোবেসেছিলেন যে কাছে আসতে চাইছিলেন... he said his mind was completely clouded, that he lost his balance for a few days, that he wanted to privately visit me... so he wants this interaction to stop for a while till he regains his balance... that he was being completely honest and truthful with me... instead of pretending to be busy... what would you have done... he himself said, 'I don't answer hypothetical question'... অথচ আমায় জিজ্ঞেস করছেন, 'what would you have done'... so I said, 'I didn't want any of that but only to be able to talk to you'... he said, 'his nose was long and he smelled us on being a slippery slope'... আমি বললাম, 'I feel guilty too because I like someone so much... someone who's not my husband... and that I had middle-class Bengali values'... so does he, he said...

পরে ভাবি জান মা, অনেকদিন ধরে আভাসে ইঙ্গিতে আমায় জানাতে চেয়েছিল ... 'Let's meet normally, without having to make excuses', বলেছিলেন ... Once I had written "Something's maddeningly spring in the air today, say whatever you want to say". And he asked me, 'what was so maddeningly spring', and I said, 'it was the book I was reading… Lady Chatterley's lover…' and he asked me what it was about… so I briefly said, 'it was about Lady Chatterley falling in love with the game-keeper of his husband's estate… his husband being an invalid'… so he asked me 'what was maddeningly spring about that'… and I wrote back saying, 'it had some very vivid description of love'… so he asked me to send some excerpts from it… I did ask him 'to find the pdf of the book from the internet… and in any case, I was busy with dinner etc., and it would take a while to get back'… but deep down I knew I would feel very embarrassed sending those parts… but he said, 'he was working and would be awake for a while'… So when I finally did have some time before going to bed, I managed to send one page of Chatterley's lover (one that I thought was the least explicit out of all that were there, that were way more so)… Nevertheless I felt very uneasy and I asked him whether he was sorry that I did… he said he wasn't and asked me whether I was…. I said I wasn't sorry, just shy and embarrassed… and he said why should I be, because 'You are a lady, are you not'… and I said, 'I don't know'… and he said, 'Okay, you are a little girl, happy?'… I was silent for a while, and then I asked him, 'You want me to be a lady?'… He didn't answer, and only wished me goodnight…

মা তোমার আনন্দদাও* হয়ত অনেক কিছু বলতে চেয়েছিল তোমায় … কিন্তু একজন কে বিয়ে করলে অন্য কারুর কথা মনে আনা যায়না, না?…

*When Parshati's mother was of marriageable age, and was having an affair with her father (would-be-husband at that time), many proposals of marital alliances had come for her. One of them was from a doctor named Anondo, who liked her mother a lot (which they had come to know later on) and had even written a letter to her, which her mother had not responded to. And possibly even did not keep to herself - she showed it to others as well. Anondo was very hurt on hearing about it. Years later, Parshati's mother had recalled the whole episode to Parshati rather pensively. Anondo was good-looking - tall, fair - very well-behaved, doctor by profession, and deeply in admiration of her mother. Any girl's dream husband, and her mother had rudely rejected him and publicly humiliated him, not purposely maybe... accidentally, but nevertheless she did.

March 19th

মা তোমাকে এই একটা কথা বলিনি ... মানে মুখ ফুটে বলিনি... তবে তোমার না জানা কিছু তো ছিল না ... আমাকে দেখেই তুমি বুঝতে, না?...

শুরু বলব না শেষ বলব বুঝতে পারছি না... তোমাকে নিয়ে, তাকে, নিয়ে জীবন একরকম ছিল ... সেটা বোধহয় শেষের পথে ... তুমি তো চলেই গেলে ... তিনিও বুঝি চলে যাবেন ... তুমি বলতে না মা, শরৎচন্দ্রের সেই অমোঘ কথা, ‘বড় প্রেম শুধু কাছেই টানে না ইহা দূরেও ঠেলিয়া ফেলে’... কেমন করে সব মনের কথা জানতে মা ...

শাঙ্গরবকে কাছে টানার সুযোগ দিলাম না বলে দূরে চলে গেল... প্রত্যয় পাগলের মতো কাছে টানতো বলে দূরে সরিয়ে রাখলাম... উদয়ন প্রেমের কবিতা শোনাতো কিন্তু ওর কবিতা শুনতে চাইনি কোনদিন... বৈশ্বানর কবিতা শুনবে বলে দেখা করতে চাইতো, আমি দেখা করিনি... সাগ্নিকদাও কাছে টানলো বলে ছেড়ে দিলাম ... ড. দাশরথিকে আমি কাছে টানলাম - এই ভাবলেন বলে দূরে চলে গেলেন?... শারদ্বতদা কাছে টানার চেষ্টা করে, কিন্তু আমি সরেই থাকতে চাই... এই দূরে কাছে টানাটানির মধ্যেই কতগুলো বছর কেটে গেল মা ...

মনের মানুষ এ জীবনে আর পাওয়া হল না... অথবা, মনের মানুষ পাওয়া যায় নাই বোধহয়... the very concept is hypothetical... perhaps because your mind and feelings and emotions keep changing... so obviously there is no one person who fits into what you want forever… খুব ইচ্ছে হয় এই শুলাম তারপর একদম অন্য কোথাও আমায় নিয়ে গেলে তুমি … এখানে আর উঠতে না হয় …

24. Yes, That Is It

(At some point, after talking to her once, Dr Dashorathi stopped writing and communicating with Parshati. Parshati felt infinitely humiliated and pained, and suffered silently for days and months at an end. She implored him to have mercy on her and just meet her once or talk to her once, just to explain why he doesn't want to speak to her anymore, but her entreaties fell on deaf ears. She felt miserable psychologically and emotionally, and why he would decide to be so, especially now that her biggest friend, her ma, was also no more, was particularly inexplicable, to say the least, and appeared to be cruelty personified. She kept writing to him often, and asked her if she could call him, but he wouldn't respond.

But deep within Parshati felt he was just as concerned and vigilant of her well-being and cared just as much for her as before, when they were on speaking terms, and quite intimately so. She felt that he just wanted to remain far away because he couldn't have her, because she'd never be his, and interacting with her made him want to have her wholly, to himself. At least that's what he told her the last time they talked. And she believed him, like always.

Here are some emails that Parshati wrote to him, around the time she sensed he was being a bit too strange, and later when he stopped communicating with her.)

Dr Dashorathi,

You know I've been going over and over in my mind as to what might have happened… but I'm so clueless… you had said that you were eager to learn about feminism, and since I would be teaching that, I remember I had offered to teach you also the last time we talked… but you refused… and you said you were on an official tour to Delhi… perfectly usual things I thought… and then you went to Darjeeling on some official errand again… and something changed so much thereafter… please Dr Dashorathi… please just consider me to be your friend this once and tell me?… because I am literally asking you as a friend… কষ্ট পেয়ে নয়, রাগ করে নয় … just as a friend who's really very perplexed… and I am neither insensitive nor stupid… আপনি যতই বলুন everything's fine, I know it isn't… আপনি কোনদিন আগে আমি কথা বলতে চাইলে বা দেখা করতে চাইলে না বলতেন কি?…

And it's the same person who spoke of how the entire society should respect poets… how I was very free to express myself to you… how I could consider you as my friend… so I know things aren't fine… why you really don't have to try so hard for whatever it is that you're trying to achieve… just tell me… can you not try to be that much open and honest with me?… tell me on FaceTime if not here?… or email me?… is it something to do with me?… don't want me to write to you?… what?… please Dr Dashorathi, whatever it is, I earnestly request you to tell me… rebuke me if I've done or said something I shouldn't have… or just tell me if you don't want me to write to you again?… I won't… but unless I know what it is, I don't know what to do… because it's hard to believe it's the same person that I am writing to whom I wrote and talked to a couple of weeks back… মানে একটুও মেলাতে পারছিনা জানেন তো … মানে হঠাৎ কি হল যে আর কথা বলতে, লিখতে চান না?… সত্যি রাগ, কষ্ট, অভিমান, সব ভুলে

গেছি জানেন তো... just want to know the truth... please tell me... I mean I perceive an abrupt drastic change in you towards me... towards being cold and indifferent... and I'm literally pleading with you to let me in on the reason... whatever it is... please...

So you tell me nothing is amiss... এটা না পুরো অশ্বত্থামা হত ইতি গজর মতো... আমাকে না স্বয়ং ভগবান এসে বললেও আমি বিশ্বাস করব না... nothing is amiss is just economically true... you know what Lawrence says... never trust the teller, trust the tale... he even says... what the blood feels, and believes, and says, is always true... and the tale my blood tells is not what you say... tell me why do you not write to me anymore or talk to me anymore?... if you don't want me to be in touch with you please let me know... নাকি সেটা আপনার ভদ্রতায় বাধে... but you did promise to be honest with me didn't you... just tell me and I won't write to you anymore... you didn't need to sympathise with me because of ma... you didn't need to be nice for any reason other than because you just wanted to be... and that's what I believed... but if that's true then tell me why do you not want to be nice anymore...

Okay, you don't have to tell me why if you don't want to, but at least agree that you're being very different and cold... and it can't be only because of your official commitments... at least acknowledge that... you don't have to tell me why...

And if everything's fine tell me when can I call you?... when will you drop in?... আমি না সত্যি এত ভদ্রতা formality বুঝি না... please tell me what is it that you're trying to tell me... please... I'll be so grateful to you... আপনার সঙ্গে কথায় কোনদিন পারিনি, পারবও না... to pin you down or win you over or even convince you of something is not within my abilities... so I can just make an appeal to your sense of compassion and mercy to please tell me why are you being so strange and cold to me… what have I done to deserve this…

Poems were never meant to be written
They stir oceans of unspoken pain
Sneak into your sleep
Shatter your peace
Snatch away your space
And ruin your solitude
Spread across your happiness
Like mould
(But very pretty mould!)
Distance you from your near ones
And just don't let you be…

And when you have got
A paltry out of you
The words stare back at you
And almost audibly shout back
Oh come on,
Couldn't you have done better
Is this all I deserve?
Oh this has nothing of the
Vastness of the ocean

You set out to depict
You'd rather not have me at all
And I beg for mercy
Let me drown in the ocean
But of course there's no going back...

❧

Dr Dashorathi,

I know this is completely unsolicited... yet you were asking about my thoughts the other day but then my mind was so totally clouded I couldn't think through anything of what you said... but now I think I will be able to state some of my thoughts... and just as truly and honestly as you... hope you won't mind...

I honestly think that if people love each other very deeply there is nothing wrong or atrocious or impure about wanting to be near each other... that is possibly a very natural consequence of being in love... not demeaning or despicable in any sense... but of course, circumstances may not be propitious for that to materialise... I do believe that you love me very, very deeply indeed... and from much before now or the letter... maybe you knew yourself or didn't... but I think you chose not to acknowledge it to yourself even keeping everything else in mind... which is fine... it may have got deeper with greater and more intimate interactions but it couldn't have started right now... and possibly that's why it hurt you to read my story... that's why it hurt you to leave me and go away... that's why you couldn't read my poems like a passive distant onlooker... but that's fine, isn't it?... I am worthy of your love... or am I not?... am I being too presumptuous?...

And I also agree, you were a bit, what should I say, domineering with me when I used to keep away from saying a lot of things... I remember you said that I wasn't telling the whole truth... and I did say what I wrote was very outrageous so I wouldn't show you but you wanted me to... I did not want to ask you about your feelings for me but you wanted me to... and I somehow had a feeling you didn't want calm waters to be resting... didn't want things to go on like they did... just me having you as my close bosom friend, my confidante, my sole succour and refuge in an otherwise lonely and cold world... like you wanted more... and you said I should have told you if I was uncomfortable... I somehow thought that you'd understand... I am very shy by nature you know... but I couldn't fathom what is it that you wanted... I still don't... but I had the feeling that something was making you very restless... something about me was making you very jittery and I didn't know what...

But maybe from the first time I ever wrote to you... and for everything thereafter, I possibly never thought that you'd reciprocate my feelings... I always thought I was too ordinary for you to even notice me... and I laid myself all open and bare and unhindered before you... and even if you haven't said anything, I know that you do reciprocate... but truly you haven't done anything atrocious, or wrong or impure you know... your mind and heart are just as pure... there's no cloud anywhere in your mind you know... I know, for our temperament, it feels too wrong to give space to anyone of the opposite gender in a close way... but you only wanted to be with me… only wanted… never did… so why are you punishing yourself and me along with it… and I know, even if we're together by ourselves, irrespective of what you want and feel, irrespective of what I want and feel, you wouldn't come near me… so many thoughts and wants cross our minds, don't they… and thoughts and feelings and emotions are really not in our control… you just feel what you feel… but actions we take evoked by them are all that we have control over… and you haven't done anything that can be criticised… you will never do anything that can be criticised… you've always been and will remain the most impeccable gentleman I've ever seen…

Please tell me you've got over whatever made you say all those things about yourself… and be my Dr Dashorathi again… please… fast…

৶

On second thoughts you know, though you're trying to keep me away to have your feelings for me wane away, I was absolutely overwhelmed at the courage and the honesty that your 'confession' (should I say) manifested… you don't know how much elevated you have become in my eyes… you're keeping me away so you don't get tempted to come near a loved one?… how blessed can a loved one be?…

And you know when you did keep asking me the other day about my thoughts, I did not say because I was too distraught to speak, but there was one thought that kept coming back… When I was very upset you know that you'd go to Harvard… and ma somehow knew everything… she had said "বড় প্রেম শুধু

কাছেই টানে না, ইহা দূরেও ঠেলিয়া ফেলে"… like implying I should happily let you go… she somehow knew all I feel for you… this is actually a quotation from Sarat Chandra Chattopadhyay's famous novel Rajlakshmi and Srikanto… their entire lives they loved each other but never got married… ma somehow knew that it was extremely painful for me and said that… just wanted to say that to you… I know you're in a lot of pain… আর মাকে না বড্ডো মনে পড়ে জানেন… especially if it's something that concerns you there is no one I can talk about it with… except you… won't you please talk to me… maybe even 'horrible things' that crossed your mind?…

And today's world poetry day you know… but all my verse and poems seem to have gone… seemed to be waiting for your return… do come back… all life's drying up within me… it's a dull cloudy dusk here in Calcutta and I'm in my office… a few lines for you…

You swim in my veins like a king

And the redness in my blood

Splashes across my body and my being

Shivering with joy that you bring

You strut across my conscience like a god

But a kindly loving god

That picks up pieces of love

That lay strewn across the

Unkempt clouds that cover my mind…

❧

Dr Dashorathi,

You know I never told you anything, never wanted anything, could never even make myself ask you anything, no matter how much I'd crave to hear something… I knew I was the lowland and you were a powerful ocean all around… so I had dykes to rein me in… because I knew there was no stopping a flood if it started… slippery slope in your terms… but I don't think I breached the dyke… I don't think you did either… nothing has been breached or broken… what's your fear then?… what are you keeping away from?… not me… you're probably keeping away from your own self?… your own mind?… our greatest enemy and our greatest friend is our conscience… and does yours feel good doing whatever it's doing?… why have you conjured up this very strange artificial regime of frost without any actual reason for doing so?… don't want me to write to you?… don't want to meet me again?… wouldn't it be much better and simpler if you just said so… like honestly between friends… like acquaintances that have known each other for almost a decade… without this elaborate hurting and humiliating mechanism… just having pity on someone who's recently been orphaned…

Dr Dashorathi,

You know my daughter is into Harry Potter these days… she's finished reading the seven books and now watches the movies… and has quizzes based on them…:-)… I had read the first book long back and seen the movies long back too… but it was very different coming back to them now… especially the character of Snape you know… silently loving Lily his whole life… and whole-heartedly thereafter protecting Harry in spite of being so wronged by his father James (and Lily to some extent) and Sirius… his patronus was also a doe which was Lily's…

And I obviously love Dumbledore… but I didn't recall some very nice dialogues he says right at the end… you know when Harry is in the realm where the part of Voldemort that resided in him goes out and he meets Dumbledore, and asks him something like "Is this real or are these happening in my head?" And Dumbledore says something like "Of course, they're happening in your head… but why should that make them not real?"… How deep isn't it… and when whatever's happening in your head is real, it's hard to distinguish between dream and reality isn't it… like what Inception was all about… we know something's a dream because there is a waking up… what if there was no waking up… not in the usual sense… and we kept dreaming… we would be thinking that to be reality isn't it… in fact dreams feel so real don't they… like you are so much living in it… and waking up makes you feel awkward and out of place…

And you know it's like every character has both dark and positive sides… Draco Malfoy for example is fashioned as if he's typically anti-Harry but in Malfoy Manor when Bellatrix Lestrange asks him to identify Harry, he doesn't (you won't recall all of this if you haven't seen it in the near past)… Dumbledore, for example, is portrayed in a positive light but he's said to have neglected his brother and sister Ariana who was very devoted to him, in his pursuit of career… James and Sirius are Harry's closest but in their youth they had been very unkind to Snape… Narcissa (Draco's mother) actually lies to Voldemort and saves Harry in the end…

So sorry about this long Harry Potter stuff but this is exactly the kind of things I love talking to you about… can we please come back to talking again?…

And I keep thinking about you the last time we spoke… and it does seem to me that you appeared kind of relieved after you said what you did… sad but relieved… just like saying it to me itself has reduced your burden of carrying it with you… like just confiding your thoughts have lessened the load of your thought… that often is true isn't it… we do sometimes want to unburden ourselves… and I think you could have said that to me much earlier if it made you feel better… :-)…

You won't write to me because writing to me reminds you of me?… and why should you try to forget me?… do you remember the "obliviate" spell in Harry Potter?… remember Gilderoy Lockhart used to use it in the Chamber of Secrets?… took one's memory away… I wish I could selectively "obliviate" all that's bothering you and just leave you with the good ones… that'd make you want to remember me… how long will you take to get over whatever you're trying to get over?… you said you'll get over it… not there yet?… when will you be?…

And didn't you say that I shouldn't take any decision because I was emotionally vulnerable… I believe you were too… so you shouldn't have taken any decision either… at least not all by yourself… you're just being one big selfish giant you know:-)…

There are lots of things about Harry Potter that I want to tell you… like Godrik Gryffindor's sword… see it's neither horcrux nor any other other soul lives in it… at least we're not told anything… yet it appears and disappears all by itself at the appropriate moments… it's like one can write a novel on the sword's journey itself!…

And I'm reading almost diametrically opposite of what Harry Potter is… Homo Deus:-)…

Take care…

~

Dr Dashorathi,

একটা কথা বলি?… unsolicited advice… at least that's how it works for me I think… if I really wanted to forget someone I would perhaps meet the person everyday, instead of keeping him away… distance only adds to the enigma, the aura, the lure of him, instead of reducing it… familiarity on the other hand lets the attraction wane away gradually I would suppose… see if it's not the case, if you really stopped loving someone you don't see, or don't talk to, you would have stopped loving Lord Krishna… or your father… but you don't… so it doesn't matter… in fact it's the opposite… you probably didn't know you loved your father so much whilst he was around… and if god did appear and stayed with you always, you'd probably not love him as much (maybe that's why He doesn't come down to visit us that often:-))… so if you're really trying to forget someone, you should try and meet the person very often… everyday if possible… that is more likely to wear out her attraction rather than keep her away you know…

And I even removed my picture from my WhatsApp profile… seen?… lest I make it difficult for you to keep me away from your thoughts…

You know it's been a few days since I bit my inner lip while eating… so hard that it has swollen up and bleeds… ma used to say "কেউ মনে করছে নিশ্চই"… and I keep thinking it must be you… who else would think of me?…

❧

Dr Dashorathi,

Tuesday is my daughter's last day of this term… she's going on to class 5… and her class teacher has asked her to bring her English literature, grammar and Maths exercise books (and one more girl for English and Maths and one other for Maths)… surely because she's been one of the best girls in her class… makes me feel so proud of her… and once again, I can never thank you enough for making Loreto happen for her… you know, I heard one of the parents say (both of them are doctors) that they actually moved to Calcutta to have their daughter go to Loreto…

And the TV was open and I heard it blaring out some news about a seven-year old girl being kidnapped and brutally killed and I couldn't bear to listen to the rest of it - I switched off the TV… imagine, seven-year old… she almost wouldn't even know what it is to be a girl… what inhuman perversion, what unthinkable animality in us…

And to talk about Dumbledore once more… you know he says right at the end, something like… words are the most inexhaustible source of magic, capable of both inflicting harm and also remedying it... have my words hurt you and injured you in any way?... would you not let them heal you too?... remember how Snape asks Harry to collect his tears in his dying moment and to use them in the "pensieve" (that showed all memories)... that's how Harry learnt how Snape had been the one silently protecting Harry... I wish you could see what my tears held in a "pensieve" too... I have never meant anything but well for you, no matter what spoken and written words have conveyed...

Dr Dashorathi,

Somehow one thing I despise about the Rowling books is that they have a lot of unnecessary demises... well, of course, she has dictatorial rights over what she wrote but given it's a children's series, couldn't she be a little more compassionate?... and she's especially killed people on the Good side... across ages... see there's Cedric Diggory, Sirius Black, Lupin and his wife Tonks, Fred (the twin brother of Ron), Moody... and all so unnecessarily... in the sense nothing would really alter too much with the plot and story if they would be around... whereas only Bellatrix Lestrange dies on the Dark side... I actually couldn't see the movies from the fourth one onwards especially because of these deaths... my daughter is reading other books by Rowling and she says they have similar events... the father mother of the children die so very often... I know that that is reality but somehow maybe we could save children's literature from it...

And I also wanted to tell you something else… when we talked the other day, you said a few times that this is why you didn't want to meet me (because I was so upset)… but there's a flaw in your logic you know… the fact that I was upset was conditioned on the other factors of our talking… that you would not meet… that you were away… hypothetically, had we met and you told me what you did I may not have been affected the way I was … the fact of you being in front of me could have buffered the pain… nothing in real life is true ceteris paribus… because it is never so…

Sometimes you know I spend whole days warming and serving things and waiting for everyone to show up… my mother needed it… my daughter also needs it, she's just a child… but he doesn't… but he very rarely will even take one bit of anything and have it himself… sometimes I so feel like disappearing for a while you know… would you mind if I tell you and my daughter (so you two won't worry) and just vanish for a few days… really like to be alone at times you know… খুব ইচ্ছে করে শুলাম আর তারপর কোথাও যেন মা নিয়ে চলে যায় এখানে আর না উঠি…

When I was younger you know I remember I sometimes used to see my mother very frustrated, very vexed at my father… and I am quite ashamed to say that I sometimes even sided with my father against her… trying to argue her into understanding… once I remember you know I told her you could have asked him (baba)?… if you wanted it?… and ma had just said… বলব কেন?… how I see myself echoing her now… why should I need to ask him for anything?… why won't he be concerned enough?…

✤

Dr Dashorathi,

I don't know when you will put an end to your madness… if at all… if I were, you know, to put a physical analogy to the kind of mental pain you're causing, it'll be like scooping out each of my organs one after the other, leaving my heart and brain functioning so I could know and feel the pain…

When you first asked me to explain the Bengali part you know, my first instinct was to say that it cannot be explained verbally, and it cannot be explained by any other means because then we'll be on a "slippery slope"… and I would never do anything jeopardising your integrity… why can't you trust me on that… I asked you to visit me when I was alone mainly to show you a few things that ma had tried to write (because she couldn't talk) when she came out of ventilation the first time… I didn't want to discuss her when my husband would be around…

I had an 'Inception' like dream the other day you know… I was dreaming… that I was dreaming… and in the dream within my dream, I was dreaming that ma was no more and I was so filled with pain… and I somehow invariably see ma in one of my grandmother's white saree the way she used to wear when I used to stay at my grandma's after school and ma used to come there after College… for many years… and then I wake up from that nightmare and find to my relief that I was wrong… that ma is still here… and then I wake up again and plunge back in the nightmare again…

I know it's highly audacious trying to translate Tagore especially for me… but given the stormy night yesterday, penned this… for one of my favourite songs…

আজি ঝড়ের রাতে তোমার অভিসার

পরানসখা বন্ধু হে আমার।

আকাশ কাঁদে হতাশসম, নাই যে ঘুম নয়নে মম,

দুয়ার খুলি হে প্রিয়তম,

চাই যে বারে বার।

বাহিরে কিছু দেখিতে নাহি পাই

তোমার পথ কোথায় ভাবি তাই,

সুদূর কোন্ নদীর পারে, গহন কোন্ বনের ধারে,

গভীর কোন্ অন্ধকারে

হতেছ তুমি পার।

It's your rendezvous on today's stormy night

Bosom friend of mine.

The sky cries like it has lost all hope, my eyes are sleepless,

I open the door my beloved, and look again and again.

I can't see anything at all

And wonder where your trail might be,

By the banks of a river far away, near some dense forest,

What fathomless darkness you tide.

25. The Month of April

April 9th

Dr Dashorathi,

আজকে ওপরের ঘরের AC টা ঠিক কাজ করছে না বলে নিচে মা'র ঘরে এসেছি জানেন ওলি আর আমি ... and I am exactly in the place ma was laid down the last time she was here... she was wrapped in a kind of white cloth and the thumbs on her feet were tied together probably to keep her body straight... and all kinds of people were coming and crying you know... যেরম এই বাড়ির সামনে construction worker এর বৌ ... মা তার ছেলের জন্য regularly দুধ, জন্মদিন-এ cake, নতুন জামা, পায়েসের গোবিন্দভোগ চাল, মেয়ের জন্য বই খাতা, etc দিতেই থাকত, অথচ several times মা-কে কত insult করেছে... তারপর মা'র এক colleague-এর মেয়ে ... সে সংস্কৃত-ই পড়েছে ... এসে প্রিয়া* বলে আমাকে জড়িয়ে ধরে কত কাঁদলো... I probably embarrassed them a lot because I think I just stared back at them... মনে হচ্ছিলো মা দেখছে দূর থেকে সবার কান্ড কারখানা আর হাসছে ... মনে হচ্ছিলো সবাই চলে গেলে, আমি আর মা যেরম গল্প করতাম, সেরম করব আবার আর বলব 'মা ভাবা যায় তুমি চলে যেতে কারা কারা এসে কি কি করল!'...

*Priya is one of Parshati's nicknames.

মাঝে মাঝে জানেন খুব ইচ্ছে করে মরে যেতে ... কত লোক তো শোয়ে আর ওঠে না ... আপনি আগে বললে কত রাগ করতেন ... last time you said you won't talk to me anymore if I said so again... but you're not talking to me in any case nowadays, so I can fearlessly say so.. সত্যি চলে গেলে, তখন তো নিশ্চই আসবেন একবার ... তখন মনে মনে অনুশোচনা

হবে না কি একবারও?... যে মিথ্যে মিথ্যে আমায় কত কষ্ট দিলেন?... কিসের জন্য আমার ওপর এতো অভিমান করলেন...

কয়েকদিন আগে মা তোমার মেঘদূতম* দেখছিলাম ... তোমার স্ক্রিপ্ট-টা অনবদ্য ... সেখানে এক জায়গায় তুমি বলছ মেঘদূত সমাপ্ত হল কিন্তু মেঘদূতের সমাপ্তি নাই ... how true... সবার অন্তরে এক অতলস্পর্শী বিরহী থাকে ... যাকে সশরীরে পাওয়া যায় না ... অন্তর দিয়েই তার কাছে পৌঁছনো যায় ...

*Meghadutam was a dance drama that Parshati's mother had written in which Parshati and her dance teacher had performed.

11th April

Ma,

আজ থেকে Oli'র class five start হলো ... তোমাকে কী যে দ্যাখাতে ইচ্ছে করছে ওর certificate গুলো যে কি বলি ... আর কেউ তো আমার ফোনের অপেক্ষায় বসে থাকে না ... school থেকেই ভাবছিলাম phone করি তোমায় ... তাই তো করতাম আগে... কিন্তু এখন আর করার নেই ... একদিন রাত্তিরে দেখি হঠাৎ জিজ্ঞেস করছে মা সব ওষুধ খেয়েছো তো?... কিসের ওষুধ ওগুলো?... আমি প্রায়ই ওষুধ খেতে ভুলে যাই বলে ওকে বলি না ডুগি মনে করবি ওষুধের কথা ... তাই হয়তো ... ওর জন্যই থাকা মা ... ও একটু বড় হয়ে ওর নিজের সংসার হোক, আমাকে তোমার বাবা'র কাছে যেতে দিও ...

তুমি থাকতে যাজ্ঞসেনী পড়িনি ...এখন পড়লাম ... বল মা আমার কৃষ্ণ কে?... আমার বন্ধু, আমার কৃষ্ণ ... সব তুমি ... in fact তুমি থাকতে তোমাকে যা কথা বলে উঠতে পারিনি বা বলতে পারতাম না ...সেই সবও মন উজার করে বলতে পারলাম এখন ...

14th April

মা,

কাল পয়লা বৈশাখ ... আগে একবার পয়লা বৈশাখে তোমার মনে আছে ... ঠিক তোমার stroke এর পরপর, আমার বর আমাকে আর ওলিকে নিয়ে Strawberry

তে খেতে গিয়েছিল?... আমি বলেছিলাম মাকেও নিয়ে যাই বা বাড়িতেই order করি বা something like that... কিন্তু শোনেনি ... আমার মনে আছে বেড়িয়ে আমি বলেছিলাম মাকে ওষুধ দিতে হত... and he said 'কাজের লোক বা আয়াহ রেখে দেবে, ওষুধ দেবার জন্য থাকবে না, আমি মেয়ে বৌ কে নিয়ে পয়লা বৈশাখের দিন বেরোব... ব্যাসা'... ব্যাস?... কিরম নিষ্ঠুর জান মা ... I remember সেদিন বোধহয় তার আগে load shedding হয়েছিল আর কোন কারণে আমাদের generator এ current আসেনি ... তুমি সেই একে তাকে phone করছিলে আর ও চুপ করে sofa এ বসে রইল... কিরম ওখানে* থাকা হয় বলে সবটা তোমার headache ... তোমাকে কী কষ্ট দিল মা আর আমি কিচ্ছু করতে পারলাম না ... সেই পয়লা বৈশাখের দিন যে কী কষ্ট হয়েছিল ... I couldn't tell you obviously even when we got back... তুমি না চলে গিয়ে কাছে এলে জান ... এখন কিরম বলতে পারি ... তুমি সব কষ্টের ঊর্ধে মা ... কোন কষ্ট পাও না তো এখন ... শুধু বলে হালকা হই আমি ...

*After her mother's stroke, Parshati had insisted that her family come and stay with her mother, in her mother's apartment. Their physician had advised for her not to be staying alone, so for a while when Parshati insisted, her mother used to stay in their apartment (Parshati's apartment), but given the location of this apartment to be a little interior, she had a hard time getting maids, cook etc., and given her mother needed some help nowadays, which were more readily available in her mother's apartment, Parshati had insisted that they come over and stay in her mother's apartment. To her, it seemed perfectly alright as an arrangement, when the priority was not to leave her mother alone.

কাল আবার সেই পয়লা বৈশাখ ... এবার ওর মা'র (মানে আমার শাশুড়ির) শরীর খারাপ বলে এখানে আছে ... গরম, ভীড়, etc বলছিল... বৌ মেয়ে'র সঙ্গে এবারে বেরোতে চায় না আর?... ব্যস, না?...

April 16

(Here are some more messages that Parshati wrote to Dr Dashorathi, when he stopped writing to her.)

April 19

You know today (April 19th) is exactly one month since we last talked on FT video (I remember since my daughter had that invitation on 19th March)… and even though you haven't written to me since, I don't think I stopped thinking about you for one moment…

I am still having fever, and it's blazing outside so maybe it's all a feverish delusion… see, "আপনাকে ভালোবাসি … প্রচন্ড … পাগলের মতো … like I didn't think any human could be capable of… for years together "… এই কথাটা আপনাকে কোনদিন বলতে পারিনি … আপনি ভালোবাসেন কিনা… এই কথাটা কোনদিন জিজ্ঞেসও করতে পারিনি … জিজ্ঞেস করতে বড় মানে লাগত… যদি আপনি বলতেন, "না বাসি না"… সে আঘাত বড় কঠিন … তার চেয়ে নাই জানলাম … সেটা অনেক কষ্টে আপনাকে শেষ পর্যন্ত যখন চিঠিতে লিখলাম, সেটাও in some other way (like what are your feelings for me etc)… and I really should apologise for all this… for not being a lady at all… at least for not behaving like one at all… even though I may have felt things inside… intuitively… আমার পুরোটাই না বই পরা বিদ্যে … so very sorry…

You really should have believed me when I said I haven't interacted with people at all… you should have made me a lady… well, I don't know if you should be guilty of anything else but you should surely be guilty of killing a poet… me… I used to write on and off in school and college but then hadn't written at all after my father left us… and then I wrote again…

almost the first time in my grown-up life when I saw you… I wrote again after ma left when you asked me to…

By the way, I left the poetry library… so I don't read poems anymore, don't write them anymore… not just that I haven't written a line in this past month, I absolutely don't feel any poetry inside too… no lines come to me… nothing wants to come out of me… the poet in me had come with you and has left with you… she's quite dead… poetry came with you and the last one I wrote was the one I sent you… the untitled one about tears… that's it… it's gone now… poetry and the poet… don't call me a poet anymore, I no longer am…

Tears have a strange nature
Sometimes they'll fill up the eyes
But not drop over
They'll roll from one end of the eye
To the other, as if looking for something
Like they're looking for refuge and relief
On one corner, but not finding them
They roll over to the other, looking for
Love and hope and succour
And again not finding them
They'll keep rolling over
From corner to corner
Over the curve of the kohl lined eyes
Wetting the lashes perhaps

Caressing the darkness

As they moisten it

But still holding on

Tightly, boldly, never to fall…

Yet knowing very well

That if they did

If they let go

Then perhaps their purpose

Will be served

The reason they were born

Will be fulfilled

If only they fell over

But they won't

They will just remain

Like unforgiving, unyielding

Remnants of purposeless birth…

April 26

It's such a sparkling sunny afternoon now… almost pleasant in my office… just the hint of much-awaited rain disappearing… just like rain-washed cobbled streets were in Edinburgh… and we're* into Lord of the Rings now… it's a little too much for my daughter right now to read the books so she didn't read them but she likes the movies… I love both… I love Strider, Gandalf, the Shire and everything… it's epic really and Harry

Potter seems kind of puny beside it... and one sees how much Rowling actually borrowed from her predecessors... the concepts of the Dark Lord, the Dark Lord returning, Gandalf (just like Dumbledore) and so much more...

(*Parshati and Oli read books together.)

Tolkien actually constructed the Elvish language for his series... amazing isn't it?... I actually remember a Tolkien fan in IIMB actually sitting down and deciphering the language just to be able to read the Elvish in the books...

Remember in Inception it was actually the husband who first tried out 'inception' on his wife... experimented with her to see if it works and planted an idea, a thought in her... when it did work, he regretted it forever... sometimes I have a feeling you know that someone did that with you... planted a thought till it grew and grew like a poisonous tree and filled you up... and I once said I am no detective, no pheluda with a mogojastro... now I wish I really was one... and could enter your mind and see what goes on in it... and even take away the thought that grows in you like poison... and prevents you from talking to me... it really was you who asked me to express myself freely... and promised me you'll never stop talking to me no matter what I said... really don't want to talk to me at all?... anymore?... ever?... it's like a layer of dream I'm in and one day I'll fall with a jolt and wake up... and see none of this is true... but those few moments in that layer is like ages here...

April 28

মা কারুর সঙ্গে রবীন্দ্রসঙ্গীত নিয়ে কথা বলার নেই ... বিপিনজেঠু একটা গান পাঠিয়েছেন, কী অসাধারণ জান... আমি রোজ শুনি ... এটা ...

জড়ায়ে আছে বাধা, ছাড়ায়ে যেতে চাই,

ছাড়াতে গেলে ব্যথা বাজে।

মুক্তি চাহিবারে তোমার কাছে যাই

চাহিতে গেলে মরি লাজে।

জানি হে তুমি মম জীবনে শ্রেয়তম,

এমন ধন আর নাহি যে তোমা-সম,

তবু যা ভাঙাচোরা ঘরেতে আছে পোরা

ফেলিয়া দিতে পারি না যে॥

তোমারে আবরিয়া ধুলাতে ঢাকে হিয়া

মরণ আনে রাশি রাশি,

আমি যে প্রাণ ভরি তাদের ঘৃণা করি

তবুও তাই ভালোবাসি।

এতই আছে বাকি, জমেছে এত ফাঁকি,

কত যে বিফলতা, কত যে ঢাকাঢাকি,

আমার ভালো তাই চাহিতে যবে যাই

ভয় যে আসে মনোমাঝে॥

I know, even attempting to translate Tagore is audaciously outrageous… still I tried… how's it, ma?…

I am encumbered in hindrances that I want to transcend,

But when I try to, pain rings.

I go to You to seek my freedom

But in your presence, I die of shame to ask for it.

I know You are the loftiest,

No riches compare with You,

Yet my home is filled with all that's old and broken

And I am unable to dispose them off.

When You are veiled, my heart gets filled with dust

And innumerable demises gush in,

I despise them with all my heart

Yet I love it.

So much is left, so much I've shirked,

A lot of failure, a lot of pretensions,

So when I go to seek what's good for me

My heart is filled with fear.

(And Parshati sent it to Dr Dashorathi as well.)

Dr Dashorathi,

Remember I sent you a Tagore song?… জড়ায়ে আছে বাধা, ছাড়ায়ে যেতে চাই… I listened to it so many times that some words came to me in English… I haven't written anything original in days, but I ended up with the audacity and timidity of translating Tagore again… I'll send you… and sending you the song again… it's from Gitanjali and I keep being surprised how I didn't know it before… it's truly unparalleled…

Dr Dashorathi,

Authoritarian dictatorial regime এ যেরম হয় না, the ruler or the dictator is not ready to listen to anyone else, আপনার সেই দশা হয়েছে জানেন তো :-)... in civilised democratic society like ours... খুব বড় criminal দেরও কথা বলার সুযোগ দেওয়া হয় না?... one hears their last wish isn't it?... one asks them if they have to say anything?... তাই না?... you'd know better... and here you are... বললেন একবার কথা বলে তারপর দেখা করবেন ... leave that alone... you won't even let me talk to you... এটা কোন dictatorial diktat?... you said what you had to say... something that you've been thinking over for quite some days I believe... just asked me a couple of times if I have to say anything, then and there, giving me no time to think... and telling me you'd get over whatever you were trying to get over in a few days and then talk to me, meet me...

You haven't kept any of your words you know... at least let me talk to you once... why is talking to a woman so despicable... I know if you haven't had mercy on me till now (and it has been so many days), it's unlikely that you'll have today... nevertheless, my entreaties to you... I still don't want to write or talk to anyone else... never will... I was in a cocoon... will be there again... just that আগে মা থাকত close by... এখন না মনে হয় ICU bed no 295 (that's where she was for almost two and a half months...) ওখানেই আছে ... মনে হয় গেলেই যেরম আকুল হয়ে তাকিয়ে থাকত না ... সেরম তাকিয়ে আছে দরজার দিকে to see me when I enter...

I don't know if you've read Coelho's By the River Piedra I Sat Down and Wept... but it had something like the woman and the man got together after seventeen years... I don't even know whether I'll be here that long but no matter how long it is, if at all... I'd never care to think about or talk to anyone else... just like I never did in all these years of my life... it's strange you know because I never did want to talk to you or write to you to begin with… it's strange how hard it is to go back to how things were… after what seems to be a slight detour… that I never meant to take…

কাল সারারাত যন্ত্রনা হয়েছে জানেন … in the toes… and everything waist downwards thighs calves were all so stiffened didn't feel like moving at all… but it was much better in the morning… I guess it gets better with rest… সেটা কোথায় হয় … and I don't have a cook now… সংসার বড় কঠিন জানেন … so I'm limping around because I have to…

And did you notice yesterday's Google doodle was Alan Rickman?… who plays Professor Snape… I love Snape… how he always loved Lily Potter…

If I asked you how you were would you tell me?… I don't ask you… I didn't even wish you on নববর্ষ … I don't believe in observing days… but I keep telling you about how miserable I am… আপনি কেমন আছেন একবারও জানতে চাই না তো … হয়ত কেউ আপনাকে একবারও জিজ্ঞেস করেনা আপনি কেমন আছেন… maybe they do, out of courtesy only… not genuinely to know about you… আপনি বলতেন না সবাই আপনার কাছে দরকারে যায়… I never went to you to ask for anything for myself… would you then tell me how you are?… হয়ত আপনার জ্বর হয়েছিল… হয়ত ব্যথা লেগেছিলো কোথাও … I don't know how you've been for days together…

আপনাকে আমি বলতাম না I have a feeling that when you want to write to me the most, that's when you're most silent… maybe that's true even now… আপনাকে বড্ড বড্ড বড্ড miss করি … আপনার কথা বড্ড বড্ড বড্ড মনে পরে… I just wish we could grow old together…

26. The Month of May

3rd May

Ma,

জানতো আমার Hotmail account এ storage কম বলে একটা gmail account খুলতে হয়েছে ... সেটার নাম দিয়েছি parshati.pursuits@gmail.com... I didn't want to use my surname or gender studies or the name of my office...

Hotmail wasn't just an email... ওটা Banerjee, তোমরা (বাবা-মা), my youth সবকিছুর সঙ্গে connection ছিল... losing it is like severing ties with all of them... plus Parshati username টা gmail এ available হয়না... আগেও দেখেছি... সেই Cuttack এ আমার maths sir তাঁর মেয়ে'র নাম রাখলো না... আরও অনেকে আলাপ হলে আমার নাম শুনে বলত রাখবে... তার মধ্যেই কেউ রেখেছে হয়ত...

আর আমি Homo Deus পড়ছি... Yuval Noah Harari... Harari's first book of the series, Sapiens is also very nice... তুমি চলে যাওয়ার পর আর একটা বইয়ের review লিখেছি ...

Dr Dashorathi,

You know I am possibly becoming more cynical because I'm reading Homo Deus (almost finished)... have you read it?... you should if you haven't because it really dwells on technology a lot... Harari talks a lot about how technology is actually taking over our jobs, our lives and even ourselves... because we're after all, an algorithm of electrical impulses (our intelligence, our emotions, our decisions, desires, everything) that artificial intelligence can do better at… so for example, taxi driver… his main job is helping people safely travel from one place to another… but AI controlled cars can do that much better… automatic cars of Google drive safely, and avoid congested roads much better than human drivers… doesn't feel tired or sleepy… but one can argue that a human driver listens to music, fills with joy when he looks at the sky and so on… but those are not necessary driving skills… and whatever is essential for safe travel can be done better by machines… think of how travel earlier meant horse carriages… totally obsolete now… taxi drivers would be potential horses in future… similar fate awaits professions of doctors, teachers etc.… in fact even music… which you'd think requires souls and emotions… have been proved to be produced better by an algorithm sufficiently exposed to Beethoven and Bach… and the book is filled with many other such examples… this morning in fact I read a paragraph specifically talking of emails… and read the one about our political inclinations… really very scary for me… I know none of these will happen in our lifetimes but nevertheless we're all bound by shared feelings for those that were, are, and will be…

In fact the "machine driver" can be trained to play the music the passenger wanted to hear too!

15th May

মা কাল ওলি'র জন্মদিনে… তোমরা যেরম কোনদিন কিছুতে quality compromise করোনি, আমিও তাই মা … Cuisine Caterers খাবার করছে … they're one of the best in the city now… ওই ও'র কয়েকজন বন্ধু আসছে আর তাদের বাবা-মা'রা …

(Parshati often used to open up about her marital woes, especially the psychological unease she felt with her in-laws, to Dr Dashorathi. When her brother-in-law, who resided in the

USA, was visiting India with his daughter, Oli's cousin and a couple of years older to Oli, Parshati once again wrote to him, even though he wasn't writing to her.)

Dr Dashorathi,

So his brother is coming sometimes towards the end of May… like other times he asked me when he'd ask them to come stay with us… I said their daughter is welcome but I don't want to meet his brother… আগে না ওরা যখনি আসতো, it was standard… ওরা এসে they'll stay just like in a hotel, and I'll make and serve them everything from morning tea to dinner… take them shopping and socialising… even when my husband had his commitments and would be away… and all I did for them and his mother was with that little bit of expectation that he'd be nice to ma… well, that pressure point is not there…

এই কদিন আগে ও'র বৌদি এসেছিল… had written to me on WhatsApp but I did not respond… his mother asked him to call her up and he did but not in front of me and I clearly told him I will not talk to her… this time I told him I don't want to meet his brother and attend him like before…if he does meet me or talk to me I will tell him exactly why I don't want to meet him… this drove him furious… অপ্রিয় সত্য কেউ শুনতে চায় না … he said I was out of my mind… was not stable mentally… that he was nice and cordial to ma… I was making everything up… that he'll divorce me and meet me in the court etc etc… I told him he was just scared that I'd expose his true colour to his family… and all that he did when ma was in ICU (he keeps saying how much he did when ma was in the ICU… what did he do?… when I was standing there the whole day, he'd pick my daughter up from school and manage the maids in the house… you know when ma was needing lots of blood and they asked for donors, I gave my blood, but he didn't…)… and I keep telling him whatever he did was really to try and atone for the unbearably painful amount of humiliation and cold indifference that he had subjected her for the last twenty years, especially after we came back to Kolkata…

বাইরের লোকের কাছে না মনে হত 'বাবারে কী ভালো জামাই, শাশুড়ি সঙ্গে থাকে!'… but I know exactly how he treated ma… and he's actually a big liar… মা বলত জানেন ও তো রাতকে দিন করে… and initially I used to think I must be thinking wrong, but when ma also felt similarly I knew I was right…

এখন কি বলে জানেন… you know he wouldn't even come near the dining table when ma used to have food… leave alone talk to her… except for when I used to be in office maybe… and he says ও নাকি মাকে খেতে দিতো, জিজ্ঞেস করত কি লাগবে etc… and you know sometimes it has happened that he didn't even know whether ma has got woken up in the morning, even when it was very late (and I was not home)… এমন ভাবে বলে জানেন যেন I am making everything up… যে মানুষটার কষ্ট হল … কষ্ট পেয়ে চলেই গেল … সে তো আর কথা বলতে আসছে না… all he needs to do is try and brain wash me… প্রচন্ড ঝগড়া করল… and he left the house… when I called up he said he was in our Sunrise apartment… came back in the night… but wouldn't have anything (I made tea which I kept for him)…

I knew he'd create a big ruckus when I'd tell him I won't smilingly entertain his brother… all my previous niceties yielded no benefits when it came to ma… so I will not return any… I know I am being horrid… but I don't want to be nice anymore… ভালো মেয়ে হয়ে কোন লাভ তো হয়নি … and his attitude is exactly that… মা তো আর নেই … যা কষ্ট দেবার etc that episode is closed for him… so I should get back to being the nice wife he wants me to be... অনেকদিন ছাড়াছাড়ি হবারই ছিল... আগে হলে হয়ত ভালো হত ... এবার হয়ত হবেও... এই মেয়েটার জন্মদিন জানেন আর মুখ ছোট করে ঘুরে বেড়ায়... she was crying when we were quarrelling... এই জন্যই আমি absolutely কোন কথাই বাড়াই না ... just when I have to... ও ইচ্ছে করেই ওর birthday র আগে এইটা নিয়ে ঝামেলা করছিe... so that I will do whatever he wants keeping her birthday in mind... that's what he's always done... but I am not giving in this time... if he does bring his brother's family over, I will leave my house you know... at least for a few days... will tell my daughter of course...

Ma,

আজকে জানোতো mother's day... সারাদিন কাগজে, internet এ সব ad দিচ্ছে... আমি তোমার আর ওলি'র সঙ্গে একটা ছবি WhatsApp এ dp তে রেখেছি... সেটা দেখে অনেকে লিখেছে ...তার মধ্যে সমর্পিতা* লিখেছে... কবে ও তোমার সঙ্গে যখন কথা বলছিল ওর M. Phil. এর সময়, তখন ভূমিকম্প হচ্ছিলো... (হয়েছিল না মাঝখানে April এ)... তখন আমাদের phone করে বোধহয় প্রথমবার পাওনি... তখন চিন্তায় খুব ঘেমেছিলে ... পরে phone এ পেয়েছিলে ... সমর্পিতা said আমাদের তুমি কত ভালোবাসতে... me too মা... অন্যদের কি করে বলে বোঝাই সেটা ... কলকাতায় আসার পর কত happy ছিলে না তুমি ... আগে Gladioli** এ রোজ University ফেরত যেতে মনে আছে ...এটা ওটা খাবার, আমাদের জন্য জামা কাপড়, কত কী নিয়ে যেতে ... তারপর কিছুক্ষন থেকে বাড়ি যেতে ... সবদিন কেমন চলে গেল ... ও কিরম তোমার ভালোবাসার কোন কদর করল না... unappreciated, unacknowledged, unwanted... তুমি and your love...

(*Samarpita was Parshati's mother's student at the University, and had been in touch with Parshati, even after her mother was no more.

** Gladioli was the apartment Parshati (and her husband and daughter) used to stay at when they moved back to Calcutta a few years earlier.)

Dr Dashorathi,

আজকে চতুর্দিকে খালি mother's day-র ad দেখেছেন … you know when we first came to Kolkata ma was so happy, almost everyday she used to drop in at our place at while returning from … would bring snacks… sometimes dresses for all of us… somehow ও কোনদিন সেগুলোর কোন কদর করেনি … all her love was so much unappreciated, unacknowledged, and unwanted… like her presence, her frequent visits were nothing but an intrusion in our lives… life is so complicated you know… just because I got married, why should a mother suddenly become less motherly?… less affectionate towards her only child?… why should my mother show less affection than she always did?… just because my husband may not like it?… in fact, this has been the attitude of my in-laws right from the beginning… বাবা-মার আমাকে বেশি ভালোবাসাটা বড় অপরাধ… যেন বিয়ে দিয়েছে বলেই দাসখত লিখে দিয়েছে যে আর আমাকে বেশি ভালোবাসবে না…

আজকে জানেন তো I told him Netaji etc all of them sacrificed so much because of an ideal a belief… আমি না হয় সংসারই ছাড়লাম… a minor sacrifice for what I believe… he makes me feel so evil so inferior… he said I was not fit to be a mother… that I was thinking only of myself… maybe I am… but it's something I learnt from him… যে কষ্টটা ও পাচ্ছে না because I wouldn't be nice to his brother… exactly এই কষ্টটা ও আমাকে আর মাকে day in and day out every moment of the last few years দিয়েছে… he's killed all humanity and nicety in me...

23 May

Dr Dashorathi,

I actually thought a lot about why I want to write to you so much… in fact, more than 'want', I think I 'need' to write to you… why do I?… well, that 'আপনাকে খুব ভালোবাসি' doesn't really answer you know, it just takes the question one level back… what is it that makes me feel for you the way I do?… I really thought very deeply you know but I think this has more to feel than to think… there are others around me who'd be very glad to talk to me maybe… why do I not feel like talking to them?… ছোটখাটো সব কিছু থেকে important সবকিছু, কেন শুধু আপনাকেই বলতে চাই?…

You know I feel this is the reason: after my parents, and my daughter is too small… there hasn't been anyone, literally, who has been as intellectually stimulating, emotionally understanding, and temperamentally like-minded the way you have… certainly not my husband and none of any of the few 'friends'… I actually pondered a lot about the words to write you know… and these are exactly what you have and no one else does… I can't define 'love' for you but am sure this has a lot to do with the qualities I wrote above… "agreeing to disagree" was a big agreement and I began to write to you after Alchemist* not because we agreed on everything beginning with God and education… but precisely because I never found anyone who'd listen with intelligent interest to my thoughts, would genuinely perceive them, and honestly respond to them… in agreement or otherwise… that's why I wanted to write poems and share them with you… I never found a reader like you… honestly passionate and appreciative of my passion… এখনও তাই জন্যই আপনাকে লিখি… even if you don't write back… there's no one else I want to write to or share my feelings with… because no one else has those qualities that you have… তাই কষ্ট হলেও আপনাকে লিখি … মাকে মনে পরলেও আপনাকে লিখি … আনন্দ হলেও আপনাকে লিখি … কবিতা, articleকিছু লিখলেও আপনাকে দেখাই … আপনাকে লিখলেই প্রাণের শান্তি … আত্মার আরাম…

I do hope your long nose has stopped smelling something wrong now (it's been more than 2 months you know… we last called on 19th March)… and it has started smelling everything fine by now…

24 May

I finished reading Go Set a Watchman by Harper Lee a couple of days back… So on the surface, it's like Atticus hasn't exactly begun to hate Negroes but he abides by the law and conventions and does not support many of the liberties like franchise etc. to be shared with them because they are still backward and have to catch up with advanced ways of life that the Whites have… so Scout discovers this during one of her visits and her whole world, built around Atticus, shatters… she's completely crestfallen and decides to leave her house and family and packs to go after unimaginably humiliating Atticus calling him names etc… but then is stopped by her uncle (he actually hits her to bring her back to her senses)… and then her uncle (Atticus' brother) says this…

"Every man's island, Jean Louise, every man's watchman, is his conscience. There is no such thing as a collective conscious. … now you, Miss, born with your own conscience, somewhere along the line fastened it like barnacle onto your father's. As you grew up, when you were grown, totally unknown to yourself, you confused your father with God. You never saw him as a man with a man's heart, and a man's failings - I'll grant you it may have been hard to see, he makes so few mistakes, but he makes 'em like all of us. You were an emotional cripple, leaning on him, getting the answers from him, assuming that your answers will always be his answers. … When you happened along and saw him doing something that seemed to you to be the very antithesis of his conscience - your conscience - you literally could not stand it. It made you physically ill. Life became hell on earth to you. You had to kill yourself, or he had to kill you to get you functioning as a separate entity. …"

In a way you know, it speaks directly to me… maybe I have latched onto my parents' consciences and think those to be mine… but I guess that's natural isn't it… every person's conscience gets shaped and directed and moulded by people they get born amongst… that's why upbringing is so important… that's why families matter so much as to who one becomes… that's why irrespective of our genes, circumstances make us who we are… nevertheless it does make you think you know… am I really just a replica of my parents… is there anything in me that was not there in my parents… probably is…

And then Scout says that he was speaking like he knew all along… and his uncle answers…

"I have. So's your father. We wondered, sometimes, when your conscience and his would part company, and over what. … Well, we know now. I'm just thankful I was around when the ructions started. Atticus couldn't talk to you the way I'm talking… You wouldn't have listened to him. You couldn't have listened. Our gods are remote from us, Jean Louise. They must never descend to human level."

So deep down you know, the book's really about the experiences of growing up… the change in feelings, attitudes and loyalties… the transition that sometimes happens naturally but is sometimes forced… in a way, it's the greatest guide to adulthood that I've ever seen… read this…

"She did not stand alone, but what stood behind her, the most potent moral force in her life, was the love of her father. She never questioned it, never thought about it, never even realised that before she made any decision of importance the reflex, "What would Atticus do?" Passed through her unconscious; she never realized what made her dig in her feet and stand firm whenever she did was her father; that whatever was decent and of good report in her character was put there by her father; she did not know that she worshipped him.

All she knew was that she felt sorry for the people her age who railed against their parents for not giving them this and cheating them out of that. She felt sorry for middle-aged matrons who after much analysis discovered that the seat of their anxiety was in their seats; she felt sorry for persons who called their fathers My Old Man, denoting that they were raffish, probably boozy ineffective creatures who had disappointed their children dreadfully and unforgivably somewhere along the line.

She was extravagant with her pity, and complacent in her snug world."

Harper Lee might as well be writing about me… and what happens when that snug world is no longer around… where do you hide… where do you find your refuge…

Remember I always told you you were god and you always said you were human with usual weaknesses… I sometimes wonder whether I owe you an apology… I kept saying I look upon you as god… I did… still do… but inwardly always wanted you to be human… well, how do you differentiate between them anyway… we only know humans… their weaknesses, their desires, their strengths… and can only imagine about 'gods'… free of all vices and sins and weaknesses… rather we just give the name 'god' to humans who we think possess these extraordinary qualities… well, in that way you are god aren't you… so I guess my conscience, shaped by the values and qualities that my parents had, was thrilled to find you… you who felt and were so much like me… meeting you literally is an experience that I'd be grateful for forever…

"She gave lip service to the world: she went through the motions of complying with the regulations governing the behavior of teenaged girls from good families; she developed halfway interest in clothes, boys, hairdos, gossip, and female aspirations; but she was uneasy all the time she was away from the security of those who she knew loved her.

…

She did not stand alone, but what stood behind her, the most potent moral force in her life, was the love of her father. She never questioned it, never thought about it, never even realised that before she made any decision of importance the reflex, "What would Atticus do?" Passed through her unconscious; she never realized what made her dig in her feet and stand firm whenever she did was her father; that whatever was decent and of good report in her character was put there by her father; she did not know that she worshipped him.

All she knew was that she felt sorry for the people her age who railed against their parents for not giving them this and cheating them out of that. She felt sorry for middle-aged matrons who after much analysis discovered that the seat of their anxiety was in their seats; she felt sorry for persons who called their fathers My Old Man, denoting that they were raffish, probably boozy ineffective creatures who had disappointed their children dreadfully and unforgivably somewhere along the line.

She was extravagant with her pity, and complacent in her snug world."

So where do you go when you don't have your snug world anymore?... I don't know if you've read প্রথম প্রতিশ্রুতি by আশাপূর্ণা দেবী... but there when her mother-in-law got সুবর্ণ married off while she was visiting her grandma's house in the village... Satya (Subarna's mother) had returned and left her home... where did she go?... she went to stay with her father in Kashi where he practised medicine (her father was a Kabiraj, Ayurvedic doctor)... and she opened schools for girls... and basically spent the rest of her days there...

Essentially therefore she renounced... and could renounce her family (she had a younger son and daughter) as a protest against Subarna's marriage without her consent primarily because she had her father, who had a towering personality, with her... I am not sure she could otherwise have done so...

In contrast you know, Subarna herself could never protest in spite of numerous such occasions arising, only because she literally had nowhere to go… her father, Satya's husband, was a complete non-entity, and could never dare stand up against Subarna's mother-in-law or husband… in a way, in Bengali we colloquially call it "বাপের বাড়ির জোর"… you know, meaning how much a girl's parents are with her in her decisions… my ma always said she never had any "বাপের বাড়ির জোর"… so whenever she had a fight with my father and felt like going somewhere, she'd say she never could because the only option was her parents' home but my দিদান and মামা were the first ones to ask her to get back to my father… without a Ramkali Chatterjee (Satya's father) or an Atticus it's hard to show your protest isn't it… আমার যেরম কেউ নেই … কোথাও যাওয়ার নেই…

So though she's hardly met her cousin, my daughter is very fond of her cousin… that's what's called রক্তের টান I suppose… দিদিভাই দিদিভাই করে অস্থির … and I can never deny her what she wants… and she's also a child so I finally had to give in… and have asked my husband to tell them to come over if they want…

But if I wouldn't… if I did want to go somewhere, where would I… my husband could go to our Gladioli apartment… it's kind of 'his' apartment… ma's apartment has been closed for so long and many of the furniture has also been brought over… I literally don't have anyone to go to… no place to go to… if I ever have to go out of my house you know, you're the only person I can go to…

You know we're getting some tiles in our kitchen so we've come to our Gladioli apartment… the last time I was here was during the pujas the year before last… remember you arranged for that appointment with the nephrologist here… and ma could go out during the pujas… and I had written to you at night… saying it wouldn't be possible without you… and thanking you… and I also wrote about the song/hymn "you raise me up"… that had a favourite line "you raise me up to more than I can be"… and I said I haven't seen god but he must have come in my life through you… and I also sent you this picture saying I would have given its title "three mothers" if I could…

আর জানেন তো আমি ও বাড়ি থেকে আনার জন্য একটা বাবা একটা মা'র ছবি রেখেছিলাম packet এ along with other packets… I was carrying many other bags… and he brought the bags from where the pictures were… but somehow you know he didn't bring that one…

And you know the answer scripts of our admission test have come… we're doing the grading scrutiny tabulation etc… last year exactly around this time, after coming back from Chennai, and after finishing my grading, I had returned from office one day… when ma said she was having breathing trouble… it was 2nd June… আর সেই যে hospital এ ভর্তি হল আর ফিরল না … দেখতে দেখতে it's almost a year see… and I remember every moment almost… we had talked that day also (2nd June)… from my office… that day you know I had a dream that ma wasn't able to talk… but I was very thankful that I could at least see her… then I suddenly wake up and realise of course… even if you don't talk to me, will you let me see you at least…

You remember I had talked about Baishwanor da… who came to listen to our Draupadi program and then asked for the script and thereafter had been in touch with me… he often comes to chat with me and the other day he was talking in my office for about two hours… he's slightly older than you… and is very frank and honest about everything… out of several things, he said that recently he's been talking to his wife Ekankika di (I know her too)… about how their life had been etc… and he said he often felt his wife was unable to meet his emotional expectations and so he did have relationships (probably still has)… not that he'd divorce Ekankika di and marry someone else but he did need them… he said he's been open and frank about them with Ekankika di too and she knows and accepts them… strange arrangement isn't it…

And he asked me whether there was someone in my life… I said I absolutely never looked at anyone… was very busy with studies etc… then I saw someone who almost made me understand what love was… and I said it's been eight years and I still haven't felt anything like it for anyone else… and I said I was very sorry I don't think I gave the time I should have… the time that would have been commensurate with my feelings… that I never went out for coffee or lunch with him… that I could never go to meet him just like that… even though I thought about him and literally was him every moment of the day… said I did not know what to tell my husband because he surely wouldn't be happy about it… because I had to tell my chauffeur etc…

And you know Baishwanor da said I should have managed better… I should have spent more time with him… he almost scolded me you know… told me there's just one life… and that we're polygamous by nature… I told him about Sapiens and how Harari says females were especially encouraged to have sex with many men when they were pregnant (before it was known that there was one father) so that the offspring would have the good qualities of all the mates (would be handsome and strong and brave etc.)… he said that what we believe to be right and wrong are all social impositions and I mustn't let them get in the way of my feelings… and you know what he said that I was physically very attractive… do you think so too?… I was pretty embarrassed and talked of something else…

And remember that childhood friend of mine Pratyay… he saw some of my Panchgani photos and said… যে আমি "দিনে দিনে আরও লাবণ্যময়ী" হয়ে উঠছি … do you feel so too?…

My brother-in-law and their daughter are coming tomorrow…

❧

Dr Dashorathi,

You know I had a strange dream yesterday… I saw that we were travelling by train somewhere (I don't even remember when I last travelled by train)… ma was not well and was lying down on the bunk on an adjacent cluster of bunks… and my cousin older sister (my masi's daughter… she's two years older to me and teaches at an agricultural university in Anand in Gujarat and is a spinster) was also with me… and I was lying down probably sleeping on one of those two berths that are perpendicular to the three on each side facing each other… my daughter was travelling too but she was playing with someone a few clusters away… and you were travelling with us… you came from where my daughter was playing and sat near the window on the far opposite side… you were in a white half-sleeved shirt… there was no one else in this cluster… just me দিদিভাই and you on the far corner… and then you look outside and hum the Tagore song

আজি বাংলাদেশের হৃদয় হতে কখন আপনি

তুমি এই অপরূপ রূপে বাহির হলে জননী!

ওগো মা, তোমায় দেখে দেখে আঁখি না ফিরে!

(I know you can't sing and I don't even know whether you know this song)… and then you keep going and coming… later on I wake up and hum a few lines of

বিরহ মধুর হল আজি মধুরাতে।

গভীর রাগিণী উঠে বাজি বেদনাতে॥ভরি দিয়া পূর্ণিমানিশা

অধীর অদর্শনতৃষা

কী করুণ মরীচিকা আনে আঁখিপাতে॥

I don't know if you know this song… but ma had it in her Meghadutam script and I know it from then… beautiful song…

Well, that was the dream…

আগে সারাক্ষন বলতেন না বরের সঙ্গে মিটিয়ে নিতে ঝগড়া হলে… to calm down… to cool down… একবার বলেছিলাম না 'he said something that I can never forgive and you said that I should try to … সারাক্ষন তো ভালো হওয়ার advice দিতেন … so remember I had once written to you যে ক্ষমা, ধৈর্য্য, সহ্য, সব virtue দিয়ে মূর্তি গড়ে কি পাবেন?… I asked you, আমি কি পেলাম ছেড়েই দিলাম, আপনি কি পাবেন?… মূর্তি, মূর্তিই আছে জানেন তো … definitely for the rest of the world… একমাত্র

আপনার কথার পরশে হয়ত মানবী হতেও পারত...'আমি'-নামক মূর্তিকে মানবী হতে দিতে এতো আপত্তি কিসের আপনার?... কি ক্ষতি মানবী হলে আমি?... মূর্তি করেই রাখবেন আজীবন?... সত্যি কোনদিন সব খোলস, মাটির আবরণ, ভেঙেচুড়ে বেরিয়ে আসতে চাই ...

27. The Month of June

2nd June

Ma,

তুমি সেই বলতে না মা মাঝ-বয়সী এক মহিলা, when her whole সংসার was settled, had left her home… এখন খুব মনে হয় জান যে তাই করি … বা vipassana meditation হয় জান buddhism এ- when for one whole month people are without phone or any kind of gadget… খুব ইচ্ছে হয় সেরম করি…. Or think of সত্য (in প্রথম প্রতিশ্রুতি)… the way she left her সংসার to stay with her father in Kashi to teach girls… সত্যি সংসার ছেড়ে যেতে চাই …

তুমি যেরম ইদানিং বলতে না ছাত্র, ছাত্রী, আমার বর, কাজের লোক, প্রত্যেকটা মানুষ যেন দু-মুখো - এক ভাবছে, এক বলছে, এক করছে… তাই ঠিক জান… এই দুদিন আগে সিদ্ধার্থকে বললাম 15th July একটা ছোট অনুষ্ঠান করে certificates গুলো দেব… আজ দেখি একজন student জিজ্ঞেস করেছে, আর সিদ্ধার্থ তাকে বলেছে next week-ই পেয়ে যাবে … when I asked him he said ও নাকি ভুলে গেছে… ভাব … এই দুদিন আগেকার কথা … এরম কথা (যে তোমার birthday-টা commemorate করে একটা convocation যেরম সব institute এ হয় সেরম করব, certificates দেব) … সেটা ও ভুলে গেল?… must be because ওর কিছু হয়ত commitment থাকবে সেদিন … but he never said that to me… did not even say sorry… I am very tired dealing with him and people in general জান …

And it turned out that he did not even come to the library from mid-July onwards, he had invigilation duties etc in North Bengal… so basically, I think he knew that earlier too… that he will not be able to come here in July and so conveniently pretended to forget what I said about holding a small convocation-like event… he could just have been honest with me, ma, couldn't he?… I wouldn't have held him physically down here against his wish, would I?….

Ma, exactly a year ago, on 2nd June মনে আছে when I came back after grading তুমি নিশ্বাসের কষ্ট হচ্ছে বলেছিলে … সেই দেখেছিলাম oxygen level 87 আর সেই যে hospital এ ভর্তি হলে আর বাড়ি এলে না মা … সেদিন infact তোমার খাওয়া-দাওয়া etc জন্য একটা নতুন লোক রেখেছিলাম … সকালে যখন বেরোচ্ছি তুমি অভিমান করে বলেছিলে, 'মা-কে কাজের লোকের হাতে দিয়ে চলে যাবি?'… খুব খারাপ লেগেছিল জান, কষ্ট হয়েছিল… but I did not know what to do… and what you said was also true… থাকতে হল না তো মা কাজের লোকের হাতে … I never could keep you so… সেই চলে গেলে … তুমি সেই দেয়াল ধরে আস্তে আস্তে হাঁটতে হাঁটতে আসতে না আমি বেরোনোর সময় … সেই browm ছাপা ছাপা জামাটা পরেছিলে… and you said খুব শরীর খারাপ…. ইদানিং সবসময়ই প্রায় বলতে … এবারে আমি ভেবেছিলাম হয়ত Chennai থেকে ঘুরে এসে tired…

সেই কাজের লোক … এক মাসের ওপর রান্নার কোন লোক নেই জানত … রোজ হয় রান্না কর না হলে বাইরের খাবার … আর সেই gall bladder এ stone -টা এখনও আছে … operation আর করানো হয়নি … তাই বাইরের খাওয়া একেবারেই যায় না … so I am having to cook…

Life has become very purposeless জান … if I'm not there জান, মেয়েটার খুব খারাপ লাগবে … she'll feel terrible but she'll get used to it… and the kind of talent she has, she'll soon have enough to do and think about to forget about me…

শুধু লেখালিখি করতে ভালোলাগে … there's a kind of honesty in it… কেউ নেই to argue and talk back and lie… just me and myself… সেই জন্যই লোকজন বোধহয় nature এর কাছে যায় … Himalaya… এই Shillong এ Umiam lake… there's no hypocrisy in there… তাই শান্তি … অগাধ … অনন্ত …

June 10

Dr Dashorathi,

Last year 10th June you know ma was put on ventilation... drs told me in the morning that she might have to be ventilated... but to me you know she looked better... she had talked to me relatively more in fact... and when I came back in the afternoon they called and asked me to come back... as soon as I could... I went back and told ma that they will put her to sleep for a while for her relief and she was in fact quite happy to hear that... পরে না when she came back again but couldn't speak anymore, she described the horror of it all... partly by writing and partly I guessed... I remember she said something like she was not asleep by then... and they had forced a tube down her throat... and she was almost reliving the horror as she recalled... সব drsদের কাছে নিয়ে গেলাম মা ভালো হবে বলে ... সবাই রয়ে গেল আর মা কেমন চলে গেল ... সেদিন রাত্তিরে when I stood beside her and she was unconscious... I had touched her eyelids you know... and as if she could feel... you know a drop of tear had rolled down from her closed eyes...

Dr Dashorathi,

See I came across this lovely quotation...

"Normality is a paved road: It's comfortable to walk, but no flowers grow on it."

– Vincent van Gogh

I may not be the nicest person you've met... I surely am not... but I am probably not the worst either... am I?... sometimes it's like I'd survive... sometimes it's like I won't... talking to you made me feel so safe... so happy... remember

I often used to tell you I wish I was bodiless... like I was pure thoughts... that I could communicate just by thinking... see how nice that would be... I wish we could just talk like we first did ... about books and education and passion and dreams... and not feel any more intimate than like two strangers meeting over Alchemist... and talking about soul of the Universe in a grain of sand... or about pursuing passions... and honestly nothing actually happened to that space you know... remember I had written that that space wasn't gendered... it still isn't...in my mind it's just a feeling of unhindered liberty not circumscribed by my gender or past or profession or opinions... or anything of yours for that matter... why should I feel that we belong to opposite camps and therefore that space is hindered in any way... what can I do that I am a woman... how can I erase all that I may have said that I shouldn't have... how can I unwomanise myself... how can I make myself worthy of your words again...

I feel I'm growing old and ugly... not only because of passing days and months... but because I'm withering inwardly... I feel unenthusiastic about life and everything around me... you haven't been the most comfortable thing in my life... in fact you haven't been comfortable at all... not a paved road (as Van Gogh said)... but you've been such a flower... the road has been all bumpy and muddy and I've fallen a thousand times but you've been such a beautiful wild flower at the end of it... that I could die just admiring it... I am not trying to convince you... but I do feel you too aren't happy about doing this with me... then why are you... you know I never expected you'd be kind to me or you'd like me or you'd dislike me or you'd feel anything for me for that matter... so no matter how you feel, even if you don't feel anything, it's all fine for me... just wanted to tell you, you take care... here's a poem for you...

Rose... that rebels

Suppose the rose didn't want to be red
All it wanted was to remain bland, white
Unadorned by love and beauty
How do we know that every rose
Wants to be red?
Maybe they don't...
This one didn't...
Every word that made her blush
The thought of his smell and caress
The memory of his words and look
Every touch of the night air
That brought his whiff
Across lakes and starry nights
Across red skies and hidden moons
Across sleepless desires
And soft solitary pillows
And drenched her in him
Had reddened her...
Had filled her up with colours
And joy and dreams
And passion and laughter...

But memory lacks colour
She feels pale within
And the bright red, remained
An assault on her privacy
On her desire to be left alone
On the shreds of love that once was…
Do roses not have
The right to be wrong?
To un-rose herself?
To look blanched and
Bereft of all rosiness?
Not once?
The right to shed all the glamour
And promises and passions
That brought lovers and dreamers
On their knees
Begging for a bit of its enticing
Enchantments…
Not today… let her for once
Not adorn crowns and bouquets
And gala receptions
And marital vows
Let my rose… rebel.

Saturday 24 June

Dr Dashorathi,

You often used to come to office on Saturdays... are you here today too?... and I often used to meet you then... you know in the grand scheme of things you don't matter... I don't matter... the few years that we knew each other doesn't matter... the few months that you're not talking to me doesn't matter... I try to lessen my suffering thinking so... rationally speaking you don't write to me because I don't matter to you... but irrationally speaking there's this huge instinct deep within me which refuses to believe that... tells me just the opposite... and even if I don't write poems anymore (not like before definitely... one in three months isn't any writing really) I still have the irrationality, eccentricity and immaturity of a poet's mind and heart I guess... so I still nurture you with that within me... and I don't think I'll ever change that... wish I could see you on a Saturday afternoon like before...

Sunday 25 June

Dr Dashorathi,

কি চান সত্যি বলবেন না?... আমি আগেও বুঝিনি, এখনও বুঝিনা জানেন তো... I have only grown in years but haven't matured enough to understand... always my peers were much ahead of me in every aspect of life except academics maybe... my understanding about everything is very bookish you know... but real life is pretty different... but I did want to become a lady... for you...

আজকে ওলি'র school এর এক বন্ধু আর ওর বাবা-মা এসেছিল... or মা'রও exactly আমার মতো অবস্থা জানেন তো ... ওর মাও ওদের সঙ্গে থাকে আর বর misbehave করে ... so somehow she really likes me... I cooked পোলাও and দই মাছ... and had my cook cook chicken and মাছের মুড়ো দিয়ে মুগডাল... and I got masala prawn from Licious... nice menu না?... they praised my dishes a lot...

And by chance I ended up wearing the dress I wore when I met you after you got the offer from the very prestigious University abroad... I somehow remember that... remember you said I should visit you so you could thank me... I said you didn't need to but you really wanted me to see you... so I managed one evening... and I couldn't go empty handed but I didn't know what to give you... so I bought a slender bouquet of flowers... it was such a remarkable feeling... you getting into the best possible place... and that too when I wrote for you... but at the same time the thought that you'd go away made me feel so wrecked... I remember I cried so much that night... we used to sleep with ma then... and they were asleep... and in the wee hours I couldn't control myself... I couldn't bear to think you'd go far away... and I thought with you getting through Harvard you surely would... I couldn't imagine you would stay back... and I didn't realise how I'd feel when I wrote the letter... তাই তো পরের বার আর লিখলাম না ... please don't leave me and go away some place... I remember you were wearing a white full sleeved shirt... and you looked so nice...

My daughter's friend's father is a clerk in the pension department of your office... আপনার অনেক প্রশংসা করছিলো ... that you don't care about hierarchy... but value inherent talent etc... I of course know that...

And remember I have a gall bladder stone?... মা যেটা নিয়ে খুব চিন্তা করত... সেই Apollo তে Dr Chatterjee র সঙ্গে appointment arrange করে দিয়েছিলেন?... I still have it... and the mother of my daughter's friend apparently had a similar stone which got infected etc she had to be admitted in hospital for ten days and later got it operated and dr actually told her that such single large stone turns carcinogenic so it was very timely for her to get rid of it... they were very anxious for me and said I should get rid of it immediately... my stone even few years back was bigger than hers... and they said it's fatal if the stone "burst"... and they mentioned someone's case they know... কি করি...

28 June

Ma,

Dr Dashorathi doesn't write and I don't write to him either... and I don't want to write to anyone else... it's so hard not to love someone you want to... and so hard to try to love someone you don't...

কাল পরেশকাকা আসবে... বাবার কাজ অনেকদিন হয়নি ... আর তুমি চলে গেছ প্রায় এক বছর হতে চলল... আজকে অনেক্ষন তোমার ঘরে একা একা শুয়ে ছিলাম ... বড্ড মন খারাপ লাগে মা ... চাই তোমার সঙ্গে কথা বলতে ...

সত্যি দ্রৌপদী যেরম অর্জুনকে পেল না, কৃষ্ণকে পেল না... যাকে পেল তাকে ভালোবাসলো না... কেউ ওকে বুঝলো না ... আমার তো তাই হল মা ... তাই কি আমার নাম Parshati রাখলে?...

ওর আদিক্ষেতা সহ্য করতে পারিনা, প্রতিবাদও করতে পারিনা... যাকে ভালোবাসি তার কাছে যেতেও পারিনা... normality আর paved road এর মধ্যেই জীবন কেটে গেল... তোমার কাছে যেতে চাই মা...

সেই যেদিন প্রথম periods হয়েছিল, মনে আছে আমাদের PT ছিল আর আমি white shorts পরেছিলাম ... I was in class four and was 10 years... সন্ধ্যেবেলা, দিদানবাড়ি থেকে এসে, bathroom গিয়ে, দেখে, আমি খুব ভয় পেয়ে এসে তোমাকে বলেছিলাম ... and you said বাবাকে যেন না বলি ...

and I remember I was smiling and asked baba "বাবা, তুমি মেয়েদের ব্যাপারে সব জান?"...

In maybe around a decade or less I will be having menopause... the end of periods... the end of my reproductive abilities... you were there when it all began but not when it ends ma... সেদিনকে একটা লেখা লিখতে লিখতে পড়ছিলাম... after 40, the periods either become heavier or lighter... before they stop... I think they have become lighter for me... আর দেখ ওলি's have begun... কিরম অদ্ভুত cycles না... the same play, only the actors keep changing... তাও I wish you just take me with you while I'm asleep...

রোজ ওলির সঙ্গে যখন শুতে যাই ওকে জড়িয়ে ধরে, মনে হয় জীবনের best part... সেরম কোনদিন আমাকে নিয়ে নিও মা ...

29 June

Ma,

আজকে পরেশকাকা এসেছিল কথা বলতে ... বাবা-তোমার কাজের জন্য ... বলল, সেটাতেও, আমার গোত্র পরিবর্তন হয়েছে বলে permission নিতে হবে... বরের... মা তোমাকে বড্ড miss করি...

28. The Month of July

13 July

Ma,

আজকে তোমার-বাবার দুজনের কাজ করলাম... দেখতে দেখতে তুমি নেই এক বছর হয়ে গেল মা... it's still so unbelievable... every morning when I go to your room just like before, it's like I'll suddenly see you smiling at me like always... I draw the curtains away like before, and the bright sunshine fills your room just like always, ma... it's impossible to believe that you've actually left me and gone somewhere...

সেদিন জান আমার বর শাশুড়িকে phone করছে, আর আমি হঠাৎ ঘরে গিয়ে পড়েছি... বলল, 'মাকে করেছিলাম, অনেকদিন মার সঙ্গে কথা হয়নি'... আমি বললাম, 'এই তো সেদিন করেছিল'... ও বলল 'হ্যাঁ, last Sunday ... আর আজকে Friday... অনেকদিন না?'... ভাব, and he's telling me...

আমি কিরম বিদেশে থাকতে কতবার তোমাদের phone করতাম?... প্রায় hourly না?... class এর আগে, পরে... এখানেও কতবার phone এ কথা হত না, আলাদা থাকতাম যখন ... তারপর একসঙ্গে থাকতাম তো... সেটাই কি কাল হল মা?... আলাদা থাকলেই কি ভালো ছিল?... তাহলে দেখা হওয়ার, কথা হওয়ার আগ্রহেই কি থাকতে?...

তুমি যদিও চলে গেছিলে পরের মাসে, বাবা'র কাজ pandemic এর জন্য গত দুবছর হয়নি ... আর আগেরবার তো তুমিই এই সময় hospital e ভর্তি তাই হলনা ... তাই আমি পরেশকাকাকে জিজ্ঞেস করেছিলাম বাবার কাজ করা যায় কি না ... পরেশকাকা বলল যেহেতু আমার কালাশৌচ তুমি নেই বলে, আগে তোমার

কাজ করতে হবে, তারপর বাবা'র ... তাই একই দিনে তোমাদের দুজনেরই কাজ হল ... আগে তোমারটা তারপর বাবারটা...

এটাও কি আমার কোন অসুবিধে করবে না বলে?... এমন এক মাস আগে পরে কি করে চলে গেলে?... baba in July, and you in August?... that too পুরো দুটো semester এর মাঝখানে... যখন semester এর পড়ানো চলছে না?... কাজটাও যাতে একদিনে কারুর কোন অসুবিধে না করে হয়ে যায়... তাই বাবা-তুমি ঠিক July-August-এ চলে গেলে?

অনেক সময় মনে হয় মা তুমি এত কাছে আছো যে এই কথাগুলো বলা redundant... you already know them all too well... আর সবকিছু তুমি আমার ভালোর জন্য সাজিয়ে গুছিয়ে দিচ্ছো... প্রত্যেকটা জিনিস that I am feeling, you are feeling as well...

তোমায় যেরম সাজিয়ে খেতে দিতাম না রোজ, সেরম দিলাম মা আজকে... তুমি যা যা ভালোবাসো তাই... fish fry, ফুচকা, কড়াইয়ের ডাল, আলু-ঝিঙে পোস্ত, ভাত, চাটনি, পার্শে মাছের সর্ষে বাটার ঝাল ... আর মিষ্টি - সোণপাপড়ি আর দরবেশ ... আর ঠান্ডা মিশিয়ে জল ... রুপোর থালায় আর glass এ ... আর বাবাকেও দিলাম but নিরামিষ (that's what Pareshkaka said, but I have no idea why... especially because baba didn't like vegetarian at all!)... কিরম মনেই হয়না তোমরা নেই মা ... তোমার, বাবার সঙ্গে দেখা হয়েছে?... কথা হয়েছে?... আমাকে দেখ তোমরা দূর থেকে?...

কালকে CC market থেকে বাজার করতে গেছিলাম ... বাপি'র* সঙ্গে ... শান্তনুর** সঙ্গে আর পারতপক্ষে গাড়িতে উঠতে চাইনা ... সেই তুমি যখন ICU তে ভর্তি ছিলে, বলেছিলাম না একটা Sunday এলোই না?... Remember, I used to go at night once too to see you?... That Sunday, I kept waiting, and not only did he not show up, he did not even receive my call when I kept calling him... so finally বর drove with Oli, who waited while I went and saw you... so basically, he does not show up, without any notice, at a time when you were admitted in ICU and he knew I was going to go to see you... imagine... next day when he came, he said something like, he'd left the phone for charging etc… I will never forgive him for that… পারলে তক্ষুনি ছাড়িয়ে দিতাম মা… but you know the kind of dependence we have on such staff…

But I decided that at some point, I am going to get rid of my dependence on him… I will start driving on my own, no matter what it takes… and it was your dream that I would be commuting myself… এখন যাই মা… নিজে চালিয়ে office যাই আসি…

(*Bapi is a chauffeur that worked for the Parshati's later, but initially worked for her mother before Parshati moved back to Calcutta. But Bapi worked only part-time for the Parshati's (mainly for picking up Oli from her school) nowadays. Shantanu was their full-time permanent chauffeur.)

আর কিরম গাড়িতে উঠে একটা phone করা যায় না, কথা বলা যায় না … কোন privacy independence নেই … আমি parlour গেলেও he will know… কেন এমন হবে?… so I've started driving myself… বাপি much better…

তোমায় কাজে দেওয়ার একটা বস্ত্র কিনেছি মা… cream আর violet combination যেরম তোমার পছন্দ … ভালো লেগেছে মা?… সব খাবার, সব বস্ত্র, তারপর পরেশকাকা নিয়ে চলে যায় … বা বলে বিসর্জন দিয়ে দিতে … কেন মা তোমার কাছে পৌঁছতে পারিনা … please এস মা আজ রাতে স্বপ্নে … তোমায় দেখতে চাই আবার …

19th July

It's your birthday today ma but you didn't turn 71… তুমি যে Pursuits-টা start করে গেছিলে, আমি ওটার একটা newsletter edit করে বার করেছি… তোমার সব ছাত্র ছাত্রী অনেকে লিখেছে … তোমাকে প্রণাম জানিয়ে … শ্রদ্ধা জানিয়ে … সিদ্ধার্থ লিখেছিল কিরম তুমি সবার জন্মদিনে cake আনতে … সবাই তোমাকে খুব ভালোবাসে মা… তুমি মিথ্যে রাগ করে চলে গেলে…

আগের বার তুমি ICU তে ভর্তি এই সময়... আমি তোমার জন্য cake order দিয়েছিলাম Monginis এ .... ওলি'র নাম করে লিখেছিলাম ... 'emamma get well soon'... সব doctors, nurses, সবাই খেয়েছিল... আর আমার মনে আছে তোমাকে যারাই happy birthday বলছিল ... তুমি কথা বলতে পারছিলেনা কিন্তু তাও thank you বলছিলে ঠোঁট নাড়িয়ে ... how well behaved you were ma... in spite of all that was going on with your body... খুব চাইলেও কি ভালো হতে না?...

29. The Month of August

August 8

Last August, around this time, your days were literally numbered. Though I think you weren't fully in your senses by now. And possibly forgot about me too - not altogether maybe but quite a bit?...

You know there was a seminar in the Department the other day and the speaker was a senior of mine... now a faculty at a UK college... he had come to Kolkata for some medical issue of his mother... in the audience there was another person who was a faculty in another UK college, and she was also here visiting her parents... ma, most people even older to me, have their parents but see I don't have either of you with me... sometimes I feel so neglected and unloved by god...

But then জান যাদের বাবা-মা'র অনেক বয়েস এখনও আছে... তাদের কথা ভাবি... অনেক সময় মনে হয় they are only waiting for death... with no real contribution in anywhere... even their sons and daughters are not really that keen to have them around... the other day, I met a colleague whose 90-year mother is still with him, and he told me, how his mother doesn't listen to him at all nowadays... the older you get you probably enter a world of your own and you shut yourself up from everyone...

So in a way ma, was it good that you left us at the peak of being loved and wanted by me?... could it ever have happened that I did not care whether you are there or not? I shudder to think…

Remember you often complained about too many medicines?… so sometimes I did not give you a couple of tablets that were prescribed… one of them was Lasix, which I later learned must have led to even further fluid accumulation inside your body… and remember, the AC in the Marriott room wasn't functioning properly… so it was always so cold and wet?… that must have affected your body and its fluids too… somehow when I look back, God let everything happen so you would not be with us after a while… so in a way, we murdered you ma… I did… my husband did… our doctors did… all of us did… forgive me…

এখনও চোখ বুজলে তোমায় দেখি মা… সেই যেদিন একদিনের জন্য বাড়ি এলে মা… সেই নীল জামাটা নিয়ে গেছিলাম… আর তুমি খাটের ওপর বসে দু হাতে ডাকছিলে আমায়… আমি জিজ্ঞেস করলাম, মা আমার জন্য wait করছিলে আর তুমি মাথা নেড়ে হ্যাঁ বললে… কি আকুল হয়ে তাকিয়ে ছিলে মা…. কখন বাড়ি আসবে বলে… সেই সকালবেলা বাড়ি পৌঁছলাম…. নিচের ঘরে তোমায় শোয়ালো… সেই দোতলায় বসার ঘরে সোফার ওপর আর এসে বসা হল না মা… ওলি কে ডেকে নিয়ে গেছিলাম… ওকে দেখতেই বোধহয় তুমি একদিনের জন্য বাড়ি এলে না মা… ওকে দেখে এবার নিশ্চিন্তে যেতে পারলে…

Dear Dr Dashorathi,

You know it's been months I've spoken to anyone… literally office যাই, class নিই, phd students-দের সঙ্গে কথা বলি, and come back… don't even talk to colleagues… I've been so cold to my colleagues that they don't come over to my room anymore… that friend from Tripura (Pratyay) took a transfer and came over to Kolkata but I have not met him or spoken with him… my daughter's friend's mom called up but I didn't know what to say and she hung up after a while… I've really not spoken to anyone besides husband and daughter for months together you know...

You often used to tell me to have friends remember... but friends aren't like pens or books that you can scout around and get a few... I just wish you would remain the way you had been for years together... at the end of distance and formality... I wish you wouldn't have me call you my friend and wouldn't have me open up to you... so I wouldn't know what it would be to have a friend, to open up to someone, to come out of the cocoon I was in... and I didn't want to come out in the first place... I never had any friend... didn't want one either... I had ma as long as she was there... and I thought I had you... I spoke to you... and that's it... that's all... now I don't speak to anyone else.... don't want to speak to anyone else...

You know before our times in this world end, please at least tell me why you don't want to talk to me anymore... why you wouldn't keep any of your words to me... I hate unexplained things you know... and this is so unexplained to me... I can't even die in peace you know... wouldn't it be so much simpler to just say that you never liked talking to me, never liked me, never liked writing to me... I did ask you so many times... why wouldn't you just say that in simple terms...

I know you have many friends and talking to me or having me talk to you doesn't make the slightest difference to you... but believe me you were, and are, the only friend I've ever had... you not only make a huge difference to me, you define friendship for me... and the Dr Dashorathi who asked me to express myself freely, promised never to stop talking to me, called himself my friend and used to be brutally honest and frank with me, isn't this Dr Dashorathi I am writing to... so I don't know what to feel... রাশি রাশি কষ্ট পাই and I feel so utterly puzzled... something's grossly anomalous... it's like your phone is being used by someone else... and I don't know how to reach you...

12th August

Dear Dr Dashorathi,

You know, today is exactly a year ma has ceased to be here...

You were the first person I had written to last year when ma was no more, and today also I wanted to write to you...

I don't know what else she may have told you when she met year last year, but she must have requested you to take care of me and look after me when she was not around anymore... because she usually said that to everyone she thought was trustworthy... she was so apprehensive about her health and about leaving me in this world...

So won't you keep her request?... still not done hurting me?...

একবার কথা বলবেন?...

And I haven't seen Ijaazat but I do know the song/lyrics of mera kuchh saman... and somehow it feels so true... like that letter I am asking for somehow seems to have bits of ma and me in it, bits of our shared pain and suffering, like laying them before you had somehow allayed them a bit... but they're still there... and if I could see my words again, I could perhaps relive back to the dusk in my office where I sat writing it (I remember you were in Delhi and I wanted to talk to you but you didn't have time so I wrote this letter... and a poem which also I don't have a copy of... but I don't want that)... and every message, letter, poem that I have written to you has bits of me... bits of my emotions and tears, maybe the silence and smell of dawn of a rain-washed night... maybe the chirping of birds in the wee hours of the morn... maybe the warmth of my pillow... maybe the droop of my eyelids after a sleepless night... you won't know because the writings never had them... but the writer knows... and the writings bring them back... so would you please somehow send the letter back to me?... I know you have so many people to carry your missives and you don't need to meet me to give me the letter... nevertheless I would like to request you to please not send it via someone else (somehow it has bits of ma in it and I wouldn't want her to be treated that way)... you could maybe just drop a word with my husband about something (I don't know what)... of when you have kept it with your office and I could go and collect it... without wanting to meet you if that's what you want... please let me have that letter back...

কেই বা কাছে আসতে বলেছিল? কেই বা দূরে যেতে বলেছিল? কেনই বা কাছে এলেন? কেনই বা দূরে গেলেন? At least talk to me once before my times here have ended... won't you, please?... You know there's often a few moments between waking and fully waking... like you're conscious of this world... but all the day's works, details of everything haven't rushed in and filled up the mind... and sometimes strange thoughts or thoughts that lay unacknowledged and hidden sometimes surface... I wish you think of me on some such moment and have a change of heart... before all your reasons come back to you...

❧

Both her ma and Dr Dashorathi left Parshati. Her mother's departure was still explicable to her (in medical terms) and no matter how unbearable the pain was, she knew her mother always loved her and wanted to be with her- this thought itself was a solace to her in impossibly difficult moments. She ruminated the times she talked to her, held her hand, touched her cheeks and face and blessed her. They were all that she had left of her now.

With Dr Dashorathi, it was different. She felt miserable that he, especially when she was so broken-hearted after her ma was no more, should choose to abandon her, even if it was for some greater good of keeping away from her. She felt her soul withering and all enthusiasm towards life wilting with every passing moment.

Oli and her work kept her busy and provided the means for her to cling on to life, even as she felt a suppressed disgust coming out for her husband, who had suddenly become very jovial and happy spending time with her and their daughter.

Life went on.

www.ingramcontent.com/pod-product-compliance
Ingram Content Group UK Ltd.
Pitfield, Milton Keynes, MK11 3LW, UK
UKHW041954190726
13854UKWH00005B/1956

9 798891 337428